"Kimberley Woodhouse once again gives ⸻ ⸻ ⸻ ⸻ thriller that kept me turning the pages, unable to put the book down until the story concluded. I've long admired Kim's writing, but this series highlighted her talents in unexpected ways. I encourage readers to pick up the entire series."

TRACIE PETERSON, ECPA and *USA Today* best-selling author of the Pictures of the Heart series

"Wow. Just wow. *70 North* is the third installment of a race to catch a killer. It's a gripping tale set in Alaska's harsh beauty, where Dr. Tracie Hunter and haunted hero David McPherson unite to stop a serial killer before he kills his next target. With its perfect blend of suspense and emotional depth, this novel is a powerful exploration of resilience and redemption—and the knowledge that while we might give up on God, He never gives up on us. Pick up this book. Read it. Live it. You won't be sorry. The only thing you'll be sorry about is reaching the end."

LYNETTE EASON, best-selling and award-winning author of the Lake City Heroes series

"*70 North* had me on the edge of my seat for the whole nail-biting ride. I strongly suggest the reader finish all their tasks before picking up the book, because dishes will be left dirty and beds unmade until 'the end.'"

PATRICIA BRADLEY, winner of the Inspirational Readers' Choice Book Award

"Buckle up, suspense fans! The intense ride that Kimberley Woodhouse has been so skillfully steering us on in the Alaskan Cyber Hunters series comes to a heart-racing conclusion in *70 North*. Plan not to do anything trivial like sleeping, eating, or even working—and figure out a way to read in the shower—because you won't want to put this book down until it's done. Having the whole team in play will delight readers, as will the sweet romance and the heartfelt explorations of addiction, grief, faith, and forgiveness. I loved every word!"

CARRIE SCHMIDT, ReadingIsMySuperPower.org

"I was on the edge of my seat and truly captivated by Kimberley's characters and all the aha moments in *70 North*. I feel fully qualified to be an amateur sleuth! The All-American Book Club gives *70 North* our seal of approval."

EDEN HILL, host of *The All-American Book Club*

70

NORTH

ALASKAN CYBER HUNTERS

26 Below
8 Down
70 North

ALASKAN CYBER HUNTERS | BOOK THREE

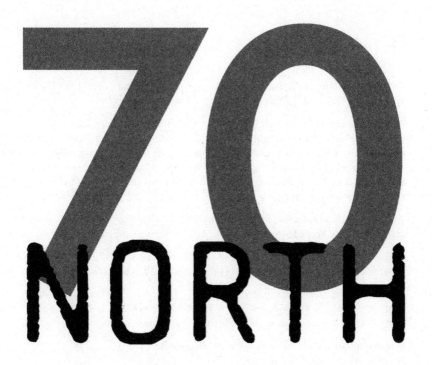

70 NORTH

KIMBERLEY WOODHOUSE

KREGEL
PUBLICATIONS

70 North
© 2024 by Kimberley Woodhouse

Published by Kregel Publications, a division of Kregel Inc., 2450 Oak Industrial Dr. NE, Grand Rapids, MI 49505. www.kregel.com.

Kimberley Woodhouse is represented by and *70 North* is published in association with The Steve Laube Agency, LLC, www.stevelaube.com.

The persons and events portrayed in this work are the creations of the author, and any resemblance to persons living or dead is purely coincidental.

Scripture quotations are taken from the (NASB®) New American Standard Bible®, Copyright © 1960, 1971, 1977, 1995, 2020 by The Lockman Foundation. Used by permission. All rights reserved. www.Lockman.org

Library of Congress Cataloging-in-Publication Data
Names: Woodhouse, Kimberley, 1973– author.
Title: 70 north / Kimberley Woodhouse.
Other titles: Seventy north
Description: First edition. | Grand Rapids, MI : Kregel Publications, 2024.
  | Series: Alaskan cyber hunters ; book 3
Identifiers: LCCN 2024019426 (print) | LCCN 2024019427 (ebook)
Subjects: LCGFT: Christian fiction. | Thrillers (Fiction) | Novels.
Classification: LCC PS3623.O665 A616 2024 (print) | LCC PS3623.O665
  (ebook) | DDC 813/.6—dc23/eng/20240429
LC record available at https://lccn.loc.gov/2024019426
LC ebook record available at https://lccn.loc.gov/2024019427

ISBN 978-0-8254-4774-7, print
ISBN 978-0-8254-7017-2, epub
ISBN 978-0-8254-6394-5, Kindle

Printed in the United States of America
24 25 26 27 28 29 30 31 32 33 / 5 4 3 2 1

*This book is lovingly dedicated to
MAJ Steven Whitham.*

*When I met your mom umpteen years ago, she was a bit lost in a
new city as your dad was on his first deployment. Little did I know
that by roping her into my writers' group and my life, I would not
only gain one of my closest friends but would then one day gain
the most incredible son-in-love.*

*Thank you for all you've done to bring this series to life. You are
seriously so stinking fun to brainstorm with.*

*But more importantly, thank you for loving and adoring our
daughter so very much. Thank you for blessing us with our first
two grandkids.*

I thank God for blessing our family with you, Steven.

To God be the glory!

PREFACE

Dear Reader,

Well, gang . . . this is my fortieth book. Kinda hard to believe. But I'm excited to share this milestone with you.

Thank you for joining me for the third book in the Alaskan Cyber Hunters series, *70 North*.

It has been quite a ride with the team from Cyber Solutions, hasn't it?

What's funny—or maybe not so funny—is the fact that all of this is all too possible. The world we live in is filled with amazing technology that changes every day.

Don't even get me started on AI . . . but I will give my two cents here. Ever since hearing that a dozen of my books had been pirated and used to train AI without my permission and without compensation, I've mulled over the fact that there are people who think that's okay. Obviously, I don't. To have my creative and intellectual property stolen makes me a bit sick to my stomach. And so sad.

Let me also say that I do not—and never will—use AI to write in my stead. Writing is a beautiful and wonderfully creative process. It's a gift from the Author of all stories. While my first draft might be a complete mess, I have been told I'm the queen of edits and absolutely love fleshing out the bones of the story. I love how the novel that comes to be in your hands takes shape over the months of the editing process. The thought of using AI to write a story for me

9

makes everything inside me turn upside down and twist into knots. I keep asking people, Haven't you seen the new *Mission Impossible: Dead Reckoning* movie? Or the original *Terminator*? I mean, really, people.

Steven calls AI an amplifier—meaning it can make things ten times better in good hands and ten times worse in bad hands. With a bachelor's in computer science from West Point and a master's degree with a focus on AI, his work with the Army Cyber Institute, and the cyber work he continues to do for the Army, he has *lots* of thoughts on it. As a creative in the trenches of this fast-moving and growing new tech, I also have a great deal of thoughts on the matter. Especially when it comes down to my intellectual property and negating the creator. But isn't that what our society has been trying to do for thousands of years? Negate *the* Creator. Makes you think, doesn't it?

Allen Arnold has written a fabulous book, *Risk the Real: How to Defy the Rise of the Artificial*. I highly recommend it.

Everything I've learned about technology through writing this series has made me seriously consider how much of it I use in my life. And yet I love it. I love the ease. I love the incredible tools we have at our fingertips. I love Scrivener to write in, Plottr to plot in, and Word with Track Changes to edit in. I love my super-fast desktop, my three massive monitors, and my laptop with its color-changing keyboard. Then there's my iPad and iPhone, with all the ways they keep me connected; and my Apple Watch that helps me communicate, tracks my health and steps and water intake, and offers its lifesaving help with my heart rate and breathing when I'm having an asthma attack.

Yeah, I do love my tech. I'm betting you probably do too.

There are so many wonderful things about technology. And so many scary things about it as well. People with ill intentions can do some awful business with it.

It made me think long and hard. Just because we invent something new in technology doesn't mean that it's always a good idea.

For instance, I "invented" a weapon in my first suspense book—*No Safe Haven* (2011)—and when I talked to some guys at NASA who were helpful in my research, we all agreed it was something we never actually *wanted* invented.

That's how I feel about many things right now in our technological world. Yes, I'm spoiled by electricity, indoor plumbing, air-conditioning, heat, computers, internet, and so on. But sometimes I feel like we've just gone a little too far. Maybe it's because of the research I've had to saturate myself in for this series. Every time Steven and I sit down and brainstorm, I cringe a bit more.

Please note: Even though Steven is an expert, I am *not*. I've used his expertise to the best of my ability but have also attempted to keep it understandable for the reader. Any mistakes are obviously my own.

In this series you've seen a character with a drug addiction. It's not an easy topic to handle. So many times we think of addicts as not being able to function, being unclean, and living on the streets. Heroin, cocaine, meth, opioids, and marijuana are the usual suspects. But there are many drugs that are addictive. Even medications that are used to treat conditions and are so helpful in the right situations can be highly addictive. And there are some people who keep their addictions out of sight and under control, sometimes for years—right up until that moment when they need just a little more. Then a little more. Then a little more. And they spiral out of control.

One thing I want to make very clear: we are in no place to judge because we are all susceptible.

It is heartbreaking to watch someone deal with a drug addiction, but please remember there is always hope—just like with any addiction. (They are all around us. Alcohol, food, TV, gaming, doomscrolling on your phone—the list really is endless.)

Griz came to life because of a friend I watched wrestle with an addiction to her meds. She recommended I use the diagnoses she was given so I could write him as realistically as possible. This is in no way to make light of these conditions or to offend or belittle anyone dealing with any of these conditions. My friend was one of the most brilliant people I'd ever met. I was often in awe of what her brain was capable of and saddened by the struggles she faced.

With my friend's diagnoses came a lot of prescription drugs and long-term use to help her balance her life. As she shared with me the reality of what an addictive personality coupled with drugs could do, I knew her wisdom and personal experience could make my character real and intense for the reader. She was incredibly excited to help create him and couldn't wait for the readers to get into his head. Obviously, she will remain anonymous, but it is with her blessing that I am able to share truths from a real addict. An amazing person, she is greatly missed, and I am so grateful for the insight she gave me into developing the character.

Griz is brilliant, just like she was. But rest assured, his psychopathic, all-out craziness is purely from my imagination. (I know, I know . . . what that says about me is a bit scary, but we won't go there. My friend and fellow author Kristin Billerbeck told me that it's "always the nicest people who kill characters. Us snarky girls don't murder." Hmm. Take that as you will. Hopefully you'll still think I'm a nice person.) Please remember that this is a work of fiction.

If you've been a reader of mine for any length of time, you know that one of my dearest friends in the whole world is Tracie Peterson. She's been a mentor and friend for more than two and a half decades, and, well . . . she's put up with me for a long time. So the female lead character in this book is lovingly named after her. Thankfully, she got a kick out of this and didn't want to toss me to the curb.

Lastly, some things you need to know about Alaska:

1. It's huge. Seriously, you need to go look at how large it is in comparison to the continental United States if you aren't aware. At more than 665,000 square miles, it's bigger than Texas (268,000 square miles), California (155,000 square miles), and Montana (147,000 square miles) combined!

2. There are only a few major highways and no interstates because it doesn't join any other states. Seward, Sterling, the Parks, Richardson, Dalton, and the Glenn are the most common highways and have been mentioned in this series. (If

you see them on a map, they might be numbered, but Alaskans know them by name.)

3. Eighty percent of Alaska isn't accessible by road. Did you read that? Eighty. Percent.

4. Because of number 3, there are a great number of pilots and small aircraft, and travel between cities is just as likely to be done by air as by road.

5. Small planes can land on wheels on paved, gravel, mud, or dirt runways, they can have skis on the bottom instead of wheels for snow or glacier landings, or they can have pontoons on the bottom to land on water.

6. When we lived in Alaska, I often heard the joke that there were more planes and moose than people in the state. In fact, according to *Business Insider*, "Today, there are six times as many pilots and 16 times as many aircraft per capita in Alaska than anywhere else in the US."[*]

If you've never had the chance to visit my favorite state and our beautiful country's largest state, I hope you can plan a trip in the future. There is truly nothing like it.

It's hard to say goodbye at the end of a series. Goodbye to the setting, to the characters, and all the things that we love most. But I'm excited to hear what you think of this final installment in the Alaskan Cyber Hunters series.

As always, I love to hear from my readers, so send me a note!

Until next time, enjoy the journey,
Kimberley

---

[*] Taylor Rains, "Why Alaska Bush Pilots Are Essential in the State," *Business Insider*, January 9, 2022, https://www.businessinsider.com/why-alaska-bush-pilots-are-essential-in-the-state-2022-1.

PROLOGUE

273 Days Until Final Judgment
32 Members Left
December 2—9:39 p.m.
Latitude: 70.193385° N, Longitude: 148.444766° W
Griz's Small Compound—off the Grid

He'd killed more people than Pedro López.

He'd made more money than Jennifer Lopez.

But none of it brought him the satisfaction he desired.

Griz reached into his pocket and pulled out the Tic Tac container that held his pills for the day. Three left. Perfect.

He wasn't an addict. He was in control. At all times.

For decades he'd managed his ludicrous diagnoses and labels ever since he'd discovered the right drugs.

High-functioning autism. The docs had no idea the scope of his brilliance—his brain was a supercomputer. Bipolar disorder—a fancy way of saying his mind was beyond the imagination of the doctors, so they slapped a ridiculous title there. ADHD—another insane way to explain the spectacular firings of his neural network.

But no matter. Over time he'd found exactly what he needed. And the increased use had only proven to make him stronger. Smarter. More focused.

He popped a small white pill and surveyed the space.

This.

This would bring him what he needed.

Stacks of handwritten notes filled the otherwise empty room. Twenty-nine stacks, to be exact. Each in absolute order. Five precise rows. Six across—except for the last one. He picked up the last stack and stared at it, satisfaction rushing through his veins.

His plan was complete.

Each stack held his outline for that particular piece of stratagem. Underneath that, a hand-drawn map. Then his brilliant, detailed step-by-step process. Everything had been checked and double-checked. There wasn't an error or loophole anywhere.

It was, quite honestly, perfect.

He'd memorized every detail. When he'd quizzed himself last night, he'd made one error. Today he'd gone through it twelve times and hadn't missed a single point.

Closing his eyes, he pictured every page, every piece of the plan. It was time.

When he'd first started on this journey, he'd been appalled at the condition of the world. The deplorable disorder of leadership in his country. The stupidity and ignorance of his fellow man.

The Members had opened his eyes in a way that he could have never imagined at the time. The cyberterror attack in Fairbanks two years ago had been brilliant. But all too quickly the world's attention shifted.

So he'd played a little game with them to show his true power. The intricacies of his mind.

Even now whispers of the 8 DOWN serial killer caused people to shiver. It didn't matter that the Alaska Bureau of Investigation announced the killer had been gunned down by an agent.

A small smile tugged at the corner of his mouth. What would the ABI think if they knew he was alive?

Everything up to this point was peanuts in comparison to what he had planned next—his final judgment. A cleansing. An opportunity for his brilliance and power to change the world.

The more he learned, the more he realized even the Members

weren't seeing the big picture. They couldn't. Not like him. They couldn't envision what the world truly needed.

Enlightenment. A true leader.

He picked up the stacks one by one. In three strides he was at the fireplace. The flames were anxious for more fuel.

One page at a time, he fed the fire and watched it lick up every last piece of evidence.

His plan was too magnificent to keep in detail on his computer. That was why up here—even in the middle of nowhere—he stayed off the grid except for the hours he worked at his "job."

The imbeciles around here had no clue who he was.

And he'd been careful to leave no trace of *anything* tied to his plan.

Less than a year from now, all the preparation would be complete. Everything would be in place, and he would see the culmination of all he'd worked for. No one would be left to stand in his way. The Members would all be gone. They might think they had birthed his genius, but his ideas were bigger. Quite simply, they'd served their purpose.

In the past he'd surrounded himself with like-minded individuals. People who could be eliminated at a moment's notice. People who were dedicated to his cause.

But over the past few years, he'd learned something amazing about himself.

He loved power. And yes, he was smarter than everyone else.

No one understood the true beauty of his brilliance—because no one else had seen the chaos. They didn't understand the thrill it brought him not only to succeed in pulling off the greatest cyber-attack in history but to outsmart anyone who chased him.

Then when the world thought they could ignore him, he showed them how powerful he was. No one was safe. He could snuff out a life with a keystroke or two.

That was when the insatiable thirst came to life. Power was one thing.

But to be the creator of chaos?

It was a high like he'd never known.

He'd *allowed* his pursuers to get close to catching him. Just to give them a taste. And to make them feel safe once again.

They thought the serial killer was dead.

Griz popped another pill.

The Members—with all their money and power—thought he had disappeared for good. That their threats had gotten through and scared him straight.

In truth, he had been planning his greatest masterpiece. And their demise.

Everyone would know who he was. Those who lived would fear him. No one would stand in his way.

It was almost time to begin.

✦ ✦ ✦

751 Days After
December 11—5:37 p.m.
Latitude: 70.25955° N, Longitude: 148.44526° W
Flow Station 1—Deadhorse, Alaska

Two years, twenty-one days, three hours, and seven minutes had passed since that monster—that crazed lunatic—had murdered his family.

Mac winced and shook his head as he leaned over the sink in the tiny restroom and splashed frigid water on his face. When he looked into the mirror, he hardly recognized himself. His cheekbones were sharp. His skin chapped and dry. His eyes hollow and dark. But it was more than just how he looked.

The man David McPherson had been—husband, father, friend— was long gone.

His faith lay in tatters. His relationships cut off. He didn't know who he was anymore. Other than the man chasing the monster . . . and failing to find him.

Twenty-one months ago—almost two years—he'd seen the man. Had him in his sights. And then he'd lost the murderer in the wilds of Alaska.

No one else believed the creep was still alive. Even Mac's closest friends thought he was crazy for chasing after a ghost. But he didn't care what anyone thought. He didn't care about anything anymore. Except for justice.

For Sarah. For Beth.

Just because the police, state troopers, ABI, and FBI all said the culprit behind the 26 Below attack and the crossword-puzzle serial killer had been taken down didn't mean he had to believe it. He knew better.

The man had taunted him. Somehow he knew Mac was following him. And then he'd had the audacity to *show* he knew it by saluting Mac's direction.

Mac would never let that go. Now all the authorities thought *he* was the crazy one. He'd heard it in their tone of voice, seen it in their eyes. Even though he'd once been their ally and cybersecurity specialist. They'd tossed him aside as a grieving man. An obsessed man.

An untrustworthy man.

Well . . . that wouldn't continue. He'd prove to everyone he'd been right all along. Not to be ugly or to receive accolades. No.

He simply wanted the monster caught. Stopped. For good.

Staying off his colleagues'—and old friends'—radar was a piece of tricky footwork.

It had been more than a year since he'd halted communication with anyone who knew him, because everyone tried to convince him to let it go. To cling to God. To grieve and heal.

But he couldn't do that. He *wouldn't* do that.

Sarah and Beth deserved better.

Every family member of everyone the monster had killed deserved better.

Once Mac found him and it was over? Then he would rest. He would mend his broken relationships. Somehow find a way to live again. Crawl his way back to God and pick up the pieces of his shattered faith. If he could.

At least he would have peace and justice would be served.

He exited the building and climbed into his truck. The anonymous email he'd received saying that what he sought was in Deadhorse had raised all kinds of alarms in his mind. But no matter what he tried, he couldn't find out who the sender was, or how they knew what he was looking for, or why they would help him.

Still, he followed the tip. What choice did he have?

The rough eleven-hour drive from Fairbanks up to the North Slope had been grueling, but the closer he'd gotten, the more his gut had churned.

The monster *was* here. In the middle of nowhere at the top of the world, hiding among the oil fields and workers. Mac could feel it. How he would track him down, he wasn't sure. But there had to be a clue somewhere.

He'd find him and—

Crack!

The force of the bullet flung Mac backward against the seat. His eyes darted to his window, but all he could see was the splintered hole in the glass. Everything else blurred as spots danced before his eyes. Fire shot through him, and he struggled for breath.

He blinked away the fog as time seemed to stand still. So . . . hard . . . to breathe.

His chest burned, while his arms and legs chilled in the frozen air.

A man stepped in front of the vehicle in all-white tundra gear. He stopped and pushed the hood back from his face.

Mac gritted his teeth against the pain, forcing his eyes to focus as blood seeped out the right side of his chest.

The man grinned, saluted, and walked away.

The monster had shown himself again.

But no one would know . . . because Mac would die here. Alone.

CHAPTER ONE

Eight Years, One Day Sober
June 3—4:29 a.m.
Latitude: 64.8455° N, Longitude: 147.5338° W
Along Columbia Creek, Outside Fairbanks, Alaska

THE DEAD BODY ON THE table opened its eyes.

A chill rushed through her body.

"You! It's all your fault. All you had to do was help them find my killer. But no. You screwed it all up."

Tracie Hunter bolted upright, thankful for the screech of her alarm yanking her from the clutches of the dream. Swiping at the sweat on her forehead, she breathed in through her nose and out through a tight O in her lips, then swung her legs over the edge of the bed.

Her Apple Watch buzzed at her. She glanced at the small screen. High heart rate. Well, no kidding. She'd just had the nightmare. Again.

It had been eons since that horrible case, but every once in a while, it still snuck up on her. Haunted her for days, until she could shake its tight fingers from choking the life out of her.

She groaned as the eerie irony hit her. No wonder the nightmare reared its ugly head again. Last night she'd gotten her eight-years-sober chip. Her dive into the drowning waters of alcoholism were only because of—

No. Padding to the bathroom on her bare feet, she blinked away the thoughts and forced herself to continue with the controlled breathing. She'd spent the majority of her life in school and had managed to calm herself through the worst of tests and exams. Medical school hadn't fazed her. Not even her residency in forensic pathology had shaken her unflappable self.

Not until . . .

A tidal wave of memories rushed in, and she closed her eyes against the flood. The promises she'd made. The evidence she'd so meticulously gathered. Her naïve confidence that justice would prevail. And ultimately, her complete failure to follow through on her promise.

She shook her head. No sense thinking about the case that had sent her careening into another career and always just one more drink. Every week her dependence on her drug of choice had increased, even as she'd moved from medical examiner to master of surgery—which had taken another two years of postgraduate work—and into the first year of her five years of surgical residency.

But then it had happened.

On a rare day off, she'd been called in for an emergency situation involving a mass-transit crash. Hurrying to race back to the hospital, she caught sight of herself in the mirror. The horrid signs of addiction had stopped her in her tracks. A litany of questions flooded her mind. What if her . . . problem . . . caused her to harm someone else?

She'd been sober ever since.

Now the nightmare had returned. And with it, her thirst.

No.

She wasn't going there.

One case. One failure. It had changed everything.

Tracie washed her face and brushed her teeth, going through the motions as her mind slogged through the memories that haunted her. After all this time, the details she'd thought were burned into her brain blurred together into a foggy display of random colors, like some kind of modern art that looked like a three-year-old could copy it.

What was the truth? More than once she'd tried to piece it all back together. Retrace her steps. But it couldn't change the outcome. It couldn't erase her failure.

She buried her face in a clean hand towel and rubbed away the thoughts.

The past was behind her. Most days she did a pretty good job keeping it there.

Today she simply needed to remind herself that she loved what she did. God had given her this chance, this new life. And He had forgiven her.

Now she was saving lives in Fairbanks at her day job . . . and traveling to remote villages to give medical care on her off days. That's what fueled her, what gave her purpose.

The past was the past.

Tracie walked to her closet to grab clothes for the day. As she passed the windows in her bedroom, the thick grove of trees caught her attention. The quiet of this little piece of land was why she had built here. Between her house and the creek, she'd seen plenty of moose, bear, and even an eagle or two over the past eighteen months.

She released a long sigh. This was home.

Finally.

Yeah, home should be where family lived, where they all gathered for holidays, but she'd had to find a new home after rebuilding and restarting her life.

She loved her family and missed them, but they were across the continent. Not that she'd intended to run away from them, but after Dad's last military assignment, her parents had chosen to stay in the DC area. Their friends and connections were there. Their church. Even her siblings had all settled within two hours. At the time it had seemed right for her to stay as well.

Until she hadn't been able to fulfill her promise to the victim's family. Then she'd gone down a path she couldn't bear for her own family to know about.

There was no thought of staying after that. Oh, she'd given them all the excuses.

It was far too crazy for Tracie. The city, the traffic, the fast pace, the politicians, the media. No thank you.

Deep down she presumed they knew the truth.

The only way she'd known how to push the incident behind her and move on with her life was to move away. Far away. To someplace remote. Where she could still do some good.

Thinking about that time in her life made her all the more thankful for where she was. Stepping into the shower, she allowed the hot water to steam away the memories. Whenever they threatened to surface, she shut her eyes tight, cranked the temperature up a notch, and turned up the volume on her Bluetooth shower speaker. Her favorite playlist did the trick.

Until it didn't.

Might as well face it—she couldn't shake the lingering effects of the nightmare. She'd have to deal with it invading her thoughts all day.

By the time she reached the hospital, she'd gone through all the facts of the cold case twice. Pulling into her parking space, she shut off her car and rested her head on the steering wheel. *God, I need Your help to put it behind me. Every time the memories or nightmares come, You're the only one who can push them back. Help me to focus on the lives in front of me that need help. Guide my hands. Help me to do everything to the very best of my ability. For You.*

Peace flooded her heart. Her mind was clear once again. She was thirty-eight years old. She had a great job, a great home, a great community.

Tracie slid out of her car, grabbed her things, locked her vehicle, and headed into the fray.

✦ ✦ ✦

By the end of the day, Tracie was wiped. Staring at her desk, she blew out a long breath. It was a mess. A perfect reflection of her day. She didn't mind the mess—in fact, she loved taming and organizing it.

Another reason why she loved surgery. The feeling of mending things, putting them back together, and creating order where chaos had happened in the human body was exhilarating. And satisfying. But more than that, she helped people. Her patients were important, dear to her. Even if she couldn't make everything better in their lives, knowing she was a part of their healing process was everything to her.

Once her desk was neat and proper again, Tracie exited her internet tabs and the hospital charting software on her laptop, then shut it down. It would be staying here tonight. For the first time in a few weeks, there was nothing pressing. No lingering details or calls from patients. Just an open evening before her to clean her house, make some dinner, maybe even read.

A small smile lifted her lips. Wow. Could life get any more exciting?

She hung her white coat on the hanger by the door and pulled her phone out of her purse. With quick strokes she unlocked it and checked the weather. A balmy sixty-three degrees. She'd be fine in her long sleeves, with no need for a jacket on the drive home.

Exiting her office, she locked it, then walked down the long hallway toward the lobby. Several lights in offices were still on, and Tracie glanced at her watch. It was only four forty-five. When was the last time she'd left work this early?

She didn't want to think about it. To leave early today meant those in her care were safe and sound. That's what mattered.

"Oh, I know, and did you see her with Mrs. Abernathy?" A woman's voice floated down the hallway from the nurses' station. "I didn't even get the chance to talk to the patient about her surgery notes before she barged in and took over."

Tracie's brows furrowed as she recognized the voice of her surgical nurse, Courtney Oliver. The woman was loud and opinionated, but Tracie had never heard her talk about someone like this before. Out in the open, where patients could hear her. Completely unprofessional.

"You make it sound like her caring is a bad thing," another nurse responded.

"Dr. Hunter doesn't care for her patients, Sherry." Courtney's voice dripped with derision. "She's *obsessed* with them. Absolutely everything has to be perfect. She's a freak when it comes to it. It's like she doesn't understand what it is to make a mistake. Won't *allow* for any mistakes. The woman doesn't have a life. We're real people too, you know."

Oh. Heat rushed up Tracie's neck and face. Irritation replaced her embarrassment. She wouldn't apologize for ensuring her patients received the best health care her office could provide. For being dedicated. And she surely wasn't going to explain herself to a nurse who had nothing better to do than complain. Just because Tracie had gotten after Courtney in the OR this morning didn't give her the right to lambaste Tracie like this. Courtney should know how even the smallest slipup in surgery could cause huge problems.

Tracie rounded the corner and paused by the nurses' station. Sherry caught sight of her first and stiffened in her chair. She rolled away from Courtney and pulled some folders together before exiting the open space like her pants were on fire.

Courtney turned, and her eyes widened. She clamped her jaw shut and looked away.

"A word before I leave." Tracie gestured to an open exam room on her left.

The woman slipped by her and into the room. Tracie followed and shut the door with a click. She turned to Courtney, arching an eyebrow high on her forehead. "Want to tell me what that was about out there?"

The smaller woman folded her arms. "I was just blowing off steam with a coworker."

Tracie smoothed her fingers down the strap of her leather purse. "No. You were gossiping. In an area where not only other nurses but any patients left for the day could hear."

"The place was practically empty. I—"

"No." Tracie cut her off, her voice firm. "I will say this only once, Courtney. If you have an issue with the way I practice medicine, you come to *me*. I won't tolerate the level of unprofessionalism and insubordination displayed today again. Is that understood?"

Courtney's gaze dropped to the floor but not before Tracie caught a glimpse of the hatred there. What on earth could have brought this on? The young woman was a top-notch nurse, excellent in surgery. Confident and sure with her hands. Tracie had recognized her among her peers more than once for her exceptional abilities. For her to get so angry about being corrected was unusual. What had gone sour between them?

"Look." She sighed and tamped down her anger. "We work in a high-pressure environment. I'm not expecting things to be perfect between us all the time. But I do expect the courtesy of your coming to me if there's an issue. I need to be able to trust you in and out of the operating room. All right? Is that fair?"

"Yes."

One word. Great. Tracie looked heavenward, asking the Lord for help. But she'd said all she needed to say. "Thank you. You can go."

Courtney stalked out of the room, and Tracie followed at a sedate pace. On the way home, she prayed for her surgical nurse, hoping that whatever was eating at the young woman would dissipate before their next surgery.

Otherwise, Tracie would have to start over with someone else.

Again.

✦ ✦ ✦

89 Days Until Final Judgment
31 Members Left
June 4—3:21 a.m.
Latitude: 58.30197° N, Longitude: 134.41035° W
Close to the Capitol Building—Juneau, Alaska

Patience was what most people lacked in this day and age of everything at your fingertips.

Patience was his greatest strength. It was also one of his greatest weapons.

He'd been a little too eager before. Four years ago his former boss had convinced him to join the ranks of the Members. Lured him with some gibberish about his computer expertise. But once he was in, it had been everything he ever wanted. A group of highly intelligent, rich, and powerful people with a vision. A vision he hadn't completely understood at first but had eventually taken on as his own. The longer he spent among their ranks, the more he realized their vision wasn't enough. It had awakened a thirst inside him. An unquenchable one.

Over time he'd moved up in authority. Then he'd eliminated his boss and taken over the whole thing. The rest of the group had failed to see why the move was necessary, but things had still gone well for him.

He understood with startling clarity now just how much he was capable of. If the authorities thought the 26 Below attack was horrific, they were about to learn the true meaning of the word. And the ABI?

He scoffed. They'd been no match for him. No one was. He was always at least twenty-five steps ahead of everyone. Patience coupled with unmatched strategy. No wonder he was unstoppable.

He rotated his shoulder, the stiffness making it difficult to find a comfortable position in his chair. That had been the one glitch in his plan. Getting shot by his own brother. He couldn't blame Peter. If he'd been in the younger man's position, he would have done the same thing.

Well. He *had* done the same thing. And won. Peter, however, showed himself to be just like the rest. Opportunistic. But not hungry enough for the actual cause. Wanting domination, but just so he could have it. Not so he could shape and create the world into his own masterpiece.

Peter had no vision. He'd simply taken the Members' vision as his own.

Unlike Griz. He'd taken the power and the money of the rogue group and envisioned something so much greater.

It was no surprise Peter hadn't seen his elimination coming. Idiot.

Griz popped another pill, then typed a string of code, his keystrokes sure. Splitting off from the Members and going alone had been the best decision he'd ever made. There wasn't room for mistakes. And he had no messes to clean up if some stupid data head screwed up his code. No . . . when he did it himself, perfection was the outcome. Every time.

Besides, the stakes were higher now. His plan was more detailed and on a larger scale than those idiots had ever dreamed. He wasn't about to risk someone else taking the credit, like the Members had last time.

In fact, this time? The plan included eliminating some of their own. Eventually it would lead to the elimination of them all.

A scoff puffed out of his lips. As if any of those stuffed-shirt cowards knew anything about what it took to get to the top. Instead of seeing the masterpiece his plan was, they'd run scared. Taken cover. Tried to threaten him with exposure. They should have known better. They knew what he was capable of, and still they tried to control him, tried to tame him.

Ice clinked in his glass as he swirled his whiskey. It wasn't as good as the stuff in Fairbanks, but it soothed him for now. He released a long breath and settled back in his chair. Things really couldn't be going any better.

He'd lain low and planned for his ultimate victory. Until a few weeks ago, the Members thought he'd disappeared—that he'd been played out or found out. Thought they could continue on without him. Unknown to them, he monitored their communications. Fools.

Everyone else thought he was dead. Especially after all this time. The world had settled back into its lazy ways.

Just wait until they found out. He'd get their attention again. Just wait until they heard of the decrease in their numbers. Of course, they'd have way too many other things on their minds than to worry about his coming back to life. But they would see.

They would *all* see.

Then fear would drive their every action.

✦ ✦ ✦

907 Days After
June 5—8:30 a.m.
Latitude: 64.83156° N, Longitude: 147.73836° W
Fairbanks Memorial Hospital—Fairbanks

Mac walked into the hospital and made the all too familiar trek to see his surgeon.

One more time. Then he could get back out there and find the maniac behind all this.

Six months ago Mac had almost died.

Technically he had . . . but they'd brought him back.

She brought him back. Dr. Tracie Hunter. Her team called her a miracle worker. She gave the credit to God.

Mac couldn't argue with either.

And even with his prickly attitude toward her, she was always kind and understanding. Well . . . almost always. When he was particularly ornery and mean, she gave just as good as he dished out, which put him back in line.

The first few days he was awake, he'd wanted to die. He'd told every hospital employee to just let him go. Yelled at them even. What was there to live for? Sarah and Beth were gone. The monster had won.

But then . . . the face that haunted him day and night would appear in his mind's eye.

The face of their murderer. The man who'd tried to kill him too.

The man who had killed dozens of people, who craved power and attention, who would seemingly stop at nothing to get whatever he wanted. The lunatic who was off the rails.

The monster had a face. He was real.

It was in those moments that Mac's will to live kicked in, if only to see that man brought to justice. He would gladly lay down his own life to catch him—so no one else had to lose a loved one.

Six months. Hard to believe it had been that long.

Five surgeries. One shattering bullet did an incredible amount of damage. To his lung, his liver, his diaphragm, a kidney, and two ribs.

Of course, two of those surgeries could have been avoided had he followed the doc's orders and not done more damage by being stupid and taking off. But he'd learned his lesson.

He'd always been stubborn. And it made him want to kick himself multiple times, knowing that he'd wasted valuable time.

Mac shook his head and picked up the pace down the long hall. What was done was done.

He had one more checkup today. One. That was it. And it was an important one or he wouldn't even be here. They simply had to remove the staples from his last surgery.

His surgeon seemed to enjoy inflicting pain on him. Staples rather than stitches. Yeah, yeah, she might have saved his life, and he was a flight risk, but she didn't have to torture him.

At least after today, he wouldn't have to be back. Shoot, he wouldn't even be here today if he could get the staples out himself. And he'd tried.

Why the woman insisted on seeing him herself in person every time was beyond him. He didn't get it. Most surgeons would have sent in their residents, nurses, assistants, anyone. Especially for a pain-in-the-neck patient like himself. But no. Not Dr. Hunter. She made sure to get in his face. Every. Single. Time.

His feet took him straight to her office. He stared at the glass door and took a long breath, a luxury that a few months ago would have riddled him with pain. See? He was good to go. Healed. Ready to be on his way. As soon as those pesky staples were removed.

He walked into the office, signed in at the front desk, and then found a seat in the waiting area.

His right knee bounced as he waited. Scanning the room, he observed each person and made a preliminary report in his mind.

A mom with a child laying his head in her lap, arm in a sling.

An older gentleman holding hands with his wife.

A kid—looked no more than fifteen—with his nose and eyebrows pierced, both legs in temporary casts.

"David McPherson?" a nurse he recognized from his many visits called from a doorway leading to the exam rooms.

He rose and took purposeful strides toward her. *Last time here. Last time here. Last time.* He chanted the words to himself and clenched his jaw.

"How are you today, Mr. McPherson?" The all too chipper nurse grinned wide as she led him around the corner.

"Fine."

"Stop here. Let's get your weight."

"Seriously? You've seen me how many times, and you want to take—"

"McPherson." Dr. Hunter's voice echoed down the hall. "Are you giving Sherry a hard time?"

His grunt was the only response. She just had to witness that, didn't she?

"You know what?" Dr. Hunter marched toward him with a sugary-sweet smile. "I'm going to handle this one, Sherry."

Great. Just what he needed. A constant babysitter.

The nurse handed over his file . . . Wait. Was that a look of relief on her face? Was he really that bad?

"Mac, you really should at least *try* to treat people like they're human beings."

Ouch. That answered that question. "Sorry." He wasn't proud of the grouch he'd become. Then again, he wasn't proud of the man he was anymore either. Losing his family had changed him. A lot. Probably forever.

With one eyebrow raised, she pointed to the scale.

He shot his gaze to the ceiling and huffed. "Fine."

"You've lost another five pounds, Mac. Have you been eating?" Without waiting for a response, she headed toward an exam room.

"Sure." He followed her and then sat on the exam table, the tissue paper crunching beneath him.

As she pulled gloves out of the dispenser on the wall, he mumbled, "Be nice." He wasn't sure if the warning was for her or for him. Last time he gave her a hard time, the staple-removal procedure was . . . unpleasant. Not that he could blame her.

Dr. Hunter wrapped the blood pressure cuff around his arm, then paused. "Well, you haven't missed any workouts, have you?"

He took a long, deep breath, refusing to look at her. "Let's just get on with it."

"You do realize that working out without getting the proper nutrition is stupid, right?"

He flicked a glance her way. "You don't mince words, do you, Dr. Hunter?"

The you-really-are-stupid look she sent him made him chuckle.

"I happen to care about my patients. Especially those I spend more than twenty hours operating on and, with the good Lord's help, bring back to the living," she snapped, pumping the cuff until it felt extra tight. He grunted, but she ignored him. "Get over it. I think you're a big boy and can take it. You dish it out well enough."

He winced. The man he used to be attempted to resurface. Scolded him. Reminded him how to treat people. But the security he'd built around his heart kept his tongue lashing out. "Can we just get these staples out?"

The air eased out the cuff, and she took notes on his vitals.

He removed his shirt.

Her gaze locked on his botched attempt. She closed her eyes for a moment and inhaled sharply. "Seriously?"

He shrugged. "You can't blame me for trying."

"Um, yes. Yes I can." As she shook her head, she turned and pulled out her supplies, arranging them on the rolling tray. Her dark ponytail wagged back and forth at him. "It's a good thing I called in reinforcements."

That made him sit up straighter. "What do you mean . . . reinforcements?" He narrowed his eyes.

"This is gonna hurt. You rubbed the entire incision raw." Dr. Hunter went to the door, cracked it, and spoke into the hall. "You can come in. I might need you to hold him down."

Irritated he couldn't just get out of there, he growled. "Nobody has to hold me down. I don't want to accidentally punch some—" His words halted as Jason Myers and Scott Patteson walked into the room and closed the door.

"Hey, buddy."

"Mac, good to see you."

He blinked.

The doc's lips twitched. Was she laughing at him? "Look at that. He's speechless." She rolled her torture tray up to the exam table. With deft movements she poked and prodded the long scar, muttering something about his pigheaded stupidity.

Then without warning, she pulled out a staple.

He flinched. "*Ow.*"

"It's your own fault." She dug out another one. A small smile lifted the corner of her mouth.

Yep. She definitely looked like she was enjoying this.

This time he clenched his jaw. "What are you doing here? How'd you find me?" He pointed the words at the two men, who appeared ready to either hug him or haul him off for a good beating.

Scott tipped his head toward the doc. "She called us."

"When?" His focus whipped back to her.

Those deep-brown eyes didn't flinch. "When they brought you in by ambulance after you'd been shot. We had to find people who cared about you. Just in case. Your insurance coverage is through Cyber Solutions with Jason and Scott listed as your emergency contacts, so I tracked them down."

Scott nodded and lifted his shoulders in a shrug. "She's kept us informed about your surgeries and your progress, since you gave permission—"

"Gave permission?" Why on earth had he done that? His cloudy memories whirled around. "I must have been delirious."

The guys laughed—obviously taking it as a joke. Oh, if they only knew.

"Delirious or not, it was a good call, man. Your doc here is top-notch. We tried to respect your wishes and keep our distance—do you remember chewing Scott out on the phone?—and we were hoping to arrive when you were a bit . . . less grumpy." Jason stared him down.

When had he chewed Scott out on the phone? Mac swiped a hand over his scratchy chin.

"And before you could escape."

Mac itched to punch the grin off Scott's face.

They knew him well.

"Why do you think I kept putting staples in him rather than sutures?" Dr. Hunter grinned. "It was the only way to ensure he'd return for the checkups. But big, strong Mac here thought he could get them out himself." She poked the healing wound. The scar that had been so neat and orderly was now mangled with his handiwork.

Jason grimaced. "Ouch. Not smart, man."

Mac rolled his eyes.

"Your shooter tangled with the wrong man." Scott leaned against the wall, his gaze intent on Mac's face. "Dr. Hunter told us they caught the guy who shot you a few blocks from here. Before you were even out of surgery."

Wait a minute. His irritation with the guys evaporated. "What did you say?" He hopped off the table and crowded Dr. Hunter's space. "A few blocks from here?"

"Get back up there, or I'll make this hurt even worse." Her order was reinforced by the metal torturing tool attached to a staple in him as she pushed him back.

He smashed his lips together as the pain hit.

"Didn't you read the police report?" She removed the staple and then shoved gauze at him. "Look, now you're bleeding. Hold that there." Shaking her head at him, she cleaned off the device, then went back at it. "They brought you the report when you were out of recovery."

He stared her down. Unblinking.

"Oh, but that's right. You were an awful patient and threw things across the room at people. So it doesn't surprise me that you never read it." The hard look she gave him preceded another staple clinking into the medical bowl.

He took that moment to move forward again. "I need to see it." Out of the corner of his eye, he noticed Scott and Jason moving closer to him.

Placing her hands on his shoulders, the doctor gave him a little shove. "Nuh-uh. There are still five staples left in you."

With robot-like movements, he scooted back onto the table, his mind swirling, trying to get everything to add up. "But I told the police what happened. I remember them questioning me."

He risked a glance at the guys. Surely they believed him?

She worked on another staple. "I allowed them to question you before I took you back for surgery, but you didn't make a whole lot of sense. Apparently they got all the information they needed from the other witnesses." She shot a glance at him. "After surgery, though, the first couple weeks? You were a bear. You earned a reputation throughout the hospital." She shrugged. "But I can assure you, the police officer who came to update you on the shooter left the report for you to read."

Mac didn't remember much from the first few days after he woke up. Only that he'd wanted to die and people wouldn't leave him alone. And one other thing. What other witnesses? What was going on? "I wasn't shot a few blocks from here."

"Um, yeah, you were." She tugged on another staple. "Why the sudden interest? You never once brought up to me that you *thought* you were shot someplace else."

How could she be so nonchalant about this? Heat filled his face, and he clenched a fist.

"Cool it, Mac," Jason warned.

"I didn't bring it up because I didn't know someone else concocted a crazy story!" He raised his voice and leaned forward. "And I didn't *think* it. It happened. Your job was to patch me up so I could get back out there and—" He slammed his mouth shut. He'd almost said too much.

Instead of backing down, she stepped closer and glared at him. "The story isn't crazy when it was corroborated by multiple witnesses. Don't yell at me for giving you the facts as I know them. And I patched you up quite well, thank you very much." She lowered her eyes to his scars. "I'm sorry, Mac. But you were shot a few blocks from here."

"No, I *wasn't*. I know where I was shot." His tone was biting and hateful.

It only took a millisecond for the guys to move. Jason held him back by his left arm, Scott by his right.

Dr. Hunter stepped backward, tapping the metal staple remover against her gloved hand. Her expression shifted from kind, as she looked at his friends, to fierce, as her eyes bored into his.

"Really? Because you were incoherent and spewing all kinds of ridiculous things when you were brought in. Then you were in a medically induced coma for several days so you could heal. I don't remember your ever saying anything about . . . well, anything. You refused to speak to anyone other than to yell at them and tell them to let you die." She spat the last words. "Don't argue with me, Mac. I think I know a little bit more about what happened than you do." She stepped back into his personal space and pulled out a staple right as he moved.

Fire shot through him. And with it came clarity.

"I was shot up in Deadhorse. Outside Flow Station 1. I saw the man who shot me." He gritted out the words. Why hadn't anyone else said anything?

With steady hands, she pushed him back to the table. "No. You weren't. There were witnesses who heard the shooting. The police questioned them right here in the hospital."

What? No. "It's not true." The words came out of him hushed. Resigned. All the air left his lungs.

That's not what happened. He'd seen the monster.

Hadn't he?

CHAPTER TWO

907 Days After
June 5—9:23 a.m.
Latitude: 64.832967° N, Longitude: 147.716854° W
Screamin' Peach Bakery and Coffee Shop—Fairbanks

MAC SAT STEWING AT THE high-top table while Jason and Scott ordered at the counter.

None of what he'd heard at the hospital about where he was shot made sense. But before he could grill the doc anymore, she'd been called into an emergency surgery. A nurse had finished up with the last two staples.

His friends had done their best to talk him through what they knew as the nurse took her time with the job, but he didn't believe a word of it.

So they'd dragged him here. To hash it all out. Again.

Why wouldn't they listen to him?

"It's really good to see you, man." Jason took a seat across from him and shoved a plate in his direction. "I got the peach for me, since that's what they're famous for, but if I remember correctly, you love lemon."

Mac was in such a foul mood that he wanted to grunt and refuse it, but as soon as the aroma hit his nose, his mouth watered and betrayed him. Something about flaky layers of pastry and lemon curd that he couldn't resist. Especially when he was starving.

By the time Scott arrived with his order, Mac had scarfed the whole thing down.

"Whoa." Jason laughed. "Doc said you'd lost weight. How long has it been since you've eaten?"

Mac shrugged and took a swig of coffee.

"It's really good to see you, man." Scott echoed what Jason had said in his absence. "Alive. Emphasis on that. We were getting worried."

"Yeah. Not cool to completely cut us off there." Jason's tone was light, but his face showed his displeasure. And his hurt. "What happened to the accountability brothers?"

Guilt threatened to sneak past his defenses. What had happened? Shifting in his seat, Mac did his best to shove his irritation aside. "Everything changed when Sarah and Beth were killed. I thought you guys understood that."

"We get it." Scott cleared his throat. "We do. Obviously, we aren't in your shoes, so we won't pretend that we fully grasp it. But that doesn't mean we can't still be brothers, Mac. Remember how we used to hold each other's feet to the fire or step on a few toes every once in a while? We've been there for each other through amazing highs and horrific lows. When one of us hurts, all of us hurt. So why'd you push us out?"

Mac leaned back, as if punched by his friend. Scott was right. *He'd* come up with the group, with their accountability commitment. *He'd* said that phrase over and over to each of the guys in times of hardship. And yet on the receiving end, he didn't like it. Not one bit. Still, it was hard to access regret about how he acted. Scott was right—until they experienced loss like his, they wouldn't understand.

"Look, I'm sorry I shut you guys out. But it was the only way to protect my sanity while I hunted him down."

"Hunted who down?" Scott shook his head. "He's dead, Mac."

Fury rushed through him. "He's *not* dead. And I can prove it." He pointed his finger in Scott's face and jumped off his chair. With fury spurring him on, he went to his old 2003 truck, yanked open the door, reached behind the seat, and grabbed his messenger bag. Then he slammed the door for good measure and to work off his anger. The only way the guys would listen was if he pulled himself together.

He strode back into the eatery and sat down. Pulling out a file folder, he commanded himself to stay calm and rational. He might know all this by memory, but they didn't. "I took these first pictures in the six weeks *after* Peter Chandler was killed."

Jason and Scott leaned forward and studied the pictures.

Scott swiped a hand down his face. "Where was this?" He pointed to the last one.

"Outside Healy. That's where I lost him. I was perched a mile away, watching him. There's nothing out there but mountains and trees and wilderness. He had a four-by-four and a snowmachine. Then he saluted in my direction and took off into the forest. Leaving the vehicles behind. He *knew* I was watching him. How? I don't know."

"He knew it was you? From a mile away?" Scott didn't look convinced.

Mac held his gaze. "He knew *someone* was watching. That much was clear."

"All right. When did you see him again?" Jason slid the pictures around on the table and continued to study.

"Not until he shot me. Up in Deadhorse."

Scott picked up another photo, a deep furrow in his brow. "You're sure it was him?"

"He looked exactly like this"—Mac stabbed the last picture he'd taken in Healy—"except he was no longer wearing a sling." Watching his friends, he could see the doubt clouding their faces. "Look, it was up close and personal. He shot me through the driver's side window and then walked around the front of the car and pushed the hood of his coat back. He wanted me to see him. Again."

"But Dr. Hunter said the police report stated you were shot a few blocks from the hospital. That an ambulance brought you in." Scott eyed him.

Jason's eyes narrowed as he began to type furiously on his laptop.

Frustration clawed at Mac's chest. He clenched his fists and released them a few times to stem the intensity of his emotions. "I heard what she said. But it's not true. I know where I was. I know where I was shot. Someone's covering it all up."

Jason nodded at him, clearly still puzzled. "What vehicle were you in?"

"My truck."

"The one out there?" He thrust his thumb toward the window.

"Yeah."

"Well, how did it get here?"

Jason's question wasn't unreasonable, but it set his gut to churning. "A nurse brought me my clothes and the keys before I was released from the hospital. That was four weeks after I was shot. She said the police or someone brought it to the hospital for me."

Scott shook his head. "The police don't have the time or the manpower to do that. And how did it get fixed if he shot you through the window? I don't see any bullet holes."

"I got a bill from a local body shop here. Paid it." The fact that he'd ended up in Fairbanks wasn't a stretch. It was the closest major city to Deadhorse—but they were still a great distance apart.

How his truck had made it here was a bigger mystery. He hadn't quite worked out that piece of the puzzle. But he would. At some point. Every bit of time and energy had gone into tracking the monster. Why he'd been in Deadhorse. Where he could be now. "Don't look at me like that. Frankly, I've been too busy trying to heal and tracking down the guy who shot me to follow up on it. This guy is good. Off the grid most of the time. But when he decides to come up for air, there are too many trails to follow to any conclusion." Mac could understand their doubt. He could. But they were his friends. His brothers. "I want to talk to the guy they *say* is the one who shot me." He could feel the muscle in his jaw twitching as he stiffened and did his best not to grind his teeth at the two guys who had once been the closest friends he'd had. Guys he trusted with his life.

Jason let out a low whistle as he leaned back. "That's gonna be a problem." Pointing at his screen, he grimaced. "He was released on a technicality, and according to the Fairbanks Police Department, he's disappeared."

"Now do you guys believe me?"

Jason and Scott stared at him, their expressions unreadable.

"Do you?" The bite in his tone was back.

Scott's gaze intensified as he leaned forward. "Let's face it, you've been obsessed with this guy for what—two and a half years?" He leveled a hand at him. "I doubt much energy has actually gone into your healing. You look terrible. But"—he placed his elbows on the table—"there's no doubt about those pictures and the guy they arrested here. It's no wonder you haven't been able to think of anything else."

"Scott's right. I think we need to go visit the body shop." Jason tapped the table.

"You didn't answer the question," Mac pressed.

"I believe you." Jason nodded. "But there are a lot of holes. We have no idea how you got here. How you survived the trip. Think about it, Mac. If it happened in Deadhorse, someone had to fly you here. You would have bled out otherwise. But according to the hospital records—and apparently, the police report—it happened only a few blocks from here. You've got to understand that we're just trying to help you figure this out."

"Seems to me"—Scott rubbed his forehead—"there's got to be someone who helped you. We just need to find them."

For the first time in more than two years, Mac felt a smidge of relief. The weight of this burden—hunting down the monster—had become heavier than he could handle. "I"—his voice cracked, and he cleared his throat—"I don't want to do this alone any longer."

✦ ✦ ✦

30 Fellow Members Remain
June 5—11:57 a.m.
Latitude: 61.302290° N, Longitude: 149.470746° W
Eagle River, Alaska

She started up the end-to-end encrypted video call and then waited for the rest of the Members to arrive in the waiting room.

One by one, the boxes filled her screen. None of the faces looked happy. She couldn't blame them.

Griz had gotten . . . out of hand. After two years, the majority had assumed he'd gone quietly into the night. Only a few believed he would once again long for the spotlight.

The latter were correct.

With two more of their own confirmed dead—and not by natural causes—it was time to deal with him. The question was . . . how?

The man had gone from being loyal to the cause to utter chaos. None of it made sense. Together they could have done so much more. Why couldn't he see that? Such a brilliant man. Quite handsome too.

She called the session to order and handed it over to the secretary to read the minutes from the last meeting.

A private message blipped on her screen. When Griz had gone rogue, they'd implemented new communications, new names, new procedures. Everyone was well aware of his hacking and cyber capabilities.

Abilities that should still be used for *their* cause.

From Z to M: They're all afraid.

She blinked a few times and pondered that.

From M to Z: And rightly so.
That's why he must be stopped.

From Z to M: I hate to voice the question,
but can we? Why not give the authorities
what they want?

With a shake of her head, she pinched her lips tightly together.

From M to Z: We want no link to
him. Our focus must stay sure to
the cause.

From Z to M: I can accomplish both.
Allow me to try?

Several seconds passed as the secretary's voice droned on with the specifics of their last meeting. If anyone in their midst had a chance . . . Before she could change her mind, she typed:

From M to Z: Permission granted. But
you must keep me apprised along the
way. That's the only way I will
allow it.

From Z to M: Yes, ma'am.

She leaned back against her seat. It was always good to have backup plans. No matter what, she had to anticipate Griz's moves well ahead of time.

Otherwise, none of them would survive.

✦　✦　✦

Eight Years, Three Days Sober
June 5—2:15 p.m.

Latitude: 64.83156° N, Longitude: 147.73836° W
Fairbanks Memorial Hospital

Tracie walked the halls of the hospital back to her office and glanced down at her watch. Two more hours and then she could head out for a run, eat some dinner, and veg out in front of the TV.

She needed a long run today. Mac's words this morning had stayed with her all day, and she couldn't shake them. Why was he so convinced he had been shot in Deadhorse? It didn't make sense.

Yeah, he'd been an absolute mess when they'd brought him in. He'd lost a lot of blood, and she hadn't been sure she'd be able to save him. When they'd brought him out of the coma, he'd said he didn't want to live. Begged people to just let him die.

That wasn't the real Mac though. That had been grief talking. She recognized it plain as day. Plus, she knew about his wife and daughter.

Over the months, she'd gotten to know the man. He was fierce, yes. Stubborn. Difficult to work with. A royal pain in her side.

But no liar.

She entered her office and sat in the chair as she pulled Mac's file to the top of the stack. What was it about this man that had her trying to find a way to . . . fix him?

A tap at the door brought her gaze up.

Courtney stepped in. "Dr. Hunter." The words held no warmth.

Tracie fought the trepidation in her stomach. "What's up? Please don't tell me there's another surgery—"

"No. It's not that. I just wanted to talk to you." She stood there with her arms folded around her middle, a scowl on her face.

Oh boy. Tracie should have expected this after their confrontation a couple of days ago. But she had hoped the corrective conversation with her surgical nurse had been enough. Apparently not. "All right." She set the file aside and folded her hands on her desk. "What do you need to talk about?"

Her nurse released a sigh. "Your obsession with your patients. It's over the top. None of us can keep up with that. I think it clouds your judgment. Like this morning. You refused to allow anyone else to take out Mr. McPherson's staples."

"I am not obsessed." She stood and steepled her fingers on the desktop. "Passionate about what I do, yes. But not obsessed. That's out of line."

"Is it?" Courtney stared her down. "You refuse to take advice from other surgeons when their opinion doesn't match yours—"

"Only when they see no hope."

"You refuse to take days off. You hover over your patients and hover over the rest of the staff to make sure we are doing what you instructed."

As much as she wanted to throw out a retort, Tracie didn't. She smashed her lips together in a thin line and waited for Courtney to finish.

"Your perfectionism is making it difficult for any of us to measure up. And I understand that we need to be as perfect and precise as we can be, but your expectations are . . . impossible." With a lift of her chin, Courtney stopped speaking and stared at her.

Irked was too tame for how Tracie felt. But it would be unprofessional to unleash on the young woman. "I'm a great surgeon. I pour my heart and soul into my patients. There's nothing wrong with that."

Her nurse rolled her eyes. "You are completely missing the point."

"Exactly what *is* your point, Courtney? To let me know your displeasure in how I do things? To reprimand me for caring too much for my patients? Or is it that you just don't like me—is that it?"

The young nurse huffed. "If you're not willing to listen to objective criticism, then I can't work with you."

The thought of training another nurse in how she liked to do things was not a pleasant one. "Let's talk about this."

"No." Courtney shook her head. "You know, I'm done talking. I'm going to ask to be reassigned."

Rather than say something she would regret later, Tracie kept her mouth shut.

"Just like I thought. You can't take it for anyone to have an opinion other than your own high-and-mighty one. I don't have to work in an environment like this." She stormed out.

Great. Another stellar day.

Tracie refused to apologize for being passionate about her patients and her work.

But she was *not* obsessed.

✦ ✦ ✦

86 Days Until Final Judgment
29 Members Left
June 7—6:22 a.m.
Latitude: 64.84746° N, Longitude: 147.71425° W
Griffin Park—Fairbanks

Griz popped a pill into his mouth as he walked the trail and found a bench. What a beautiful morning.

The perfect morning to celebrate. Three hindrances were out of the way. He picked a small piece of lint off his forearm. Good riddance.

It was time to get the ball really rolling. If they didn't know already, the Members soon would.

He was alive and well and ready to deal the deck.

Every bit of the plan was laid out, with contingencies for every possible situation and outcome.

There was no way to stop him.

No one was even capable of *trying.*

The Members—and not just one or two—would be in pursuit. But not for long. He laughed out loud at the thought.

He glanced down at his phone and reread the message he'd received last night.

We know who you are, Griz.
Don't forget that. These games
you're playing are ridiculous.
Perhaps you should clear your
mind and remember the power
we wield. You don't want us as
enemies.

Oh, but he did. They didn't understand. They never would.

"They're not games," he whispered to his phone. "And you'd best understand that right now. I have no qualms about killing every last one of you."

He knew they had someone tracking him. Knew they'd sent someone to Deadhorse, where his small compound was located. He would have no problem getting rid of the guy—whoever he was.

It wasn't a coincidence that their numbers were dropping. Surely they knew that. Was this a last-ditch effort to show their bravado? To show their strength in numbers?

It was ludicrous. They saw what the world had become.

The news of late was flooded with the world dividing itself left and right. Social media was filled with vitriol. People were focused on upcoming elections. One in the US. One in Europe. Which made the timing even more perfect.

Everyone's attention was focused on getting their opinions heard. Shouting louder than their opponent. And it didn't hurt that they all hated one another.

Yes, he'd made the right decision.

Griz popped another pill. Leading people from a government position was stupid. There would never be power in that realm ever again. Not even if some demigod from outer space decided he wanted to rule the planet. He chuckled. Those old movies sure did make him laugh.

The only thing that truly brought people to their knees was fear.

He'd made enough money for ten lifetimes forcing people to cough up a ransom for their precious devices.

He had the resources to do whatever he wanted.

Yes, it was a beautiful morning indeed.

Lots of lovely people out and about.

People who would never know what hit them or where the attack came from.

His grin widened. Time for another distraction.

Now, let's see. Who. Should. I. Choose?

The woman pushing the jogging stroller?

Or how about the older couple out walking, holding hands, moving slower than molasses?

There were plenty of joggers. All ignoring one another, their earbuds tuning out the world.

A man jogged up the path next to him.

Now there was a determined stride. No earbuds or accoutrements of any kind.

The man glanced his way. His eyes widened. Fury filled his eyes, and he headed straight for Griz.

What was this? Entertaining, for sure.

The man reached him, grabbed his collar, and yanked him to his feet. "You!"

CHAPTER THREE

909 Days After
June 7—6:28 a.m.
Latitude: 64.84746° N, Longitude: 147.71425° W
Griffin Park

NEVER IN HIS LIFE HAD Mac felt this much rage. Never.

"You!" He gripped the man's collar, growling out the word again. It would be so easy to snuff the man's life out. Right here. Right now. Mac was no killer, but he could do it. Years of pent-up rage radiated out of his fingers as his grip tightened.

This wasn't a man anyway. It was a monster.

But the man only studied him. "Yes. It's me. And you are?"

Like a lightning bolt had zapped him, Mac released the monster and stepped back a few inches. "Who am I? *Who am I?* You killed my wife and daughter with your explosion at the pipeline. Then you taunted me. Then you shot me!"

The man only blinked and straightened his jacket. Flicked off a piece of lint. Like none of it mattered. "Oh. Well. I've shot a lot of people. You'll have to forgive me." Then he grinned.

Grinned. The gall of the guy.

Rage bubbled up like a volcano ready to explode. Mac grabbed him again. "How dare you act like their lives didn't matter. *You* don't matter." The criminal's profile rushed through his mind. This guy thrived on attention and power. "You're a peon. Nothing! And I'm going to squash you like—"

"Is there a problem here?"

The stern voice yanked Mac's attention away.

A Fairbanks police cruiser was on the road adjacent to the jogging trail. An officer in the passenger seat had his window rolled down with his elbow on the doorframe.

Mac frowned at the officer. If they knew who he held in his grasp, they'd help him string the guy up the nearest tree.

"*Is* there a problem?" The monster spoke, his voice calm. Almost tranquil.

Rage blurred Mac's vision. His jaw ached with how tight he had it clenched.

The man's grin was wide as he stared at Mac, an expression of false innocence dramatically portrayed.

"Sir!" The officer shouted this time. "Do we have a problem?" A car door slammed, a sure sign the officer was headed Mac's way.

As much as he wanted this guy hauled away in handcuffs, Mac realized he had no proof. No reason for the man in his grasp to even be arrested. "This isn't over." Mac spat the words, then released the monster. He whipped out his iPhone and snapped a picture.

"Oh, it's not. It's only just begun." The monster's eyes narrowed at him, and then he waved at the officer. "Just having a little fun, sir. We won't take up any more of your time." He backed away.

Mac's only choice was to watch. He turned, and the police cruiser was still there.

The officer driving studied him, gaze intense, while the other officer climbed back into the vehicle. Mac nodded at the man, but it couldn't change the fact that *he'd* been the one doing the assaulting when they'd driven up. If he tried to tell the officers now what he knew . . . they wouldn't believe him. And what proof did he have? His own friends had a hard time believing him.

He looked back to see if that man was still around, but the sidewalk was empty. The tension in the air that had sizzled like electricity when the monster had been in his grasp dissipated, taking all his energy with it. That man had taken away everything Mac held dear. He'd taken countless lives. And he was walking around carefree, ready to destroy someone else's life.

The cruiser slowly rolled away.

The fact the killer had been in his grasp made his hands tremble. The monster hadn't recognized Mac. Which only proved even more that the man was a deranged psychopath.

Mac released a breath, unaware that he'd been holding it ever since he'd let go of the killer. It wasn't fair that the monster could roam free without a care in the world. Not caring about all the lives he'd ruined.

All while Mac's focus had been on one man for more than two years.

The world crashed in around him.

Nothing felt right. Not the air. The sounds. His insides.

He turned in the direction of his apartment complex and forced his feet into a jog, doing his best to stop the swell of emotion. But it didn't work. The faster he pushed his feet, the more the swells grew and threatened to drown him in the crashing waves.

By the time he reached his tiny apartment, his heart was beating way too fast. His lungs ached, and he couldn't catch his breath. His eyes burned.

Unlocking the door, he panicked and gasped for air. He kicked the door closed and leaned against it, feeling weak in the knees. "Get it together, Mac." With his jaw clenched, he closed his eyes.

Nothing felt right.

Nothing.

"You're losing it, dude." The lack of oxygen made his brain swim.

This was more than losing it. Tiny fingers of fear pricked his conscience.

What was going on?

This was more than anything he'd ever felt, even after the loss of Sarah and Beth.

The realization was like a sucker punch, and he bent over his knees and forced his lungs to pull in air. But even as the air made its way into his lungs, the rest of his body revolted.

What was happening to him?

Heat pulsed through his face and limbs until he wanted to shred every piece of clothing. But it wouldn't stop. It just kept rising.

The intense anger in him made him want to smash something. To yell as loud as he could. To hurt the man who did this.

More than hurt. Torture. Inflict as much pain as possible.

His vision blurred, and he closed his eyes. His heart clenched in his chest.

When he opened his eyes again, spots danced before them, and he fell to his knees. He grabbed his water bottle off the side table and dumped water over his head.

But it couldn't quench the fire that raged.

He attempted to blow out and relieve the pressure building inside him, but his lungs wouldn't release their steel grip.

God . . . help!

Everything went dark, and he collapsed face-first into the carpet.

Then, from somewhere deep, *deep* inside him, the sobs took over. He sputtered and choked as the tears welled up and he sucked in great gasps of air.

Pounding the floor with a fist, he screamed his pain into the carpet until he was hoarse and spent.

Face smashed into the floor, Mac pulled out his phone and dialed Scott. His arm felt like it weighed five hundred pounds.

"Hey, man, what's up?"

"Please . . . help . . ." He croaked the words. "I saw him." Everything hurt. His throat burned. "He's here. In Fairbanks. I can't let him kill any . . . more . . ." He dropped the phone as his chest clenched again, and he gritted his teeth against the pain. A groan escaped.

Scott's voice sounded far away. "Hang on, Mac! We're coming!" Too. Far. Away. They'd never reach him in time.

✦ ✦ ✦

Eight Years, Five Days Sober
June 7—11:04 a.m.
Latitude: 64.83156° N, Longitude: 147.73836° W
Fairbanks Memorial Hospital

Opening the door to Mac's room, Tracie surged in, with Dr. Magnus behind her. She spoke over her shoulder. "Be prepared for an escape attempt."

The seasoned cardiologist chuckled.

The man she'd operated on five times lay on the bed, huge black circles under his eyes. His skin was pale, with a sheen of sweat visible under the unforgiving fluorescent lights. But more than that, his nostrils were flared and he was huffing like a bull with a matador's red flag in his sights.

"Hey, Doc, what's the word?" Jason met her at the end of Mac's bed.

Dr. Magnus peered at the monitor's display beside the bed. "The good news"—he tilted his head to one side and looked at Mac— "is your heart appears to be fine. Dr. Hunter was wise to check it with the symptoms your friends explained and your history this past year." The older doctor shoved his hands into the pockets of his white coat. "The other news, I will let Dr. Hunter explain. But allow me to say one thing."

"Go on." Mac didn't appear to care one way or the other about what the doctor might share.

"You need rest, and lots of it. From your chart and what Dr. Hunter has shared, I can honestly say that if you keep this up, you'll find yourself in an early grave." With that, the cardiologist left the room.

Tracie resisted the *I told you so* perched on her tongue as her gaze locked with Mac's. It was good of Dr. Magnus to come, even when she could have conveyed the results herself. But Mac needed to hear the severity of his condition from someone other than her. Whether he would listen was another matter. At least Mac's friends would know the truth and that she'd been thorough.

This time Scott moved forward. "So that means . . ."

She clasped her hands in front of her white coat and raised her eyebrows. "Mac . . . it appears you've had a massive panic attack."

The big guy shifted his legs over the side of the bed. "See? I'm fine."

Jason shoved him back, keeping a firm hand on his friend's shoulder. "She's not finished."

It was so tempting to laugh, but she refrained. Having backup to deal with him was nice. "Jason's correct. The health app on your smartwatch showed just how intense this attack was. Under the circumstances, it's completely understandable."

Mac's gaze snapped back and forth between his friends. "You told her?"

"Of course we did." Scott walked up to the other side of Mac's bed and grabbed the blanket draped over the bed rail, throwing it over Mac's legs.

The man looked too stunned to notice the gesture. "Everything?"

Scott stepped back and shrugged. "Most."

She felt a tad bit guilty at the look on Mac's face. But she needed to calm him, not enrage him further and send him into another attack. "I'm not interested in invading your privacy. But I needed to know what went on."

He grunted at her.

This time she didn't keep the smile off her face. *Go ahead and grunt, big guy. You don't scare me.* He wasn't going to win today.

"The good thing is, it wasn't a heart attack or angina. My first thought was pulmonary embolism, but it wasn't that either. I don't see any clots anywhere. That's good news. Especially with all the scar tissue around your lung."

He stayed silent.

Tracie resisted the urge to roll her eyes at his pouting. "But you've put your body through an immense amount of stress. Couple that with the fact that you saw your wife and daughter's killer, and your body decided it was taking charge and put you in a tailspin. Running an all-out sprint back to your apartment after you saw the guy wasn't smart."

"How'd you know?"

She lifted her wrist and pointed to her own smartwatch. "Technology."

Mac sat forward in the bed, his gaze intent on her face.

She recognized the look as one of intimidation. He should know by now his glowering stares didn't work on her. But she would hear him out.

"Look. I'm fine. Yeah, it was intense. But I'm fine now."

Scott shook his head. "I don't think you are."

"Me neither," Jason chimed in.

"Come on!" Mac slapped the bed with his hand.

For a second Tracie wanted to take pity on the man. But only for a second. "You simply need rest. That's it. Rest for your body, yeah, but also for your mind and heart. Panic attacks aren't anything to be toyed with."

"I did *not* have a panic attack."

It was her turn to move in closer. She'd been dealing with this guy for months. She'd come to care about him. Just like all her patients. "Look, I'm not about to allow you to ruin all my good work getting you back into tip-top shape after some lunatic shot you. Don't sabotage yourself, Mac. Admit the fact that what you went through this morning was intense. God designed our bodies to do amazing things, but they can only take so much."

He looked down at the thin blanket covering him. He clenched and unclenched his jaw. "I was angry. Angrier than I've ever been. So I ran faster than I have in a while and cranked my heart up too far. My lungs simply hurt from the exertion."

She could tell from the look on his face that she'd pushed too hard. He wasn't going to admit anything now. His pride was battered. That hadn't been her intention. But how did she help him see that he would do his body and mind serious harm if he didn't make some changes immediately?

She put a hand on his shoulder. "I understand that. I wouldn't have wanted to run into you after that altercation. I can only imagine what you must have felt. I've got quite a temper, but I've never had to deal with something of that magnitude." *Please help me help him, Lord.* Inhaling through her nose, Tracie released the breath slowly before gentling her voice. "You are here though. Scott and Jason brought you in after they found you unconscious on your floor."

"In a puddle of drool," Jason tossed out.

Mac at least laughed at that.

She continued, determined he would hear the facts of how bad this attack had been. Even if he wouldn't actually *listen.* "You can't ignore the fact that your body underwent a great deal of stress in a short period of time today. Your lungs are still not one hundred percent, even though you sure did push them to their limits." Oh boy, he wasn't going to like the next part. "And because of your surgical history, I'm going to keep you overnight for observation."

"What!" His yell surely echoed out into the hall.

She held up a hand. "If you behave yourself and we don't see any other adverse effects from this . . . *event,* then I will see to it that you are released first thing tomorrow morning."

His chin lifted in defiance. "I don't want to stay."

"Too bad. I didn't give you a choice." Two could play this game.

Jason settled back into the chair. "Good thing we came prepared." He patted a backpack beside him. "We're staying too."

Mac groaned and leaned his head back, covering his forehead with his arm. "Don't you guys have wives to annoy?"

"Give it a rest, Mac." Scott chuckled. "We're here, and you can't get rid of us."

Tracie nodded at the guys. "Good. I'll be back in a few hours to check on your progress." She gave Mac one final glare. "Don't even think about detaching any of those wires either. I need to keep an eye on everything. And you wouldn't want to prolong your stay, now would you?"

As she walked out of the room, she heard Scott and Jason telling Mac that even though he had to rest, they could make the best use of the time.

She pulled the door shut. It must be really nice to have people like that in your life.

Once upon a time, she'd had that too. Her throat tightened with the sudden burn of tears.

Oh, she had a nice community up here. Plenty of people here at the hospital. And she was on good terms with a few people from church. She winced. Not that she'd been to church in a while.

Still, she couldn't say she was all that close to anyone. The most interaction she had was with patients and nurses. She frowned, remembering the conversation with Courtney. Now she would have to find a new surgical nurse. Not a pleasant thought.

Pressing her lips together, Tracie kept her head down and nearly ran to her office. Most of her prayers today had been about filling Courtney's position. Maybe she should ask for a friend while she was at it.

That wasn't asking for too much, was it?

✦ ✦ ✦

86 Days Until Final Judgment
29 Members Left
June 7—4:21 p.m.
Latitude: 64.83156° N, Longitude: 147.73836° W
Fairbanks Memorial Hospital

He'd wanted a target, and he'd found one. Griz watched the doctor walk out of the hospital as he popped a pill into his mouth.

David McPherson's surgeon. The woman who'd saved his life. More than once.

It hadn't taken much to get the necessary records. He *was* on the hospital board, after all. Under a different name of course. Sure, he could have hacked the records. But this was more fun. Interacting with people without their knowing he held their lives in the palm of his hand.

The thrill never got old. He took a swig of water from his water bottle. The records still couldn't explain how the man he'd shot up in Deadhorse had managed to be treated in Fairbanks. Something he'd have to investigate.

Mr. McPherson hated him. That much was certain. Enough to follow him all the way to the North Slope.

Another fact that came into play . . . The Members hadn't sent McPherson after him. He'd been on his own mission for revenge. Or justice. Or whatever he wanted to call it. Which meant Griz still had at least one more tail that needed eliminating.

He shook his head. That could be dealt with at a later date. Right now he'd found himself an adversary up to the challenge. For the first time in a while.

The fire in the man's eyes had been intense. Exactly what Griz loved to see. So he'd done a little digging.

Mr. McPherson—or Mac, as his friends called him—was the man behind Cyber Solutions. That sad little company that had done their best—*twice*—to stop him.

Oh, they'd tried.

And failed.

But he was wise to them and their tricks.

Now Mac had led him to Dr. Tracie Hunter. Failed medical examiner. Recovering alcoholic. There was just too much fun to be had here. Even more fun than eliminating the Members one by one.

He watched the doctor as she jogged to her car and then back to the building. Interesting. So she parked on the other side of the parking lot? To what purpose? Was she a health nut? Or did she give up her spot for someone else?

Oh, this was too good. She was one of those, huh? Always paying penance for her past mistakes. It made him chuckle.

She was *perfect.*

He'd found the right target for the next distraction.

After watching and studying her for a few weeks, he'd pounce. Already he could see that she was a creature of habit. Someone who enjoyed bringing order out of chaos. Just like him. He needed to find every little behavior, nuance, and ritual.

Once he documented all of it, he could put the next step into play.

Pulling up his favorite illegal search engine, he went to work. Within minutes he knew a lot about Tracie Hunter.

Wait. What was this? He clicked on a link.

He'd struck gold, and he hadn't even been looking for it.

This was going to be even better than he'd thought. And would keep McPherson and his friends busy for a while.

He exhaled, feeling his mind lock into laser focus.

Let the games begin.

CHAPTER FOUR

909 Days After
June 7—5:16 p.m.
Latitude: 64.83156° N, Longitude: 147.73836° W
Fairbanks Memorial Hospital

THAT GRIN.

It haunted Mac.

What he wouldn't pay to wipe it off the guy's face. How dare he act like taking lives didn't matter? Like Sarah's and Beth's lives didn't matter. His jaw clenched. His body teemed with anger.

People like that monster needed to be locked up for life. No parole. Ever. No benefits for good behavior. Just throw away the key.

It wasn't forgiving or Christlike, but he couldn't help the way he felt toward that murderous wretch of a man.

Mac tried to shake the thoughts away. The more he worked up his mind, the more exhaustion overcame him.

Scott was channel surfing. Jason had made another run for food.

They'd hashed and rehashed every detail of what they knew since the 26 Below attack started.

Instead of the energy Mac usually felt putting pieces together and trying to get his friends to see what he did, the whole exercise had worn him out. As much as he hated to admit it, this morning had done a number on him.

He closed his eyes and forced his limbs to relax. One breath in through the nose. He counted to four and slowly let the air out through pursed lips. Sleep clouded the edge of his mind. *Finally.* It would be nice to ignore the world for a few hours.

His hands held the collar of the man he hated most. The man who had killed his wife and daughter. The man who took lives without a single thought. The man was evil.

With dark-brown eyes that were almost black in the bright sunshine, the man studied him. Like a predator after his prey.

Mac wasn't about to become another victim. He wouldn't allow anyone else to be hurt by this monster. He couldn't allow anyone else to be sacrificed.

He couldn't. So he squeezed for all he was worth. The man didn't even flinch. All he did was laugh.

And grin.

"Mac! *Mac!*" Scott's voice screamed in his ear, accompanying the crazy beeping sound.

Strong hands held his shoulders down. They pushed. Hard.

What was happening?

He couldn't open his eyes. He wanted to shout to whomever was there to let him go. He had to stop the murderer.

A cacophony overloaded his eardrums. Lots of people. Several poking and prodding him.

"Mac? Can you hear me?" That was Dr. Hunter's voice. "If you can hear me, squeeze my hand."

She was holding his hand? He didn't even realize it. Then he squeezed.

Something around his other arm tightened. That stupid blood pressure cuff. He wanted to yank it off. But his whole body felt like lead. Like he weighed several tons and was just sinking into the bed.

"Mac. You've got to calm down." The doctor's voice softened. "I know there's a lot going on around you, but we're trying to help. Please. Relax."

Something in the way she said it made him realize how every muscle in his body felt like it was stretched and strained to capacity.

"Breathe, Mac." Her breath was on the side of his face.

He battled against the tension in him and took a long breath.

"Good." She pressed something against his chest. "Keep breathing."

He tried, but in his mind, all he could see was his nemesis. Desperation clawed at his chest, straining his muscles. He had to end this. His lungs burned, and his heart pumped frantically.

"Mac, if you don't calm down, you're going to end up having a heart attack. Do you hear me?" Gone was the soft and soothing voice of Dr. Hunter.

He squeezed her hand. He heard her. But he didn't know how to make it stop. *God, help!*

The next few seconds passed with the beeps and squeals and whatever machines they'd brought into his room.

"His blood pressure is still rising." A bland male voice he didn't recognize. "Two eighteen over one thirty-five. He's hypertensive. Could stroke out."

Mac sensed movement close to his right side. Why were his eyelids so heavy? His body felt like it was stuck in quicksand.

"You listen to me right now, Mac." The doctor spoke into his ear, her tone firm. "You need to breathe and calm down. Long, deep breaths. All right? Let's do it together. Breathe in."

He forced his body to obey.

"Good. Now a long, slow exhale."

Sarah's and Beth's faces replaced the monster's in his mind. They were smiling.

"Come on, Mac. Focus. Breathe. You can do this."

The frenetic beeping around him faded as he cried out to the Lord. *God, I can't do this anymore. I can't.*

"Breathe in . . ."

I miss them so much. It hurts. Every single day. And then to see . . . him? I can't take it.

"Breathe out . . ."

"My grace is sufficient for you, for power is perfected in weakness."

The all too familiar passage struck him hard. Paul, too, had been afflicted by a thorn in his side. The Bible didn't say what it was, but it had to be pretty awful for Paul to beg three times for it to be taken. Mac inhaled and pressed the breath out again.

"Good job, Mac. Keep at it." Dr. Hunter's voice broke through his thoughts.

His mind wandered back to after he'd been shot. A nurse had prayed for him after he told her to just let him die. She was a tiny thing but quite a spitfire. She hadn't backed away in fear, like so many others. She'd stayed and talked to him. Prayed for him. Told him that God obviously wasn't finished with him yet if he was still here.

I want revenge, God.

The admission broke him. His body shook and his eyes burned.

He's in my mind all the time. Take this rage and grief away . . . please.

The plea in his prayer was so intense, he felt it in his gut. Like a deep groaning clawing its way through his insides.

The beeping around him intensified while the voices faded in the strident, high-pitched screams of the machines. With his eyes closed tight, he could see his wife's and daughter's graves. He squeezed his eyelids against the stabbing pain the image caused.

"Breathe, Mac."

With a sharp inhale, the picture cleared, and he was sitting on the front pew of his childhood church. Elbows on his knees, Mac stared at the floor. The doc who'd saved his life kept speaking into his ear. Low and calm.

He lifted his face to the familiar scene. The place where he'd given his life over to God. Why did he keep snatching it back?

I can't do this anymore. But for some reason that I don't understand, You still want me here. Why?

He pushed the question aside. He knew what he had to do.

Take it, God. Please take it from me. Forgive me for my hateful thoughts . . . You're going to have to change my heart and mind.

The church disappeared, and the voices around him penetrated the fog. Jason. Scott. Dr. Hunter. The bland male voice rattling off numbers. The weight that seemed to press him into the bed began to release.

"You're doing good, Mac. Keep breathing. Nice and deep. Whatever is causing this tension, you have to let it go."

Let it go.

An overused phrase if ever there was one.

"Don't make me sing the song, buddy." Jason's voice came from his left side. "'Cause you know I will, and you know I stink at singing."

He wanted to laugh, but his chest felt too heavy. His lips turned up though.

"Look at that." A loud thump. "I think he's laughing at the idea of your singing." Scott's voice was near Mac's feet.

All right, God. You're in control. Don't let me yank it back. Change my heart, Lord. I'll get the guys to help me . . . to hold me accountable. I can't do this anymore. Just please . . . take it. But please . . . that man needs to be stopped. Please.

"Another deep breath . . ."

Was the good doctor going to talk him through his breathing for the rest of the day? Comfort flooded him as he took the next breath. He wasn't alone.

The vise grip in his chest released. Then his muscles loosened. The long breaths came easier now.

When the band on his left arm tightened again, he could feel the collected breaths being held.

"It's coming down." The male voice held a hint of excitement this time. "One eighty over ninety."

"Okay. You're doing great, Mac. But we're not out of the woods yet. Long, slow, deep breaths." A pat on his right shoulder. The doc continued to encourage him, even doing the exercises with him.

After at least a hundred breaths and more pleading with God, Mac felt lighter. The weight pressing down on him had completely released, and he forced his heavy eyelids to open. With a hazy glance around the room, he saw Jason and Scott standing by the bed, along with a male nurse on his left and Doc Hunter on his right.

The room was quiet.

The doctor released a long sigh. Her hand squeezed his before letting it go. "Don't you go scaring me like that again, big guy."

✦ ✦ ✦

Eight Years, Five Days Sober
June 7—6:42 p.m.
Latitude: 64.83156° N, Longitude: 147.73836° W
Fairbanks Memorial Hospital

Was she obsessed?

Tracie walked toward the cafeteria and realized her stomach couldn't handle any food. She stopped and put a hand to her middle. What she really wanted was a drink.

She paused. That was the second time in a week the urge had bubbled to the surface. An urge she hadn't struggled with in a long time. Why now?

Why did she feel like she was losing control?

Three times today she'd thought for sure she was going to lose a patient. Three times she'd fought tooth and nail to make sure she didn't.

Redirecting her stride, she headed back toward her office. Between stubborn Mac and opinionated Courtney, her mind wouldn't stop spinning. Tracie rubbed her forehead, willing away the oncoming headache. She probably needed to listen to her own advice to Mac. She needed to rest.

Mac. She shook her head, the rush of adrenaline and fear still lingering. Her patient's blood pressure had skyrocketed and had wreaked havoc on his system. She'd never seen anyone get that high without stroking out. But thankfully, the Lord had heard her prayers and stepped in. Perhaps she needed to speak with Mac about some rehab other than physical. But at least his friends were here with him.

Praying for him. Keeping an eye on him. That kept her from camping out near his room.

Yeah, okay. Maybe she was a tad obsessed. With keeping people alive. Taking care of her patients. Doing the very best she could do.

Then there was the fact that her nurse had been talking behind her back. That was more than a little disturbing. Especially for Courtney to just up and quit without any notice. What had happened to the work ethic in this country?

It used to be that a surgeon found their surgical nurse and they worked together for years.

Tracie had been through five. In two years. What did that say about her? *Was* she the problem? None of her other nurses had ever said anything. Most had moved away—either because their husbands were active military or they were tired of the Fairbanks winters.

But it did make her examine herself.

"Dr. Hunter, may I speak with you?" Sherry headed her direction. It was clear from her tense shoulders and reluctance to meet Tracie's gaze that she was nervous.

"Of course." This better not be another nurse telling her how obsessed she was. The pain in her head was sneaking into her shoulders. *Help me, Lord.* She glanced down the length of the hallway. Empty for now. Hopefully Sherry would be brief.

The blond nurse scrunched up her nose and winced. "I haven't had a chance to apologize for what you overheard the other day."

A tinge of relief helped Tracie relax. "I understand you weren't the disgruntled one."

"But I was still there. Listening. And that was wrong." Sherry twisted her fingers together, finally looking Tracie in the eye. "I'm not good at being up front with people when they start to gossip. I've always had a problem with it. People think I'm a participant because I'm a good listener, and that's not who I want to be." She cleared her throat. "The participant, that is. I don't mind being a good listener."

The younger woman's discomfort radiated off her in waves. Tracie placed a hand on the nurse's forearm, hoping her sincerity would ring true in her tone. "Sherry, you have been a terrific nurse and an outstanding part of my department. Don't ever doubt that. I appreciate what you've said, and I understand how hard it is to be put in those kinds of situations. You and I will both have to work on things, won't we?"

The young woman's shoulders visibly eased. "Thank you, Dr. Hunter. I really do enjoy working with you. And I'm sorry. Again."

"It's all right. I appreciate your coming to me."

Sherry nodded and began to walk away, but Tracie caught her arm. "May I ask you something and hopefully not put you in an awkward position?"

"Anytime." Her head bobbed up and down.

How should Tracie put this? "Have any other nurses or any other staff had the same complaint as Courtney did about me?"

A deep V formed in Sherry's forehead. "Never. The rest of us really appreciate how much time and effort you put into your patients. You are a good example to all of us. The reminder that this isn't just a job to get through, no matter how bad our day has been. Every patient is a human being in need of the best care we can give them. They have families and friends who love them. We should care as much as we would if they were our own loved ones."

Tracie gave her a slow nod. That was encouraging to hear. "Thank you. Not that I was seeking praise, but if I needed to work on an area, it's best to know. We all have our blind spots."

"That's true. But I have not heard anyone else say anything like Courtney did." Sherry fiddled with a pen in her pocket. "I will say, many nurses appreciate that you aren't afraid to get in there and do whatever needs to be done. Whether it's learning a new technique or helping out with one of the nurses or taking out a patient's staples. You go above and beyond. You don't act like you're better than anyone else. We notice that."

Heat filled Tracie's cheeks. "Well, I appreciate the encouragement. Thank you."

The small portable phone in Sherry's pocket went off, and she pulled it out, glancing at the screen. "I've got to take this. Duty calls." Sherry waved and was off.

Maybe it was just Courtney after all. How sad that one person could be so unhappy.

But still . . . the *obsessed* accusation hit a little too close to home. Sure, she had some obsessive tendencies. She liked things a certain way. Was specific about procedures. And yes, she pushed for every single patient. It was important for her to do her very best.

Except when she failed. The little doubt niggled at the back of her mind.

That had always been her mantra, to do everything to the best of her ability so that she could bring God glory. And after what had happened all those years ago, she'd become even more passionate about it.

Yes, she wanted to honor her Lord.

But she also couldn't stand to fail.

Not again.

She hadn't lost a patient in several years. Which was unheard of. But her hospital administrator said it was because of her tenacious nature.

Which was *partly* true. She refused to give up.

But God was the Great Physician. She relied on Him, didn't she?

If her tenaciousness helped to keep people alive, then good. If her obsessive personality helped make sure she kept her promises, right on. And if she had to lose a gossipy surgical nurse because of how she did things, oh well.

But even after the little pep talk, she didn't feel any better. This restlessness was making her feel . . . unsettled.

So she took the long way back to her office and ventured toward some of her patients' rooms.

Something was really off with her lately. And she couldn't put her finger on it.

It wasn't just the nightmare coming back. Maybe it was because she hadn't been to church in several weeks, because of her schedule.

Well, not her mandated schedule. The schedule she *chose* because she wanted to check on all her patients. She frowned at the thought.

Okay. Maybe there were hints she was a little obsessed.

She stopped outside a patient's door and shook her head. Without even thinking about it, her feet had brought her straight back to Mac's room. The man was a conundrum. Not that she could blame him for wanting to find the man who'd killed his wife and daughter, but he had pushed his body to the limits. She'd never seen anything like it. And now she needed to help him heal again. But how? She was in uncharted territory.

Lifting her chin, she stared at the door. She was a good doctor. People depended on her every day to make them feel better. How could she do that without exercising some control?

Enough! Tracie shoved the thoughts aside. There were patients who needed her help. With a deep breath, she knocked and pushed the door open. "How are you feeling?"

✦ ✦ ✦

28 Fellow Members Remain
June 7—10:15 p.m.
Latitude: 61.302290° N, Longitude: 149.470746° W
Eagle River

> From M to Z: Two more confirmed dead?
> You're certain?

Not the news she'd wanted to hear this evening. The sun still shone through the slats of her wooden blinds as she shifted her gaze to the window.

Her computer dinged and brought her attention back to the screen.

> From Z to M: Yes, ma'am.
> As of fifteen minutes ago.

A frustrated groan escaped her.

> From M to Z: Unacceptable.
> You said you could handle this.

> From Z to M: These things take time.
> I need a few more days.

> From M to Z: You've got 48 hours.
> That's it.

The cursor on the screen blinked. No response. She tapped her fingers on the desk. What was he up to? Not having an inkling of what he had planned made her skin crawl.

Still no response. She grunted at the computer and poured herself another cup of tea from the pot on its warmer.

The little dots wiggled on the screen, showing that he was typing a reply. About time.

> From Z to M: Good evening. I'm sorry to
> say, your little assistant here won't be
> able to help you any longer. He's dead. Go
> ahead. Drink that cup of tea. You're going
> to need it.

Heat rushed through her. She disconnected and shut the computer system down. How was he always a step ahead?

CHAPTER FIVE

910 Days After
June 8—9:09 a.m.
Latitude: 64.83156° N, Longitude: 147.73836° W
Fairbanks Memorial Hospital

MAC SAT ON THE EDGE of the hospital bed, unencumbered by wires or anything else. He stared at the floor.

As soon as the guys came back, he would do it.

The Lord had done a number on his heart throughout the night. Not just the physical muscle. He had shown Mac all the ways he'd taken matters into his own hands for the last couple years. And it had to stop.

The only way to do that was to ask for accountability.

For the first time in a long time, he felt more at peace.

The ache of losing his family was still there. That would probably never go away, but the rage that had him constantly thinking of revenge was gone.

Only God could do that.

"Look who's up!" Jason made it into the room first, carrying a tray full of coffee and bags of something that smelled so good it made Mac's stomach rumble.

Scott followed Jason, holding two more paper bags. "Smells good, huh?"

Mac nodded. "Whatever it is. It's making my mouth water." But he held up a hand. "Before you guys dig into the food, I've got something to say."

Jason set the tray on the hospital's large overbed table and took a seat. "Sounds serious. Did the doc come back?"

"A nurse came in and ran her checks. My heart is fine, and my blood pressure is back to normal."

"Well, that's a miracle." Scott set his bags down and sat as well.

"Yeah, pretty sure God isn't finished with me yet." Mac swiped a hand down his face. "But I can't do this alone. I've been trying for more than two years, and it's obviously not working."

The guys nodded and kept their eyes fixed on him.

He shifted on the bed, embarrassment and shame warring with the determination to be honest. But he needed to be vulnerable. To stop locking everything and everyone out. "I need accountability. More than I've ever needed it before. I can't do anything alone. God knows I've tried. And my heart and mind have been filled with revenge. That has to go too. I know I'm going to struggle. I know we've got to do something to stop this guy, but you can't let me go back down that road. It wasn't pretty."

Jason stood and clapped his shoulder. "We're here."

"You can count on us." Scott gave him a smile.

"I know I can. But I had to admit it out loud. You needed to hear me say what I'm struggling with." Mac looked both men in the eye, hoping they could hear the sincerity in his voice. "And you need to hold my feet to the fire when I'm slacking. Or smack me upside the head. Whatever needs to be done."

"You got it." Jason grinned. "I'll take the smacking-you-upside-the-head part. That sounds enjoyable."

The laughter helped with the weight of the moment, but Mac was convicted to go on. "It seems I've stressed my body out. When my blood pressure went nuts yesterday? I was dreaming that I had my hands around the guy's throat and was squeezing as hard as I could. Because I didn't believe there should be any second chances. I wanted him gone. Plain and simple, I was willing to kill him."

Scott leaned forward and placed his elbows on his knees. "What happened? In your dream?"

Mac shook his head. "Nothing. He wouldn't die. Just kept grinning at me. Like he did when I saw him in the park."

"Yeah, I think we need to make sure that you don't have the opportunity to put your hands around the guy's neck again." Scott stood and opened the bags. "Glad you told us. But you should know that Jason and I have already decided we won't be leaving your side until we see this through. We'll either both be here or trade off—whatever it takes. No matter how long."

"What do Carrie and Darcie have to say about that?" Mac's heart pinched when he thought about the guys' wives.

"They're the ones who encouraged us to come in the first place." Jason handed out food. "They're invested in this too and want the guy caught for good. But more importantly, they care about you, Mac."

He dipped his chin in a nod and stared at the foot of the bed for several moments. "Sarah wouldn't want me obsessing over the guy. But she would want us to catch him—so that no one else can be hurt."

Scott's and Jason's phones both buzzed at the same time. When Scott pulled his phone out and read the screen, his shoulders slumped. "Looks like he's finally decided to come out of his little hidey-hole. The Juneau office just sent this." He held up his screen so Mac could read it.

Juneau's water system had been hacked and was undrinkable.

✦ ✦ ✦

85 Days Until Final Judgment
27 Members Left
June 8—11:23 a.m.
Latitude: 70.193385° N, Longitude: 148.444766° W
Griz's Small Compound—Deadhorse

The drivel on the news stations these days was pathetic.

People surely had to miss the excitement he had brought to their lives. After all, they loved the gory, the obscene, the disgusting. They'd completely eaten up his killing spree. Both entertained by the way he was able to eliminate people and living in fear that it could happen to them next.

Too bad the media wasn't connecting the dots of recent murders with him. Granted, they were all over the state and had died in different ways. But each death was someone powerful and rich. Which should evoke a morbid sense of curiosity from the general public.

Soon enough he'd be back in the headlines, and they'd panic in a way they never thought possible.

Patience was once again a great strength.

Griz reviewed the rest of his plan in his head. Now that he'd started, he couldn't wait until the ultimate finale.

Judgment day.

He could implement it all with his eyes closed. Wouldn't this be fun.

A flashing alert on the TV screen caught his attention.

He turned up the volume.

"The water in our great state's capital is undrinkable, thanks to a cyberterrorist attack on the water system."

What was this? He couldn't help but laugh. So the Members had finally done it. They'd used his malware to attack.

"In an attack reminiscent of the failed attempt on Tampa's water system back in 2021, the hackers changed the levels of sodium hydroxide—otherwise known as lye—from one hundred parts per million to over twenty thousand parts per million. Unfortunately, unlike Tampa, this attack was not stopped before it released into the water. Until further notice—"

Griz turned down the volume.

The Members were such fools without him. Did they really think he wouldn't be watching? This little game of cat and mouse was ridiculous.

He studied the scrolling information on the screen.

They really had used his malware. Couldn't they even be original? It clicked. They were trying to set *him* up to take the fall.

Did they think they could get rid of him so easily? After all this time, they should know better. Parlor tricks weren't going to get him out of the way.

He'd seen and heard their chatter. It was the same old rhetoric.

Hmm. Their chatter. He stood and paced the room. There'd been nothing about hacking the water in Juneau.

He chuckled. "Wouldn't you know . . ." He let the words hang. "They're actually getting smart after all."

They must suspect that he'd been monitoring their communications and changed things up. Good for them. Besides, he could use this to his advantage. Not only to step back onto the stage in a grand manner but to also let the Members and everyone else know that he wasn't to be trifled with.

His phone buzzed in his pocket.

He tapped the screen to place it on speakerphone as he put on his chipper voice. "What's up?" His persona as the IT guy for the North Slope had given him the cover and the access he needed. Since most people worked a rotational schedule up here, he could slip in and out with ease. Besides, everyone loved him. And why wouldn't they? He was fun loving and made sure they all had internet access—the lifeblood of civilization.

"I'm so glad I caught you." The manager of the Aurora Hotel sounded relieved. "We've got a major issue here with the internet."

"I'll be right there, good buddy. Don't you worry one bit."

"Thanks. I knew I could count on you. You're the best tech guy we've ever had up here."

"Glad to help. See ya in a few." Griz ended the call and smirked. If he wasn't so good at what he did, he could've had quite the career as an actor.

✦ ✦ ✦

Four Weeks Later
Eight Years, One Month, Four Days Sober
July 6—4:28 a.m.
Latitude: 64.83156° N, Longitude: 147.73836° W
Fairbanks Memorial Hospital

As Tracie drove into the hospital parking lot, she took a long swig of coffee. The unexpected phone call half an hour ago had woken her up long before her alarm and had her scrambling for the day. The on-call surgeon had taken ill with horrific food poisoning, and Tracie was needed for an appendectomy on an eight-year-old. They'd asked her to be there within the hour, and she would get there ahead of schedule. She hated the thought of a small child suffering.

She'd hopped in the shower while her coffee brewed, dressed quickly, and shot a text to Mac to tell him she couldn't meet him for coffee that morning as planned.

The thought of him caused her to grin. Was it patronizing to be proud of him? Tracie hoped not. Over the last few weeks, he hadn't missed a checkup. Hadn't missed a rehab appointment. Hadn't missed the simplest test or blood draw. Even though they suspected the man behind the water contamination was the same man who'd murdered his family, Mac had remained calm and hadn't taken off on a half-crazed chase like they all expected. His demeanor had changed for the better, and his eyes held more peace. The improvement was wonderful to see. The grief and tension of his circumstances were still there, but he seemed to be healing. Which was much needed after the last couple years he'd endured.

It had been nice to get to know him as more than a patient and not have to constantly remind him to take care of himself.

Thankfully, Jason and Scott had taken over that role.

She giggled as she thought of the way the guys ribbed each other. No holds barred, they were blunt and cut to the quick. At the same time, the deep camaraderie was something she longed for in her own life.

Had she ever witnessed a group of guys with that kind of friend-ship? She couldn't think of any . . . ever. Which fascinated her all the more.

They'd stayed true to their word. One of them was always with Mac. Always. They'd take turns going to their respective homes and spending time with their wives, but they always returned.

Carrie had come up from Anchorage once, and Tracie had in-stantly connected with her. Darcie showed up more often since she and Jason lived in Fairbanks. The curly-haired Emergency Opera-tions Center director was quieter than the ABI investigator, but Tra-cie couldn't blame her. The weight she carried on her shoulders at the EOC was huge.

Getting to know these cyber guys and understanding what they did for a living had been eye-opening. The more she learned from them, the more she wished she could abandon all technology. Of course, that wasn't practical, especially in her field of work. Technol-ogy helped her save lives, but . . .

Such a shame so many people used it for evil. A chill raced up her spine as she parked her car, and she did her best to shake it off.

She locked up her vehicle and headed in to work. She dumped her things in her office and made her way to the OR. But thoughts of the killer she'd learned far too much about in the last couple weeks made her stomach turn. Prayerfully, Mac and his friends could help the au-thorities catch the guy once and for all.

Glad to find the women's locker room empty, Tracie changed into a fresh pair of surgical scrubs. With quick movements she tucked her hair into her favorite red cap and tied the strings tight at the nape of her neck.

At the scrubbing station, she grabbed and opened a scrub-brush packet, set it on the ledge, and began her prewash. She pumped soap into her hands and rubbed the liquid over her hands, fingers, and forearms and then scrubbed. Pressing the foot pedal, she quickly and thoroughly rinsed the soap off. Grabbing the scrub brush, she started her five-minute scrub routine and recited the faith chapter—Hebrews

11—which always took her about fifteen seconds extra. The ritual helped focus her mind on the patient. She couldn't have her brain running the gamut of possibilities that some criminal mastermind might unleash on society when she should be completely honed in on the job she had to do.

Once gowned and gloved, she stepped into the OR, and all her experience and skill took over. This was her sanctuary.

Thankfully, the appendectomy held no surprises.

A new-to-her surgical resident had joined her for this routine surgery and handled herself beautifully. Tracie made a mental note to speak with the doctor later and praise her for a job well done.

But for now she was about to close up and go speak to the parents.

A tap on the glass of the OR brought her attention up, and she found the hospital administrator waving at her. "Dr. Hunter, I need a word." His voice came through the intercom.

The nurse hit the button for her to respond. "I'm almost finished."

"Dr. Richards can close up. This can't wait."

Tracie stared at her boss through the glass for several seconds. His eyes were serious. She glanced back at the resident. "Don't mess up any of my good work now, Dr. Richards, all right?" She tried to keep her voice light, but something weighty dropped into her stomach.

This didn't bode well.

Dr. Richards's eyes crinkled behind her surgical glasses. "Sure thing, Dr. Hunter."

Tracie exited the OR and removed her surgical gown and gloves and began to clean up. "What's going on?"

The hospital administrator leaned against the large sink. "It's not good, Tracie."

Apprehension prickled her skin. Now she really was worried. "Okay." She laced her fingers together and waited.

"News reports are leading with a story that you helped cover up a murder when you were a medical examiner in DC. They're saying it was politically motivated and that you were paid a hefty sum."

Shock rippled through her. "What!" Placing her hands on her hips, she paced the room. "I never covered up any murder!"

He sighed. "They're also saying it's why you left DC and changed careers."

Her breath caught in her throat. Sweat broke out over her body. No. This couldn't be happening. While she hadn't covered up a murder, the other part was true. Not that she wanted anyone to know that. "The Sanderson case?"

"That's the one."

She closed her eyes for a moment. Her nightmare was becoming all too real.

"How'd you know which case?" Suspicion laced his tone.

Well, she wasn't going to feed into the lies. Honesty was the best policy, and she'd been up front with him when she came here. "Because it was a wealthy family. I promised them—I know, I know, that was stupid—that I would help find their son's killer. I was young and thought for sure that there was enough evidence on the body. I had no idea that Mrs. Sanderson would become a congresswoman. Years later, mind you."

"Thus the political angle." He nodded.

"I met them when they came to identify the body. The parents were distraught, and I was the only one giving them hope at the time. You know how it is in the big cities—law enforcement is always overwhelmed with case after case. I wanted them to know that someone cared. I know now that was a mistake." Tracie rubbed her forehead, trying to separate what really happened from the nightmare that haunted her. "On top of making a promise I couldn't keep. But I'd been so convinced. All the evidence I collected and submitted . . . was insurmountable. Or so I thought. The detective said it wasn't enough to prove guilt, though, and the suspect was released on a technicality."

The director tapped a file folder against his palm. "I'm sorry I had to pull you out of surgery." He released a heavy breath. "But the board held an emergency meeting. They voted just a few minutes ago, and you are being asked to take immediate administrative paid leave. Until the media frenzy dies down." Her boss straightened. "We really don't have any other choice."

"Paid leave? Media frenzy?" The words stuck in her throat.

He took a moment before he replied. "It started on the East Coast early this morning. The news outlets in Alaska have already run the story with your picture and the fact that you are a surgeon here. The phones are ringing off the hook. The press want interviews. They want me to make a statement. Then there are all the people calling in because you are their family member's surgeon. Good and bad. People worried you are corrupt. People calling in to say how wonderful you are."

As the depth of the situation settled into her mind, she felt . . . unbalanced. Like someone had ripped the earth out from under her and she was about to fall into a bottomless chasm. She closed her eyes and breathed deep. "Can't we just ignore it and continue on? I've got nothing to hide!"

He shook his head. "I suggested the same thing. But the board is adamant that bad publicity cannot touch the hospital. I told them you are my best surgeon and we couldn't lose you. But they think it's best if you just take some time and distance yourself from the hospital."

"Then everyone will think I'm guilty!"

"Not if it dies down as soon as I hope it will. People forget very quickly." He stepped closer. "Look, you never take time off. This is a good opportunity for that. Don't worry—I still need you here. Your job is secure." A flash of doubt flickered in his eyes. "Unless, of course, you did what they're accusing you of?"

Not what she wanted to see or hear. "I didn't." She crossed her arms over her chest.

"Well then, there's nothing to worry about." He headed for the door. "Take six weeks off, Dr. Hunter. I'll see you when you return."

Everything he'd said swirled in her mind. Her picture was all over the news?

In the time span of one surgery, her world had turned upside down.

As he disappeared out the door, the rest of the team entered from the OR to clean up. The surgery was over. Patient would be sent to recovery. What must that little girl's parents be thinking?

Before anyone could ask questions, she ripped her scrub cap off her head and made her way out the door and down the hall toward her office. She refused to make eye contact with anyone and pretended to be studying her hands as she walked as fast as she could back to her private space. What would the staff think? They wouldn't believe she was capable of this, would they?

A million different thoughts rushed into her mind, and panic tightened her chest. Her well-appointed life was spiraling out of control. None of it was in her grasp anymore. None of it.

Not her reputation.

Not her job.

Not her future.

She barely made it to her office and closed the door before tears pricked her eyes. Leaning up against the solid door, she slid down until she was sitting on the floor. This couldn't be happening.

A little niggle at the back of her mind told her she was thirsty.

No. She wasn't.

She banished the thought. Right now she couldn't afford to give in to weakness. She had to defend herself.

Allowing a swell of anger to rise from her middle, she latched on to it.

Who would say such a thing? And why?

Courtney's words hit her mind like a rock thrown full force.

Had other people she'd worked with over the years felt the same way? Could someone be after her just out of spite?

There wasn't any other explanation. She hadn't done anything wrong.

She *hadn't*.

What was she going to do?

Tracie scrambled to her feet and went to the laptop on her desk. It probably wasn't the best thing, but she had to see for herself. To find out what people were saying.

You're obsessed. The words echoed in her mind.

The more she read, the more her heart sank. Her parents' address *and* phone number were listed. Her old phone numbers. The hospital she worked at now. Was there no common decency any longer? It was a good thing her parents were traveling right now. What would she tell them when they got home? She'd have to prepare them before they arrived, because surely the press would camp out on their front steps.

She scrolled through a mass of documents about the case. About the congresswoman. About her son's death.

Everything traced back to the log-in Tracie had used as the ME back in DC. More than a dozen years ago.

Someone had used that log-in to cover up a murder. And it wasn't her.

CHAPTER SIX

938 Days After
July 6—9:44 a.m.
Latitude: 64.832967° N, Longitude: 147.716854° W
Screamin' Peach Bakery and Coffee Shop

MAC WATCHED THE SCOWL ON his friend's face deepen. Scott had called his wife at the Anchorage ABI office for an update.

"Thanks, Carrie. Love you." Scott laid his cell phone back on the table, shaking his head. "The ABI, the state troopers, the FBI . . . no one has any idea where their suspect has gone. They're pretty certain the seven high-profile murders from the last several weeks are his handiwork as well."

"And they have evidence that all the victims were part of the group that was originally behind the 26 Below attack?" Mac didn't like that thought. Not at all. Four weeks ago, the authorities wouldn't give him the time of day whenever he said things were connected or that the man who killed his family was still alive. The world had been convinced that the cyberterrorist and serial killer was gone. But now? His monster was at the top of everyone's most wanted list. Mac almost hated being right.

"Yep." Scott opened his laptop. "The more I hear about that group, the more spooked I get. Then I remember that the guy behind all this was once part of them, and . . . what? They weren't good enough for him? Didn't want to kill enough people? And I get creeped out even more."

"You and me both." Jason tapped his cardboard coaster on the table. "Darcie and I have been cleaning up the mess they made for more than two years. Not only that but trying to prevent anything else like that from happening again. Every time I have to read the reports and dive back into it, I shiver at what they almost accomplished. What *he* almost accomplished."

"Let's not forget what he *did* accomplish." Mac's jaw was clenched as he said the words. He hated giving the guy any credit, but facts were facts. Irrefutable. Life changing. Life *ending*. "And how many people he killed in Anchorage as well."

"Something I know better than to bring up with my wife unless she needs to talk about it and vent." Scott typed something on his laptop.

His *wife*. Mac's stomach clenched. At least Scott had a wife.

Mac's was gone. Forever. Because of this cyberterrorist murderer. He stood up from the high-top table and went to the window, cringing at his own thoughts.

"Man . . . I'm sorry." Scott's voice behind him cracked. "That was thoughtless of me."

Mac closed his eyes. Ever since that fateful day when he'd almost killed himself with a panic attack, Mac had done so much better. But there were still triggers. "I wouldn't wish you to go through this agony ever. But don't apologize for talking about your wife. Carrie has done wonders for you." He turned back around, hating the pity he saw in both his friends' eyes. "Let's focus back on what we know. There's got to be something we've missed. Something everyone has missed." Every law enforcement agency in the state had been working this case, but they'd all stalled. Mac was determined that no matter what, he would see this through.

"This is our guy." Scott pointed to his laptop screen, where he'd uploaded the pictures Mac had taken. He put them side by side with the sketch they had from Anchorage. "After the cyberattack up here, just a few short weeks later, he became a dreaded serial killer down in Anchorage. He seemed to shift his ultimate goals and focus. He wanted us to know he's smart. Wanted us to know he's powerful. That he has no qualms about taking lives. But then he went silent. Why? The profilers tell us it was because he was creating his magnum opus—his master plan. Not one of them can say with certainty that they can predict what he has planned, but it's big."

Mac studied the screen. What had everyone missed?

"After the water attack in Juneau, he hacked the paper. He took credit for the 26 Below attack. He took credit as the 8 DOWN serial killer and then claimed he was behind the water attack as well. He signed off by saying we had seventy-eight days before his grand finale. That was twenty-one days ago." Scott leaned back in his chair and stared at the screen. "I mean . . . the more I read this, the angrier I get. How many times does he say that he's smarter than everyone else? How many times does he say he'll never be caught? It's just one big taunt."

Mac understood all too well what it felt like to have this guy take everything and then when there was a tiny bit of relief—thinking he'd been caught—the rug got yanked out from under him.

He'd learned his lesson. The second time he hadn't believed it, but he'd been the only one. There'd been tons of evidence supporting the fact that Peter Chandler was the mastermind. The victims' families had known peace for the last couple of years.

Now?

Well, he knew the horror of realizing the criminal was still out there. And with the guy taunting them, the wounds of their losses wouldn't just feel like the scab had been torn off—it would be more like they were getting stabbed over and over again.

He shot up a quick prayer to heaven because that was all he knew to do. The only way he could help the families was if he helped to stop the coward.

The man who hid behind his arrogant taunts.

This time the killer's op-ed hadn't made it to the paper because he'd kidnapped the editor's kid. No. This time he'd hacked the system and inserted the article into their online edition himself. From there it went viral.

Once again the world's eyes were on Alaska, and they were equating the crazed lunatic with Batman's Joker, who just wanted to watch the world burn.

Was that what this guy wanted now?

How had he gone from wanting to overthrow the government to this? Unlike the previous attacks, this time he hadn't asked for anything.

Dread built in Mac's gut. "This guy is off the rails."

"Tell me about it." Jason studied his computer screen. "We don't know his motivation. We don't know what he's got planned. We don't know what he'll do next."

"That's a huge problem." Scott tapped the table. "Carrie sent me a file from the profiler at the ABI. They've been studying everything from the past two years. The 26 Below attack that happened here a couple years ago—they're certain there was a group behind that. A group focus. All the testimony portrayed that. So yeah, our guy might have been the leader or maybe one of them, but they were driven by a cause."

Scott shuffled some papers, pulled out another file, and continued. "Same thing when he started in Anchorage. But there it became clear that he'd gone a different direction from the group. He began acting on his own. Does the cause no longer matter? What is driving him now? The profiler believes this guy is power hungry, arrogant, and caught up in his own delusion."

Jason scowled. "On top of being brilliant and well-versed in the cyber world. I really hate how he stayed ahead of us for so long."

"Times like these, I wish I were a specialist in law enforcement too"—Scott's eyebrows pinched together—"or a psychiatrist so I could understand his mind."

Mac digested all of that for a minute. "A psychiatrist . . . His *delusion*." He whispered the words.

"Huh?" Scott grabbed a pen and spun it around with his fingers. "What are you thinking?"

"There's something we're missing."

Jason released a frustrated sigh. "Yeah. Like Scott said, we're lacking the skills in all the areas to understand him. We haven't caught the guy yet. I'm guessing there's a million somethings we're missing." He chucked a wadded-up piece of paper toward the garbage.

Mac scanned the room. The coffee shop and bakery was full, just like most coffee shops this time of day. He studied the people. Most were young, with headphones over the top of their heads or earbuds in their ears. No one was sitting around having conversations, like him and the guys. They all had their noses in their computers and tablets.

"Whatcha thinking?" The pen in Scott's hand was still spinning. Back and forth.

"What makes someone go off the deep end and just start murdering innocent people? For the fun of it?" Mac rubbed his jaw.

"Someone who is not right in the head," Jason threw out. "Sorry. That sounds terrible, but we know it's true. There's got to be a disconnect. This guy is too smart to not know right from wrong."

Mac nodded. "The thing is . . . the guy knows. And that's it—he doesn't care."

"No empathy." Jason sat up straighter. "What is that? Psychopath? Sociopath?" He typed into his computer. "Psychopath—little or no conscience. Sociopath—limited to no empathy. At least, that's the simple explanation."

"Our guy fits into both categories, don'tcha think?" Scott shook his head. "Carrie asked the same question before."

"So we're looking at a brilliant psychopathic sociopath? Whatever that means." Mac blinked at the guys.

Scott shook his head. "Didn't Carrie accuse him of being one or the other, and it infuriated him?" He looked down at his phone. "Let me text her. Maybe it will help."

Mac nodded. "Ask her if she knows any criminal psychologists we could talk to as well."

Not that they had officially asked to be on the case. Cyber Solutions might have helped with the cyberattack in Fairbanks and the serial killer case in Anchorage a couple years ago, but this was different. Would the FBI step in again and say it was their jurisdiction? Had they already? And if so, would they allow Mac and his team to help?

He hoped so. But doubted it.

Scott held up his phone. "She called him a psychopath, and he didn't like it. After her mentor from college studied the case in and out, the expert labeled him a psychopath because he seems to have no conscience." His phone dinged again, and he scanned the screen. "And a narcissist."

"Huh." Jason flexed his fingers. "Why would a guy who does horrible things really care what he was called?"

"Simple." Mac tipped his chin up. "He wants everyone to think he's brilliant, not crazy."

Mac's cell buzzed. He reached into his pocket and pulled it out. Dr. Hunter. He held up a finger to the guys. "Hey, Doc. Ready for that coffee? We're at the Screamin' Peach right now and would love to have you join us."

"I need your help, Mac." The tone of her voice didn't even sound like her.

"Tracie?" His stomach dropped like a rock. "What's happened?"

"I can't"—she choked on the word—"talk about it over the phone. Can I come see you?"

"Of course. The guys are with me."

"Good. I probably need all of you." She sounded breathless, choked up, almost like she'd been crying. "I'll be there in a couple minutes. I'm just down the street."

The call ended, and Mac looked at his friends. "Dr. Hunter is on her way. Says she needs help."

"Um, about that." Scott turned his laptop around so Mac and Jason could see it.

At the top of the page was a lovely picture of Dr. Tracie Hunter in her scrubs and doctor's coat, smiling for the camera. But the scathing article below it was anything but complimentary.

The farther Mac read, the more the heat built in his gut.

"Hey, guys." Tracie plunked herself down in the chair next to Mac. Her eyes darted to the computer screen, then back to him. "I see you've read the news."

"Yeah. Just saw it." Mac wasn't sure what to say. He hadn't seen her outside of the hospital. He was used to her hair up. A white coat. A stethoscope. And a no-nonsense attitude. Outside the hospital she was dressed like the average person, and it was . . . weird.

She placed her hands palms down on the table. "Let's just get this straight right now. I did not cover up a murder."

"Glad to hear it." Scott crossed his arms over his chest. "Now, how can we help?"

"I'm not sure. But since you guys are the computer geniuses, maybe you can figure out how someone used my log-in as the medical examiner to cover up a murder. More than a dozen years ago."

Scott whistled, and Jason leaned forward, his brow deeply crinkled, and asked, "Who would have a beef with you, Doc?"

"The first person to come to mind—" She clamped her lips tight. "No, it couldn't be her."

"Who?" Mac's cell buzzed again. He glanced at the screen. Unknown caller. Somehow that didn't sit well. But still . . . He swiped to answer the call. "Hello?"

"I see Tracie has come to you for help." The robotic voice reinforced that odd feeling.

He jumped out of his seat and strode to the window behind him, searching every other business and the sidewalk and street.

"You're not going to find me, Mac. It is Mac, isn't it? Isn't that what your friends call you?"

"You are not my friend." He gritted the words out. "What do you want?"

"You and your friends can't stop me, you know."

"Can't stop you from what?" Maybe if he played innocent.

"Nice try. Why don't you try to clean up the little mess you made for Dr. Hunter."

"I didn't make that mess." Reality struck. "But *you* did."

A horrible screeching sound came over the line, and Mac had to pull the phone away from his ear.

When it stopped, he brought the phone close to his face again. "You haven't answered my question. What. Do. You. Want?"

"This is a fun little game, isn't it?"

Mac turned and faced the guys and Tracie. They were all watching him, their curiosity palpable. "A 'game'? Is that what you call it?"

"You messed with me. Now I'm going to mess with you. Dr. Hunter seemed like a good choice. Did you know the poor thing is an alcoholic? I wouldn't want to push her over the edge if I were you."

Mac should've known. He couldn't protect anyone in his life from this lunatic. "I'm not playing your game." He spat the words this time. More than anything he wanted to reach through the phone and throttle the guy.

"Tsk-tsk. That's not good for the blood pressure, Mac. Better keep an eye on that."

✦ ✦ ✦

57 Days Until Final Judgment
25 Members Left
July 6—10:09 a.m.
Latitude: 61.164531° N, Longitude: 149.975689° W
AKOP Helicopter Services, Ted Stevens Anchorage International
Airport—Anchorage, Alaska

Griz shoved his phone back into his jacket pocket and switched laptops. Didn't people realize how easy it was to hack into a computer and watch them through their webcam? Surely these Cyber Solutions guys were smarter than that.

His face hardened as the second laptop came to life. It was one thing for Mac and his little team of cyber dummies to try to keep up with him. Another thing entirely for one of the Members to ignore his threats.

No matter how many bodyguards or private security people they hired, they weren't safe from his reach.

Perhaps taking out the six weakest Members wasn't enough of a sign for them.

They'd turned a blind eye to his last threat. Then that simpleton thought he could catch him.

He didn't last long, now did he?

Today the rest of the Members would have to pay attention. Or pay with their lives.

He didn't simply offer threats. He made promises. Maybe as their numbers dwindled, they'd get the point.

The noise of the air traffic overhead was loud, but they were far enough away from the runways for it not to be deafening. Why his old friend had decided to have a press conference here was ridiculous.

The man stepping out of the helicopter had been a favorite ally—right up until yesterday, when Griz had tracked the man's encrypted email to all the press in Anchorage. A trusted friend. A multibillionaire who loved donating to politics. Many even thought of him as the next great politician. The Members had intended to use that to their advantage.

The man had a great voice. An impeccable record. And he was good-looking, with a perfect little family.

He walked up to the bank of microphones, the press surrounding him. "Thank you all for coming today. As I stated in my email, I have some grave information to share with you. I have discovered, over the last few months, that I know the identity of the man called the Typhon Killer."

The press had dubbed Griz with that name yesterday morning. It had a nice ring to it—he'd give them that. Greek mythology, father of all monsters. He kind of liked it.

"I must admit that fear kept me from coming forward like I should have. This man has threatened the lives of many people to keep them quiet, and we have seen what he is capable of. However, I am done living in that fear. That is why I will be handing over everything I have that will help the authorities catch and prosecute this criminal. I have asked for—"

Griz tapped the Enter key, and the helicopter behind the little rat exploded. Then the car next to it. Then the podium. Then a news van. The chain reaction continued until there was nothing left but fire, rubble, and bodies burning on the pavement.

"Let's just see if anyone else thinks they need to speak up." He closed his laptop, watched the fire burn for a few seconds, and then drove off before the firefighters arrived.

CHAPTER SEVEN

Eight Years, One Month, Five Days Sober
July 7—1:00 p.m.
Latitude: 64.8455° N, Longitude: 147.5338° W
Along Columbia Creek

TRACIE PACED HER KITCHEN AND tapped her hand against her thigh. Mac, Jason, and Scott were all with her, trying to piece together what they could. "I can't believe the Typhon Killer is the guy you think doxed me." Would he go after her patients? "Why me?" Everything about it made her uncomfortable. This wasn't some peon doing this for notoriety or money. This guy was legit disturbing. Had he been behind the murder of the congresswoman's son? That was a long time ago, but she wouldn't put it past him. He wasn't just a murderer . . . he was a serial killer.

She wrapped her arms around her middle as a chill raced up her spine. For the second time in as many days, she felt the urge to drown her problems in a drink or two. Or five. It wasn't like she would be going to work anytime soon, so who would care?

She swallowed hard. Sobriety the past eight years had been relatively easy. The destruction her dependence on alcohol had caused, distancing herself from almost everyone in her life so they didn't find out how far she'd truly fallen . . . She bit her lip, trying to stem the shame burning in her chest. She couldn't focus on the past.

What was important was that she'd overcome. For years. Teaching herself to lean on God and making sure she went to every AA meeting had helped. Staying busy and not even thinking about it had made overcoming the urges seem like a breeze. But now? With temptation lurking around every corner? Overwhelming her in her most vulnerable moments? Now she was beginning to understand the struggle of her fellow alcoholics in a whole new way. Yesterday she'd grabbed ahold of her anger.

Today she was weary.

Mac sat at her island bar with the other guys and grunted. "I'm sorry, Doc—"

"Stop calling me that," she snapped. "It's Tracie, remember?" She cringed. Amazing what even the thought of diving back into her vice did to her. "Sorry. I didn't mean to bite your head off. But I'm on administrative leave, and I'd prefer not being reminded of my job that I'm not allowed to do." Or the fact that she'd just been considering returning to alcohol.

"I get it. It's weird seeing you away from the hospital. But I'm glad. Might help us catch this guy." He went to refill his coffee mug. His shoulders rose and fell, as if the weight of the world was on his shoulders. He turned slowly back to her. "It's my fault he came after you and that you're on administrative leave. At least, that's what we can deduce. He said as much when he called me at the coffee shop—he came after you because I confronted him in the park. I'm sorry, Tracie. You can blame me for ruining your life." He walked to her and stood there with an arm out.

She stopped her pacing and stared, amazed he'd even suggest she lay this at his feet. "I'm not going to blame you for what this crazy guy is doing." Without another word, she stepped into his side hug.

"Doesn't change how sorry I am." He voiced it again and went back to the guys.

She rubbed her arms, missing his warmth. "Stop apologizing. It's not your fault." She leaned over the island toward the three guys she'd barely known six months ago. The fact they were in her life and could help her through a crisis of this magnitude was humbling. God was so good. But it didn't change the seriousness of her situation. "I hate this. I really do. I can't believe I'm not allowed to see my patients. Not even the ones in the remote villages. It doesn't make sense that they would keep me from going out there. It's separate work from my contract with the hospital. No media."

Jason took a swig out of his mug. "It all has to do with the fact that you've been accused of wrongdoing. The hospital board is covering their backside because they don't want anything coming back to bite them later."

"I know that." Logically, she did. "But until then, I'm guilty? The Community Health Aides rely on our help. Especially if they have a stubborn patient who refuses to be transported in for health care."

Scott's phone buzzed, and he walked out of the room to take it.

Mac sighed. "They can't risk any patients filing lawsuits. And you're not guilty. You're just on leave."

Jason set his empty cup down. "Is there someone you trust who'd be willing to go out to the remote villages on your behalf? Most of them might not even have the news, so they wouldn't be wary of you sending someone in your stead."

Hope flared in her heart. That was the best, most positive idea that had come forward all day. Tracie almost smiled. Almost. "I'll call Sherry. She's one of the nurses who works with me. I bet she'd be willing to go and check on my surgical patients and respond to calls from the CHAs." She grabbed her phone and sent the nurse—and hopefully her friend—a text to call her when Sherry got off work.

Scott strode into the room like fire was on his heels. "That was Carrie. The FBI, the ABI, the Alaska State Troopers, Fairbanks Police Department, Anchorage Police Department, and Juneau Police Department have all asked for Cyber Solutions—specifically Jason and me—to help out with the investigation. After the devastation at the airport yesterday, they are desperate to stop this guy, and this time for good."

Mac nodded, a muscle jerking in his clenched jaw.

Jason's shoulders tensed, his lips a thin line. "As much as it's an honor to be asked to assist, I'm concerned. That means they're not having a lot of luck tracking this guy down. That doesn't bode well. Those departments combined have a ton of resources. Have they hit a dead end, and we're their last hope?"

Silence reigned for several moments. Tracie darted her gaze from one cyber guy to the next and raised her eyebrows. "But it's a good thing that they asked you to help, right?"

"Yes." They all answered at the same time.

Mac took long strides across the room and grabbed his bag off the table. "We've got experience with this guy. The three of us can head this up, but I don't think I have to tell you that we are going to need every person we have on the job." He glanced at Scott. "Who was it that brought you the crossword clue?"

"Kyle." But Scott winced. "Hold up, Mac. You're one of the victims. They've put me in charge."

Mac stiffened and straightened, his jaw clenching. "I'm still the head of Cyber Solutions."

"Yeah. You are. But you're too close to this. Everyone knows it."

Tracie glanced between the three men. *Fierce* was too tame a word to describe their shared looks.

"But you took leave, remember? The man killed your wife and daughter and then shot you." Scott wasn't backing down. Good for him.

"Let me back in. You need my help." For the big bear that Tracie knew Mac could be, his voice had remained relatively calm.

She slipped over to the island and took a seat. No way she wanted to get in the middle of this.

Scott glanced at Jason. Some unspoken communication passed between them. "All right. You can help. But you have to promise that you will stay out of the way. I can't have the feds thinking that we have compromised the case in any way."

Jason stepped closer and put a hand on Mac's shoulder. Miraculously, the big man didn't swat it off.

"We're in this together, remember?" Jason tipped his head toward Tracie. "You can put all your expertise into tracking what he did to her and seeing if there's any way to fix it." He sat back down at the island in front of his laptop.

"I'll call Kyle. Just in case he has any insight after helping us with the crossword clues." Scott sat between him and Tracie.

Jason's fingers flew over the keys. "I'm emailing everyone. Asking every team member to work in shifts so we have people on this around the clock."

Scott bumped Tracie's shoulder with his own. "Don't worry. We're going to figure this out."

"Are you sure? He sounds like he's gotten away with a lot already." She looked from Scott to Mac, whose face was like stone. The knot in her chest tightened. "Ruining my life and career in the process doesn't seem like it would mean much to him."

That brought Mac's gaze up. His face softened. "Let's go over absolutely everything you know about the cold case in your past. I am not going to allow him to burn everyone in his wake. I'm not. Especially not you."

She blinked. The intensity in his gaze overwhelmed her. Heat crept up her face, and her heart sped up for a completely different reason. All she managed was a nod, trying to remember the last time someone had shown her so much care. Outside of her family, it had been a while.

Whatever emotions warred within Mac slipped from his expression as he winked at her. "You saved my life, remember? I owe you one."

✦　✦　✦

56 Days Until Final Judgment
24 Members Left
July 7—2:32 p.m.
Latitude: 61.079113° N, Longitude: 146.348939° W
Valdez, Alaska

Griz swiped a hand down his face. The exhaustion from all his planning was catching up to him. Things had been easier when he had a never-ending supply of puppets to help him. But he could no longer trust anyone else.

He'd had the occasional use of a disposable helper, but he hadn't let anyone into his inner circle since he'd killed his brother and left Anchorage. No one was smart enough or capable enough. So it had to be him.

In control. Always. And he'd never felt better. Ever since his performance yesterday morning, he'd been getting hateful correspondence from the Members.

That brought him so much happiness, it couldn't be quantified.

Before he responded to them, though, he wanted to finish the minute details that had to be put in place here. The Valdez Marine Terminal was the southern terminus for the Alaska pipeline. Millions upon millions of gallons of oil were stored here and flowed through this location.

By the time he was done—in fewer than fifty-six days—the US economy would come screeching to a halt. After that he'd go after China. And Russia. And anyone else who tickled his fancy.

Fear would rule. Country would be against country, all thinking the other was behind the chaos.

Then he would take center stage. Yes, one man could wield that much power. Oh, this was fun. He pulled out his pills and popped two of them. He needed the boost. This was going to require every bit of brilliance he had.

Once he was satisfied with his work, he exited the bunker and climbed into the waiting airplane.

On his phone, he typed up a simple yet straight-to-the-point message.

> Dearest Members,
>   After yesterday, I think you have learned that I keep
> my promises.

I have no problem killing all of you, your families, and everyone you know.

Stay out of the way, please. I did say *please*.

This is your last warning.

Eight down. Twenty-four to go.

✦ ✦ ✦

939 Days After
July 7—2:46 p.m.
Latitude: 64.8455° N, Longitude: 147.5338° W
Along Columbia Creek

"What exactly did you promise the family?" Scott had been typing up everything Tracie said about the cold case.

Mac watched her closely. The bags under her eyes gave away her lack of sleep. But the determination in her was a thing to behold.

"That I would do everything in my power to help catch the killer." She bit her lip. "It was a rookie mistake, but it wasn't completely out of order. As the ME in a smaller town outside DC, I worked closely with the detectives and prosecutors on each case. Often testified in court." She rubbed her jeans with her palm. "I should never have promised anything, but all the evidence was there."

"Let's go through the evidence one more time." Scott's voice was kind as he urged her on.

Mac stood by the window, watching the scene play out. Tracie was tired, but she kept at it. Her phone had been ringing nonstop all afternoon with friends and former coworkers calling her and checking in, and the barrage was taking its toll.

Mac had seen her at the hospital when she'd already been there more than twelve hours and still had the vitality of the Energizer Bunny.

Her phone buzzed again, and she glanced down. She leaned her head back and released a long sigh to the ceiling. Holding up her phone, she looked at him. "The call I've been dreading. My parents."

He frowned. "You haven't talked to them yet?" That was odd.
"No." She stared at the phone. "They were on a river cruise in Europe." With a glance to her watch, she grimaced. "Yeah, their plane landed about thirty minutes ago. Just enough time for them to hear all about it." She tapped her phone. "Hey, Mom." She rose and left the guys sitting at the island with their computers.

Scott was the first one to speak up. "I'm worried about her. I hate to say it, but this guy is good. He must have used AI to create the deepfake videos that are out there. She could be in some serious trouble if we can't figure this out. Once something like this is all over the TV? Even worse if social media trolls and bloggers find out." He shook his head. "I mean, what if it goes to court and he's doctored up all kinds of other evidence? Doesn't matter if she's proven innocent. It could be the end of her career as a doctor."

Mac had been afraid to voice it but knew it to be true. "Which means we've got to do something before they come after her to prosecute her."

"Exactly." Jason shifted his screen in Mac's direction. "It looks like the press gave him that nickname to feed his ego. Here's hoping that works and he does something stupid, thinking he can't be caught. It's worth a shot."

All Mac could do was stare at the screen. The Typhon Killer.

Typhon. The father of all monsters. The name made him cringe. For two and a half years, he'd thought of the guy as a monster. The longer he stared at the name, the more his head hurt. But then he shifted to Scott. "Hey . . . we have pictures of this guy. Surely between all the law enforcement agencies hunting for this guy, they could get a hit on who he is."

His friend's shoulders slumped. "Carrie gave your photos to the FBI. They've been run through every face-recognition database in the world." Scott didn't have to say the rest. His face said it all.

Somehow, this guy had erased himself. Okay, fine. "Well, why don't they post them? Get them out to the general public? People have seen him. It's not like he's a hermit."

"Yeah . . ." Jason's grimace wasn't encouraging. "The FBI has said no posting of the photos for now. There's too much of a resemblance between him and his brother, Peter. They don't want any confusion between the two. They're not willing to take any risks. Public panic over a serial killer still being alive is not going to help them catch the guy."

"But I got a shot up close and personal! They *know* that's the guy." With everything in him, he worked to keep his frustration at bay.

"I hear you, man. I do." Scott scratched the side of his jaw. "But remember . . . up close and personal because you were in the guy's face. Two officers witnessed you assault him. And while the world might cheer you on because that was the man who killed your wife and daughter, the feds aren't going to take any chances. They don't want to taint any part of this case if they want to put him away for good."

Jason leaned forward, his face serious as he tapped the counter with his index finger. "This isn't just a capital murder case. This guy is a terrorist. A serial killer. Someone who has threatened the very government of our state and country. Someone who could be planning to blow up the world, for all we know. There's too much at stake."

"Exactly—there's too much at stake! Who cares what the public thinks—we should be doing everything we can to catch this guy!" Mac barked his displeasure. "Someone has seen him. Somewhere."

Scott held up his hands. "I get it. But you and Carrie are the only ones he's shown himself to in this context. To everyone else, he's just a normal guy."

Jason shook his head. "Not necessarily. His group—the original ones behind the 26 Below attack—they know who he is. He blew up a chunk of the airport to silence the guy speaking out against him. Maybe we need to find that group. Or maybe the FBI already has. We should ask."

"Let me call Carrie back and have her ask." Scott picked up his phone and moved to a quiet corner of the room.

"Why would this mysterious group even help?" Tracie asked as she entered the room, a lot paler than a few minutes ago. "They don't want to be prosecuted for the cyberterror attack. How would the authorities know they could even be trusted?"

"She's got a point." Jason studied the ceiling with his hands on his head.

Scott came back to the island and opened his email. Flipping his computer to the group, he pointed to the open message. "Hey, look. The guys in Anchorage have a lead where our guy originally set up the op-ed to go out. They're following that."

Mac stood straighter. "After what he did at the airport, maybe he's still there. Reveling in his masterpiece. We should all go. Just to make sure we don't miss anything. If we hit a dead end in Anchorage, we'll fly to Juneau."

Tracie stepped closer, and there was no denying the tearstains on her cheeks nor the agony in her eyes. The news must not be good from home, but by the tiny shake of her head, he understood she didn't want to talk about it yet. "I'm coming with you," she said. "There's nothing I can do here except twiddle my thumbs and worry about my family and my patients. So please. There's got to be something I can do to help?"

His heart softened at the expression on her face. He knew that look. That feeling of helplessness. "I—"

"Hold up. Word just came in from the Juneau office. More than fifty people have died. Dozens are still in the hospital." Jason read his screen.

"Maybe I can help *there*. Please?" Tracie pleaded and looked at Scott and Jason before turning her gaze back to Mac.

Jason nodded to him. "We flew up here in Scott's dad's plane. We've got room."

Mac ran a hand over his scalp. How could he deny her the very thing he'd wanted for two years? A chance to *do* something. He sent a glance to Scott with a brief nod.

Scott released a long breath. "Okay. Looks like we're headed out. Everyone pack as fast as you can and meet at the airstrip. I'd like to be in the air within the hour."

CHAPTER EIGHT

Eight Years, One Month, Six Days Sober
July 8—6:30 a.m.
Latitude: 61.174133° N, Longitude: 149.887813° W
Hyatt House Hotel—Anchorage

LIFTING HER FACE TO THE showerhead, Tracie closed her eyes and allowed the hot water to wash over her in rhythmic pulses. Jason had offered to give up the couch at Carrie and Scott's small place, but she'd declined. These people had all been friends for a while. Besides, she needed time to herself. Even if staying in a hotel during tourist season meant the prices were ridiculous.

The setting on the showerhead was intense, drilling her, but it helped ease some of her tight muscles. Now that she'd gone through her morning ritual, she relished the time to simply stand there and pray for liquid heat to rid her mind, body, and soul of all the ickiness that threatened to push her over the edge.

Yes, *ickiness*. A young patient of hers had used the term a couple months back, and rather than allow her mind to traverse the ugly vocabulary of this world, Tracie decided to adopt the use of it herself.

During the plane ride here, she'd given the others a brief summary of the call with her parents. The team had way too much other stuff to deal with than to listen to her whine about her troubles. And even though Dad was tough and no nonsense with his military background, Tracie could read between the lines. Since her parents' address and phone number had been released to the world, they were getting harassed. A lot. And they'd just returned home from what had been their dream retirement vacation.

So much for that . . . Tracie's past had managed to ruin it all in one fell swoop.

She ran her fingers through her hair, closing her eyes tight against the shame. These thoughts weren't healthy. Of course, she understood that.

The defamation of her character, the accusations, and the deep-fake videos about that long-ago case were one thing. Because they were about *her*. But the jerk had brought her family into it. Probably because he knew how much that would get to her. Which put the blame squarely at her feet.

The whole thing made her sick to her stomach.

In light of what the guy had done and threatened to do, the attack on her was the equivalent of spilled milk. She knew that. But that still didn't mean it didn't hurt.

Her Apple Watch buzzed with a notification, and she glanced at the screen. She really didn't need to keep wearing her smartwatch in the shower now that she wasn't on call, but it was a habit. To always stay connected and prepared.

The message was from Mom. Telling her they were fine. They loved her. Heart emoji.

If her mom could keep her chin up, so could Tracie. She shook off the melancholy. Time to do something productive and get her thoughts off herself. She turned off the water, slid the shower door open, and grabbed a towel. It was a new day to stop the maniac, and she would do everything she could to help.

She was dressed and ready to head out to meet the others at the ABI office, when a sudden urge crashed over her senses. She stopped in her tracks.

That unquenchable thirst pushed its way into the forefront of her mind.

She closed her eyes and went through her toolbox of resources. The first was to pray.

God, I need You more than ever to fight this and stay strong. Take it away . . . please.

In the middle of the hallway, she pulled out her iPhone and typed into the calendar reminders to find a meeting. Today. If she was feeling the need for a drink at 6:45 in the morning, she was in trouble.

By 7:30 she was camped out at the ABI.

Tracie glanced around the conference room and almost laughed. It looked nothing like any of the high-tech rooms on her favorite crime shows. A long dark-brown table took up the majority of the room, with comfy office chairs scattered around. One wall at the end held a whiteboard with halfway erased notes on it. The blinds over the high windows on the west wall were open, allowing the summer sun to filter through. Another wall was a plain gray with a row of chairs shoved up against it.

And the last wall held the door that ABI Special Agent Carrie Kintz walked through. Tracie made sure to keep reminding herself that even though Carrie was married to Scott Patteson, she kept her maiden name on the job. The world had known her through media, thanks to the serial killer they now chased, and she had no desire for the world to know her new name.

"I brought us coffee!" Scott's wife announced and slid two stainless-steel insulated tumblers with *ABI* etched on the side onto the tabletop. A bottle of chocolate syrup, a plastic bottle of nondairy creamer, and a bundle of sugar packets spilled from her arms. "At least I didn't drop the important stuff."

Tracie jumped up. "Let me help you!" She scurried over as Carrie righted the sugar, syrup, and creamer.

"Oh, no worries. I realized I didn't know how you took your coffee. And then decided that I could make it to the conference room with all these items." The blonde let out a snort. "Poor decision-making on my part, but I'm also the woman who thinks she will be fine without a cart in the supermarket."

Tracie couldn't help the laugh that slipped out. It felt good. Opposite of the panic about her career and reputation that was her constant companion. And the urges from earlier coupled with fear that seemed to dog her heels at every turn. She grabbed a cup of coffee. "Ooh, I must be special. I get to drink out of an official ABI mug."

"Shh, don't tell the guys. They don't get the insulated ones." Carrie pulled the lid off her full tumbler and squirted a healthy amount of chocolate syrup into the steaming coffee.

She caught Tracie's gaze and shrugged as she set the bottle on the table. "I know, Doc. Probably not good for my health. But it's the only way I can survive. I need a little caffeine with my chocolate."

"No judgment here." Tracie nodded her thanks and took the bottle, adding a healthy dollop to her own coffee. "My diet hasn't been the greatest the last month. Lots of surgeries, which meant more patients in my care, some struggles with my surgical nurse—oh, who, by the way, called me obsessive, then quit—and then add in the last few days . . . I'm sincerely amazed I'm upright."

Carrie stirred her coffee and took a seat close to Tracie's. "Yeah, Scott shared what's been happening to you." Her brown eyes were warm and gentle. "I'm so sorry."

Tracie fixed her gaze on the swirl of coffee, chocolate, and creamer in her mug. The kindness in the other woman's voice was almost her undoing. She hadn't completely lost her mind . . . yet. But her grip on sanity felt less and less sure the more this situation dragged on. "Thank you," she finally whispered and sat down.

A warm hand covered her arm, and Tracie looked up. Carrie gave her a squeeze. "I know we don't really know each other." She chuckled. "Well, we don't know each other at all, but I have been praying for you since you called Scott and Jason about Mac."

"Lord knows I needed those prayers." Tracie watched the tiny bubbles in her coffee swirl. With everything that had happened the last few months, Mac's surgery seemed like a lifetime ago. "Mac was a bear."

Carrie pulled back and sipped her coffee. "*That* I can imagine. I didn't know Mac before the 26 Below attack. But I've seen Scott's grief over his friend the last two and a half years. It's been heartbreaking. Seeing him now?" Tears glinted in the agent's eyes. "It's a work of Jesus. And He's used you in that process."

The encouragement settled over Tracie like a warm blanket. Sure, she'd heard compliments about her work many times. But for this kind of encouragement to come from another believer . . . It meant more than she could express. She sniffed and tried to laugh off the tears. "Your husband and Jason were pretty instrumental too."

A large grin bloomed on Carrie's face. "Oh, I'm sure. Those guys have a tight thing going, and I'm not about to stand in the way of something good like that. I believe in the power of prayer. Of intercession. And I know we've all been doing that for Mac the last couple of years." She shifted in her chair. "But that's enough about him for now. I'd like to get to know you."

Dread flooded Tracie's chest. How did she answer that question anymore? What was there to know about her? She was a recovering alcoholic. A washed-up surgeon being framed for murder. An obsessive perfectionist who apparently cared too much about people. It was what kept landing her in hot water. None of that sounded like qualities anyone wanted in a friend.

Carrie released a light laugh. "I wasn't trying to interrogate you. I promise."

Tracie's face must tell a sad tale. "Sorry. I was just trying to pick which one of my most desirable qualities to share with you. Accused accomplice to a murder? Or a useless surgeon? How about failed medical examiner?"

"If the guys or myself believed that you were any of those things, you wouldn't be here. Were you an accomplice to a murder?"

"No." The word ripped from her with force. Why did a question from an actual agent feel so intimidating?

"Are you a useless surgeon because you've been sued for malpractice? Is it true that no one ever wants you to operate on them?" Her new friend's face was blank, except for the arched eyebrow on her forehead.

"I know what you're doing."

Carrie's face didn't change, and her tone stayed even. "But can you answer my questions?"

Tracie took a sip of coffee and then leaned back in the chair. "Yes. The answer is no."

"And does caring about a hurting family in the darkest hour of their lives make you a failure as a medical examiner?"

Pain shot through her heart. "It does if you make promises you can't keep," Tracie whispered, and inhaled a shuddering breath. A single tear slipped down her cheek, and she swiped it away. She couldn't cry here. Not now. If she started, she wouldn't stop.

Carrie scooted her chair closer and leaned forward, her hands clasped. She tilted her head and caught Tracie's eye. "I know this is difficult to remember when you are in the middle of a storm. Lies, no matter how public they become or who believes them, are still lies. They are the tools of the enemy. They aren't from the Lord."

"But these lies have been spread everywhere." Frustration laced every word. "It's so overwhelming. And I feel completely helpless."

"I know how that feels." Carrie rolled her coffee tumbler between her hands. "I know how *he* can make you feel."

Tracie bit her lip. She wasn't the first victim of the Typhon Killer.

Carrie took a deep breath. "I'm sure you saw on the news or heard the guys mention the crossword-creepy serial killer?" At Tracie's nod, she continued. "I was the lead investigator on that case."

"That's right." The words whooshed out on a breath. Tracie remembered it all too well. Her love of crossword puzzles had been permanently quenched during the case. A thought from a conversation with the guys resurfaced. "You're the one who called him a psychopath."

"That's me!" Laughter shook the woman's shoulders. "And, ooh boy, did I get in trouble for that. He was so angry. But I spoke the truth."

Tracie leaned forward again, feeling comfortable with this woman, as if they'd known one another for years. "Do you mind telling me what happened? I mean, I followed the news, but you know how accurate that can be."

"I don't mind, but it was tough. I was a rookie for the ABI." Carrie's tone was one of self-deprecation. "I think I'd been in this department for a red-hot minute. My boss, Kevin Hogan, was the best. He trained agents for each aspect of the job and rotated us through every position, even being the lead.

"My first case as lead detective was a multicar pileup in the middle of winter. Two people died. It was horrific." She shook her head. "Our killer hacked the traffic lights. Everyone thought their light was green, and no one stopped."

Tracie's eyes widened. What was the world coming to? How could people be so intent on taking life? On destroying people just for the . . . fun of it? "That had to be awful."

Carrie nodded, and to Tracie's surprise, a smile softened the woman's face. "It was. But it's also how I met Scott. You want to talk about being put through the fire?" She fanned her face. "It was like being thrown into a volcano. Had we known what was coming after that first case . . . I'm sure Scott would have gone running."

As Carrie took another sip of coffee, light glinted off the small diamond on her left hand. Tracie studied the ring, admiring its simplicity and the love it so clearly represented. She bit her lip. Would she ever have a love like that? She shook her head. Not if she couldn't let go of things.

"So was that when the creepy crossword-puzzle dude started sending the clues?"

"Pretty much. It started with a sinister phone call, threatening death after death if I didn't figure out clues the killer left behind." Carrie shook her head and looked toward the ceiling. "It was maddening. And I felt exactly what you were talking about. Helpless. Frustrated. Like the weight of solving the case was only on me. I was so prideful."

That confession shocked Tracie. "Prideful?"

"Yup. I was new. Obsessed with being the hero of the team, of bearing the whole responsibility for making sure that maniac was caught. Like I was the only one who could do it—even though I *knew* I couldn't." Carrie rolled her eyes. "As if God could control the whole universe except this one case. Kevin and Alan were amazing. They kept talking me off the ledge and holding me accountable. I had to learn to do what I *could* do to the best of my ability and let everything else go."

The words were like an arrow into Tracie's heart. Was that part of her problem? Pride? Courtney's accusations came roaring back. Obsessed. Perfectionist. Unwilling to listen. The accusations still stung. And while she didn't think Courtney was right about everything, maybe there had been something to what she said.

Her youth pastor when she was growing up had said that pride was the basis of all sin. She'd thought about it many times over the years but had never used herself as the example. It had always been *look at so-and-so's sin*—yep, that was pride. Look at someone else's sin—pride. Everyone else's sin—pride.

It struck her hard as she thought of her own selfish nature, but she tucked the thoughts away for later, when she'd have time alone to examine them. "So how did it resolve? Are Kevin and Alan here? I'd like to meet them."

Sorrow dimmed the light in Carrie's eyes. "I wish you could." She cleared her throat and lifted her chin. "Our serial killer was hacking into crossword puzzles that were published all over the country and changing the clues for 8 DOWN. Instead of regular clues, they were clues for how he was going to kill his next victim."

"I remember. As a doctor, it made me sick to my stomach to see some of those clues."

"Yep." Carrie licked her lips. "He shortened the timeline between publishing clues and killing once we were onto him. And it got personal. In the middle of the case"—her voice cracked—"um, Kevin went up to Providence Hospital. He'd broken his leg a few weeks before and was on crutches. Our killer was waiting for him in a car. Plowed into him as Kevin crossed the street. He didn't survive."

Oh. Tracie's heart thudded as her breath caught in her throat. She plucked a few tissues from the box in the middle of the table and pressed them into Carrie's hand. "I'm so sorry."

Carrie wiped her eyes. "It was devastating. He was like a dad to me and had been such an incredible mentor. That's why when we thought we finally got the guy, it was such a huge win. Not only was a serial killer off the streets, but we'd caught *Kevin's* killer. Now . . ." Carrie shook her head. "Now we know he's still out there. And it's like ripping into an old wound all over again. No. It's worse than that. It's ripping into the old wound and pouring salt into it."

The depths of sorrow and evil were so devastating, Tracie could scarcely take it in. The ripples from this wicked man seemed unending. And now her own life was in his sights. Yet knowing there were others who understood what she was going through took away some of the loneliness she'd been struggling with the last month.

Carrie tossed the tissues to the side and sat up. "This man is a monster. That stupid nickname the press gave him is appropriate. Every single thing he does is evil in some of its most awful forms. But"—she rapped the table with a knuckle—"we've learned a lot about him in the past few days. We've gotten smarter in our pursuit. With God's help, we'll catch him this time. You can't let him into your head, Tracie. Even though everything seems so dark and hope is impossible to find . . . cling to Jesus. Hold on to Him with everything you have. He will sustain you."

Tracie ran her fingers across her chin, wiping away tears. She could hear the ring of truth in Carrie's voice. The experience, the sorrow, the pain . . . and the hope. "Thank you for sharing all of that with me. It means a lot. To know I'm not alone." The last word came out on a whisper.

Carrie put a hand on Tracie's shoulder. "You are most definitely not alone. We all care about you and will do whatever is in our power to help you through this." She paused. "I'm totally a hugger in an office of non-huggers. Mind if I give you one?"

Tracie let out a laugh and nodded. Carrie slipped an arm around her and gave her a tight squeeze.

It was so much like one of Tracie's mom's hugs, comforting and warm. Some of the tension eased out of her body as she hugged Carrie back.

They pulled apart, and Tracie swiped her fingers under her eyes. Though their talk had been heavy, it had also been hope filled. Jesus was with her in the middle of this. She knew it with every fiber of her being, but the lies had gotten so loud. *Thank You, Lord, for the reminder that Your truth is what has to be loudest in my life. Help me to hold on to You. And thank You for these people You've brought into my life.*

Carrie's phone buzzed on the table, and she read the message. "The FBI finally got back to me about the Members. Apparently they're frustrated, trying to get an accurate list without our UNSUB killing them all first." She huffed. "In other news, the guys should be back shortly." She shot Tracie a look. "They're bringing the good stuff from Golden Donuts. I hope you're hungry. And if you're not, grab one for later. Otherwise you'll lose out."

Tracie chuckled. "Thanks for letting me know."

"We girls have to help each other. I mean, I love my husband, but if I don't stake out pieces of pizza or the jalapeño-cheddar cornbread at our favorite restaurant . . ." Carrie shook her head. "I'd starve."

The two women shared a laugh, the heaviness of their conversation easing.

"The fun has arrived!" Scott announced as he strolled into the room, several boxes in his arms. He slid them onto the table and plucked a bright-blue box off the top. "Donuts, as promised." He bowed and put the box between Tracie and Carrie.

Carrie flicked open the lid and grinned at her husband. "An old-fashioned cake donut!" She plucked the baked good out of the box. "You really do love me."

"Always." Scott dropped a kiss on her head.

"Hey, no PDA on the premises," Mac growled as he walked in and made his way to Tracie. "No one wants to see that."

"It's true," Jason agreed. "No workplace romance."

"It's a little late for that," Carrie and Scott said at the same time, then laughed.

Tracie stifled a chuckle and reached for a chocolate glazed donut.

"Don't laugh at their antics," Mac whispered. "It only encourages them."

She glanced at him, unable to keep a grin off her face. "I think they're hilarious."

Mac hummed. "Carrie, maybe. Scott, definitely not. Hand me the bear claw, will you?"

She picked up his preferred treat and put it on a plate. He took it and pulled out the chair beside her.

"Sorry for leaving you in the lurch here. Did you and Carrie have a chance to get to know each other?" He booted up his laptop.

"Yeah, she shared some things with me about her case a couple of years ago . . ." Her voice trailed off as she studied Mac's profile. How could she be so careless? Carrie wasn't the only one who'd been impacted. Mac had lost his wife *and* daughter in the first attack. Tracie bit her lip. She'd been so focused on her own pain, she'd lost sight of what her friend had lost too.

Mac didn't seem to notice her sudden silence. "I'm glad she shared it with you. For many reasons. I—" He stopped midsentence.

Tracie looked at him, then his screen. "Mac? What's wrong?"

Jason, Carrie, and Scott turned to Mac as well.

"You okay, man?" Jason asked.

The look in Mac's eyes was haunted. "I just got an email. From the same guy who told me the monster was in Deadhorse. Where he tried to kill me."

CHAPTER NINE

940 Days After
July 8—9:34 a.m.
Latitude: 61.1802913° N, Longitude: 149.7792549° W
Alaska Bureau of Investigation—Anchorage

I know who he is. I can help you stop him.

Mac had read it over and over, and the team had done the same.

"What are you going to do?" Tracie voiced the question that dangled in front of everyone.

He glanced up and then back at the screen. "Why can't I shake the feeling that this is some sort of trap?"

Jason grunted. "Because the last time you followed the guy's lead, you got shot?"

"But he *did* lead me to him." Mac rubbed his jaw. "The only question is, did he do it because he wants the guy caught or because he wanted to set me up?" He glanced over at Scott. "Any luck?"

"Nope. Can't trace it." The fierce scowl on his friend's face wasn't encouraging. "He used a VPN, a throwaway email address, and a foreign server."

Mac released a long sigh, studying the faces in the room. Time to make a decision. "Okay. I'm writing him back. It's the only way." He clicked on the arrow for Reply, and steadied his hands over his keys.

Yeah, and last time I followed your lead, he shot me.
How do I know you didn't set me up?

After hitting Send, Mac leaned back in his chair and folded his arms. Now to wait. Which could be brutal. Maybe he should get another cup of coffee, stretch his legs, and grab another donut.

But a chat window opened. From the company's Gmail—*his* email—to his personal. "Um, guys?" He waved Scott and Jason over.

They rushed over and watched the screen.

I'm sorry about that. Truly, I am.
But haven't you wondered how
you ended up in Fairbanks?
Alive?

"Don't you have two-factor authentication on?" Jason's hushed question over Mac's shoulder had been exactly what was on his mind.

Mac grabbed his phone, swiped it open, and went to the Google authenticator app.

Don't bother checking your
email or the authenticator.

I cloned your phone.

"Well, he's got our attention now." Jason munched on a donut.

You cloned my phone? How
nice of you. When?

After I saved your life. In the
hospital.

You're saying you're the
one who helped me get to
Fairbanks.

Yes.

Carrie lifted a hand from the side of the table where she'd been working. "I've got the police report, and I'm going to follow up with the ambulance drivers. Keep him talking if you can. In case I have another question."

Mac nodded at her as another response came in.

You weren't supposed to get
hurt. But he knew someone
was getting close to him. That
was me, but he thought it was
you. Sorry about that. I've had
to go into hiding for the last
six months. But he's planning
something huge, and he's got
to be stopped.

Adrenaline rushed through Mac's body. Was this for real? An actual lead? Mac thumped the table with his fingers. "All right, guys. What do we think? Do we trust him?"

Scott spoke up first. "I would press for details. So you know he's not setting you up." He looked at his wife. "Got anything?"

She had the phone up to her ear. "Nope. Neither the ambulance driver from that night nor the EMT work there any longer. Apparently they've both left Fairbanks. And all the report says is that Mac was picked up a few blocks from the hospital and brought in with a gunshot wound. Witnesses heard a shot and called 911."

"All right then. Let's ask him how he got me to Fairbanks."

For me to trust that you aren't
attempting to set me up,
possibly again, I need
details. How did you get
me to Fairbanks alive?

No one spoke as they waited for the source's response.

Check into Denali's Best
helicopter services. They are
an executive charter. The
owner owed a debt, and I
arranged for you to be airlifted
out with EMTs as soon as I
saw that he shot you. Yes, I
was there. I witnessed it. You
had just come out of Flow
Station 1. Griz was dressed in
all-white Arctic gear. He shot
you through the driver's side
window and then walked to the
front of the truck. I was worried
he would shoot again, but he
didn't. He just pulled back the
hood of his coat and stared at
you.

Mac couldn't stop his eyes from going over the small section of
text again and again. "*Griz.* Is that his name?" His voice was barely
above a whisper. Then he blinked several times and caught Tracie's
gaze. "That's what happened." He shook off the emotion of having
a name to go with the face and nodded to the screen. "Okay, so
he was there. He says he got me to Fairbanks." But his mind kept
spinning.

What about my vehicle?

I arranged for it to be fixed and
cleaned up there in Fairbanks
after I had one of my associates
drive it down. They were to bring
you the keys at the hospital.
Look, I couldn't allow Griz to
kill you. And I couldn't allow for
him to be onto me. That's why I
arranged for the story that you
were shot near the hospital and
had someone take the fall.

Enough of this. By this time,
you have what you need.

I don't have time to play games,
Mr. McPherson. None of us
do. The media hasn't pieced it
together—at least it hasn't been
aired—but Griz is methodically
killing every one of the Members.
Eight are already dead.

If anyone can stop him, it's your
team. But you're going to need
my help.

I am part of the group called
the Members.

Griz betrayed us. He has done
some horrible things that we

do not condone. He needs to
be stopped. But I need your
assurance you will not come
after me.

Check the Juneau water hack.
The malware that was used
has his digital fingerprint. He
created it for us to use.

I'll be in touch. Pay attention.
134.729

What were those numbers? When Mac looked up from his screen, the guys were already on their computers. Scott and Jason were typing furiously, looking determined.

"You need to be careful." Carrie shook her head. "We don't know a lot about his group, but they're the ones this guy Griz apparently started with. They're not above doing horrible things themselves. They planned the cyberterrorist attack up in Fairbanks."

His gaze connected with Tracie's again. She grimaced and lifted her shoulders. "The enemy of my enemy is my friend."

✦ ✦ ✦

55 Days Until Final Judgment
24 Members Left
July 8—1:13 p.m.
Latitude: 61.539307° N, Longitude: 150.112825° W
A Remote Cabin—Big Lake, Alaska

> *My dear friend Mac,*
> *By now you and your friends are frantically*

trying to find a trail of breadcrumbs that will lead you to me.

While I am sure you are much like me and love a good challenge, I do have to give you fair warning. As much as I enjoy the chase, and it is greatly entertaining for me to watch you struggle in your incompetence, there comes a time for the losing team to concede.

Every time you insist on tracing my footprints, you put lives on the line.

If you get too close, you will trip one of many traps I have set that will then put people in imminent danger. I know this isn't something you want. Your desire to protect is noble, even if it is shortsighted. By trying to protect them from me, you're only putting them tiin more danger.

Allow me to give you a piece of advice: stop now while you're ahead. You'll never beat me. You have fifty-five days and counting down.

Final judgment is coming, my friend. Let's watch it together.

Sincerely,
The Typhon Killer

He held up the paper and marveled at his own genius. Mac wouldn't be able to resist taking the bait.

Who needed wars and elections to divide the population? All people needed was anger and fear.

✦ ✦ ✦

24 Fellow Members Remain
July 8—10:00 p.m.

Latitude: 61.302290° N, Longitude: 149.470746° W
Eagle River

"When was the last time you were in contact with your brother?" She twisted the thick, solid-gold bracelet around her wrist and pursed her lips.

Kirk Myers stood in front of her solid mahogany desk, his hands clasped in front of him. "Not since I was in jail."

"Do you think he'd be a good asset for us? Would he believe you if you went to him in a time of crisis?" Crossing her legs, she set one elbow on the buttery leather arm of her chair.

"I could be convincing, if needed."

With laser-sharp focus, she analyzed him. "Are you clean, Mr. Myers?"

He didn't flinch. "Yes, ma'am, you know I am."

"For how long?"

"Eighteen months." His gaze never left hers.

"Even as Griz's supplier, you've managed to stay clean? That's impressive." She didn't offer praise often, but the guy deserved it. Especially since he had stepped up and handled every assigned task with precision, never balking, and with the utmost respect for her. That included an intense rehab program she'd put him through. Grueling and without mercy.

Kirk had proven himself time and again. She could trust him. She knew that now.

"Do you want me to reach out to my brother? I'm pretty sure he thinks I'm dead."

"Not yet." She bobbed her foot up and down. "But soon. First, I need to hear your report on our Mr. Chandler."

"Yes, ma'am."

"When was your last drop?"

"Two days ago."

"What kind of condition is he in?"

He looked off into the distance. "That's a tough question. He's an incredibly strong, willful, and smart human being. But that being said, he's also . . ." His head wagged back and forth, as if he was trying to find the correct term. "Deteriorating."

"In what way? Is he vulnerable?"

"No." Kirk grunted. "He's far from vulnerable. But I do think he's beginning to crack. He thinks he's in complete control of his meds. He knows what makes him feel great and think faster, but he's upped them to an amount that could very well send him over the edge. He's still in control, but for how long? That's anyone's guess."

Well. She could work with that. "Leave me a list of his new dosages. I'll have the good doctor advise me on the best way to proceed."

"Griz'll know if you mess with his meds, ma'am." Kirk's warning was clipped. Concerned.

"Oh, I know. I'm not planning on doing that, but it would be prudent to know what potential symptoms or weaknesses our adversary might display that we can exploit."

His nod was slow, his brow still furrowed.

"You're worried about me, aren't you?"

"He *is* killing us off one by one."

"True." She couldn't hold his gaze, and shifted her eyes to the window. Nothing but blackness greeted her. "But Griz will save me for last." She rubbed her forehead. No matter what, she had to make sure she stopped him before that happened.

CHAPTER TEN

941 Days After
July 9—7:31 a.m.
Latitude: 61.1802913° N, Longitude: 149.7792549° W
Alaska Bureau of Investigation

MAC PACED THE CONFERENCE ROOM. He hated tight spaces. Especially after the last two years, when he hadn't worked in an office at all. But this was what he had to work with. The monster—*God forgive me for my thoughts toward him*—the *man* called Griz had to be stopped.

The big question hanging over everyone's head was *how.*

Scott and Carrie had flown to Juneau yesterday afternoon to see what they could find. If what their source said was true, there had to be some evidence on-site there somewhere. A USB drive still plugged in. Something. Of course, the folks in Juneau might have already found it, but now that they knew they were looking for Griz's digital fingerprint, then maybe—just maybe—they might have some luck. He sat for a moment, burying his face in his palms. *Please, Lord.*

Tracie had offered to go in case she could offer some medical help, and they'd welcomed her along. Mac now felt alone without her presence. It had been a long time since he'd wanted someone around.

He hadn't realized how much she'd gotten under his skin the last few months.

He'd given her a tough time every step of the way, but he'd really gotten used to having her in his life. The last couple days reinforced that. Spending so much time with her away from the hospital made him appreciate her even more.

Man, he hated that she'd been dragged into all this.

Because of him.

Griz had obviously attacked her because of him. It made Mac feel like a heel, but he'd just have to fix it. And catch the guy for good.

Sarah and Beth had been innocent bystanders. They hadn't even been on this guy's radar. And he'd taken them anyway. Tracie . . . she was in his sights.

Mac hated him.

For all he'd taken away.

No. Stop.

He bolted out of his chair and headed straight to the men's room. This train of thought had sent him spiraling down before. He wouldn't go there. He couldn't allow hate to win.

God, help me. Mac splashed water on his face and scrubbed at it. If only he could scrub his thoughts the same way. *Please . . . I need Your wisdom and help more than ever.*

Why did all his prayers of late seem to be the same? Pleading for help.

He examined the old guy in the mirror staring back at him. At almost forty, he looked like he'd aged a decade in the past two years. That's what grief and getting shot would do to a man. He tried to laugh it off but couldn't.

All right, Lord. I'm listening. I know I keep begging for Your help, but that's because You are Almighty God and I'm not. I might not have any words to say other than help, *but You know. You know my struggles. You know my failings. You know my inner thoughts. I can't do this on my own—I've tried and failed. So yes, God, please help.*

No zap of lightning or grand answers from heaven came flying through the window, but a peace he couldn't have fathomed a few months ago pressed on him like a weighted blanket. Soothing.

Calming. Just enough to recognize it was there. Mac dried his face and took one last glance in the mirror, then headed back to the conference room.

At his computer, he checked the spreadsheet he'd shared with the guys at Cyber Solutions around the state. Each person had tasks assigned to them in addition to the tasks that the entire team was working on. If anyone had a new piece to the puzzle, they were to place it in the secure drive for everyone to see. This helped because many times, it took the collective brainstorming of the entire group to figure out each facet.

But as he made his own punch list, Mac didn't like what he saw. Too many details pulled at him.

The new clue from the water hack in Juneau that might help trace Griz.

The source from the Members. Could that person be trusted?

The fact that Griz had hacked into their computers in the coffee shop and watched them through the cameras. They'd all upped their own security, but still. The man seemed to get into anything and everything.

The doxing of Tracie. Mac couldn't allow her to lose her career because of him.

The thought of Tracie brought his thoughts back to earlier. In his grief, he'd never thought he could care for another woman again. But something tugged him toward—

"Mac?" One of the detectives—Alan—leaned around the door. "A messenger just delivered a letter for you. You're gonna want to see this."

Mac surged from his seat and followed Alan to a desk in the middle of the big squad room. Several others from the team had gloves on and surrounded the note.

Alan spoke up. "The messenger brought it to the building and said it was from Griz. It's dated yesterday. After your source named the guy, we had forensics take a look at it first."

"When did it arrive?" Mac leaned forward to see the missive.

"About three minutes ago."

The calligraphy was perfect. Like John Hancock had penned it. Mac read the letter, and his stomach sank like a rock to the bottom of a lake.

"Great."

Alan's hands were on his hips. "What are you thinking?"

Too many thoughts warred in his brain. Mac took a deep breath to calm the anxiety clawing at his chest. "We know this guy is brilliant. We know he understands the cyber world all too well and can navigate his way through just about anything. He's a master hacker. After all he's done, these aren't empty threats. Which means tracking him will have consequences."

"But we *have* to." The words from Alan's mouth carried the weight they all felt in that moment.

"Yeah . . ." Mac put both his hands up to his head and squeezed. There wasn't any way around it. And Griz knew it. He'd *planned* it that way. "Okay. What about this countdown? Would he really be that arrogant to tell us when he's going to do something?"

Alan shook his head. "This guy is scarier than any other suspect I've gone after. I don't think it's just arrogance. It's blatant taunting. He's using it to instill fear."

If they left him alone, he'd cause destruction and probably many more people would die. He'd get more attention, which would fuel his thirst. On the other hand, if they pursued him, he promised to set off who knew what kind of chaos that would no doubt also be destructive, and people would die.

It was lose-lose. No matter what. And this guy loved it.

Mac's cell phone buzzed in his pocket, and he dug it out. Scott. Good. "Hey, whatcha got?"

"We've got the drive that triggered the hack here. The FBI handed it over when we told them what we knew. Running it through our software now to search out his digital fingerprint. It might take a while, but at least we've got it."

"How are things there?"

"Water systems are fixed and back online. But, Mac"—Scott's voice was heavy with sorrow and anger—"there are lots of sick people in the hospital. Five more have died. A hundred or so are critical, but they're hoping for the best."

"Even after all this time? It's been a month."

"Apparently." Voices were muffled in the background, then Scott was back. "Tracie can explain it better."

Some shuffling sounded. Mac's heart lifted with even the thought of hearing her voice.

"Mac?"

"I'm here."

Her sigh traveled across the line. He knew that sigh and braced himself for her news. "The situation's not good, I'm afraid. The amount of sodium hydroxide that was released into the water was extreme. It can cause massive damage if swallowed. Mouth, throat, esophagus, stomach, even eyes, lungs, and nose are vulnerable to being affected. But, Mac . . ." Tracie paused, and dread crept up his spine. "It doesn't stop after the victim stops drinking the contaminated water. The damage can continue for several weeks after ingestion. Fatalities can still occur a month later. Possibly more when it's such a significant amount of poison. But the medical facilities here are amazing and handling it well. We'll know the full extent in the next few weeks."

He closed his eyes. More casualties. He hated it. Griz was winning. Again. "All right. When do you head back?"

"Let me give you back to Scott."

Another muffled exchange. "We'll leave within the hour, Mac. Unless there's something else you need us to do down here?"

"No. We need all hands on deck."

"Got it."

The call ended, and Mac updated the ABI team. He glanced around the room, watching the impact of the news. Anger. Sorrow. Shock. The weight of *another* attack, of more lives lost, was almost too much to bear.

Alan placed a hand on his shoulder. "We'll work on finding out what we can about the letter. Let forensics handle it. You get back to doing what you guys do best."

With a nod, he headed to the conference room.

His cell buzzed again. A local 907 number. Huh. "This is Mac."

"Mr. McPherson? This is Ken from the Aurora Borealis Apartments?"

When he'd left Anchorage more than two years ago on the manhunt for Griz, he'd put all his things into storage and sold his house. Ever since, he'd lived out of hotels or even his truck during the summer. But coming back to his hometown during tourist season made it almost impossible to find a hotel for a longer stay that was affordable. Thankfully, he still had connections, which led him to these little apartments. He really didn't want to sleep in his truck for another night. If the guys found out, they'd string him up. Worse. What if Tracie found out?

"Hey, thanks for getting me a place so quick. What can I do for you?"

"That's the problem. Your credit card was declined. Could you come down to the office? The number you gave us over the phone didn't work, and our business office says you have to bring a different one in person."

"Sure. I must have given you the wrong number." He shook his head. There wasn't time for this. But he needed a place to stay. He closed his laptop and headed for the exit. "Hey, Alan, I've got to go handle something so I have a place to sleep. I'll be back as quick as I can."

"Got it." Alan gave him a thumbs-up, his phone pressed to his ear. He frowned and spoke into it. "What do you mean it's been declined?"

What? Mac stopped in his tracks. Another member of the team had something declined? He caught Alan's gaze, and the recognition was clear.

This *wasn't* a coincidence.

✦ ✦ ✦

54 Days Until Final Judgment
24 Members Left
July 9—10:53 a.m.
Latitude: 61.539307° N, Longitude: 150.112825° W
Outside a Remote Cabin—Big Lake

The hateful correspondence and threats had continued even though Griz gave them fair warning.

It didn't matter that they knew who he was. Pretty soon the whole world would. When it was time. But not until then.

If they thought they could get at him, even stop him? They were delusional.

Eight were gone. The remaining Members were out of their minds if they thought they had a chance.

She should know better than anyone.

Ridiculous.

He twitched and blinked against the dryness in his eyes. Such a nuisance. He had a job to do. A mission.

Still his eyes wouldn't cooperate. He pressed the heels of his hands against them for a moment, then focused again and watched the blip headed across the screen.

He'd arranged this little meeting of a few of the higher-ups. The Members were joining forces with other organizations to boost their strength. Or so they thought.

They really had no idea what they had started.

Well, it was time to send another message. They obviously weren't paying attention.

He pressed three keys on the keyboard and hovered his index finger over the Enter key. The blip crept closer to his location.

He let his finger drop to the key.

The blip disappeared.

Just like that.

What a wonderful feeling.

Sliding out of his vehicle, he glanced up at the sky and saw the flaming pieces of debris fall to the earth.

He was beginning to really like explosions. Time to head back to Deadhorse.

✦ ✦ ✦

Eight Years, One Month, Seven Days Sober
July 9—11:07 a.m.
In the Air over the Gulf of Alaska

Tracie's knee bounced up and down in the small plane as they flew closer and closer to the mainland shores of Alaska.

She'd missed the AA meeting and couldn't get ahold of her sponsor. That worried her. In all of the eight-plus years of her sobriety, she'd never *once* had trouble getting through. Immediately.

On top of that, she'd never been in the position she was in now. Desperate for a drink. Desperate for escape. Desperate for something to take it all away.

What if the mastermind behind all this knew about her . . . problem? Could he have done something to Susan?

Concern gnawed at her. She knew Susan's parents and brother relatively well. Maybe she should just get in touch with them. Make sure the woman who'd been a rock for her all these years . . .

"We're starting our descent now." Scott spoke into his headset and glanced over his shoulder at her. "You okay?"

His wife swiveled around at his question, catching Tracie's gaze.

Both looked at her with worry etched on their faces. She couldn't add to their stress. They had a criminal to catch and didn't have time to worry about her. Tracie pasted on a smile. "Yeah, I'm fine. Just tired."

✦ ✦ ✦

941 Days After
July 9—12:28 p.m.
Latitude: 61.1802913° N, Longitude: 149.7792549° W
Alaska Bureau of Investigation

Every single person in the ABI was affected by the same thing. Jason too. When Mac called the Cyber Solutions office, it had happened there as well. Bank accounts locked up. Credit cards declined. When Scott, Carrie, and Tracie returned, Mac had a feeling they would say the same.

Was this one of the traps Griz had alluded to? Or was he just messing with them?

The fact that it had happened right after the team had found Griz's code in Juneau and begun to look for his digital fingerprint could not be a coincidence. It couldn't be.

Several from the ABI had raced to their banks or homes to handle things for their families. One spouse got stuck at a gas station and couldn't pay. Another spouse was at the grocery store in the checkout line. Pregnant, and twins in the cart. They needed food.

For once Mac was thankful he was alone. At least this only affected him. So yeah, it was a nuisance. And he wouldn't have a place to stay. He'd bunk at . . . Scott and Carrie's? Jason was already there, and they didn't even have room for him. Well, there was always his truck. His neck and back tensed. Where he'd sleep was the least of his worries right now.

As he sat back down in front of his computer, his mind raced through all the facts they had gathered.

The question reverberated. Was this one of the traps?

No one had died though. And Griz had made it clear lives would be on the line.

So maybe this was just him flexing his hacker muscles and taunting them all.

A distraction.

Mac leaned back in the chair and propped his feet on the table as his thoughts ran through it all. That had to be it.

Griz understood there would be multitudes of people on the case now. Not just Mac and his team. Every law enforcement agency in the state was working on stopping him.

So distractions would be key.

But the threat was out there. Meaning that whenever any one of them got close, Griz would set off . . . something.

A good thing. And a bad thing.

Good in that they would know they were on the right track. Bad in that they had no idea who he would hurt. No one wanted to take the risk, but in the grand scheme of things, they had to if they were going to stop him.

There had to be another way. There had to be.

But no matter how hard he thought it through, he couldn't find any other path than the one they were on.

Mac stretched his arms up over his head and closed his eyes for several seconds. It burned him up that there was no other conclusion than more people losing their lives because of this monster.

He needed to change gears. Shift his thinking.

Mac stood and walked into the squad room. He spotted Alan speaking with another agent. Their faces didn't look like they had good news.

Alan's frown deepened when he spotted Mac. "There's been an explosion at a small airstrip outside of Willow. Six people plus the pilot were on that plane."

CHAPTER ELEVEN

Eight Years, One Month, Eight Days Sober
July 10—1:34 p.m.
Latitude: 61.1802913° N, Longitude: 149.7792549° W
Alaska Bureau of Investigation

THE CONFERENCE ROOM SMELLED LIKE stale pastries and potato chips. The walls seemed to be inching closer and closer to her, hemming Tracie in with no escape route.

Today was not going well. At all. Even though she'd had an encouraging phone call from the detectives in DC, it hadn't changed her current predicament.

She swiped mindlessly through the apps on her phone, not really seeing what was on the screen. No one would talk to her. Not her old colleagues in DC. Definitely not Congresswoman Sanderson and her family.

Not that she really expected them to talk to her. But she needed to do *something* to clear her name.

The Cyber Solutions guys were working overtime not only to help everyone clear their credit—she couldn't begin to fathom how they were going to untangle *that* mess—but also trying to find anything from the water-tainting attack that would help them trace their mystery man in the future. To stop him before he could unleash something else.

One thing was certain—he knew how to create time-consuming distractions.

A fact that had Mac back into his fierce-bear mentality. She didn't mind that kind of intensity when it wasn't directed at her. He was a fighter, and she appreciated everything he and his team were doing.

Two new Cyber Solutions guys she hadn't met before were camped out in a little closet-size space, doing their best to find the source that had contacted Mac. That was their only focus because everyone had resigned to thinking that their best bet right now was to link arms with the crazed group that called themselves the Members. How to accomplish that was the question.

Griz—whoever he was—had been their leader, as recently as two and a half years ago. *Someone* must have information that could help them.

She refused to call him the Typhon Killer. The name was everywhere in the media. The amount of coverage he received was infuriating. Obsession with what he would do next was at an all-time high. The papers. Cable news stations. Social media. The stories were everywhere.

As she scrolled on her phone, she blew out a breath. Well, there was a bonus. The story of her covering up a murder seemed to have fallen out of the news cycle. Now that she thought about it, she hadn't received one phone call today requesting a comment about the cold case. Her parents left a message yesterday saying the press was no longer camped out on their street, begging for statements about their daughter.

Tracie clicked her phone to sleep and shoved it to the middle of the table. Doomscrolling was doing nothing to help her. She leaned back in the chair, stretching her arms over her head. Maybe she should call her boss and see if the board would be willing to let her come back to work early. Their whole reasoning for this long hiatus had been bad press.

Well, now there was no press. Right? Everyone was caught up in the hype of the maniac.

Hope rushed through her. She needed to go back to work. Mostly because the urge to dive back into her vice was too strong when she wasn't focused on her job and staying busy.

Yeah, she'd call her boss. Maybe get some normalcy back to her life. But she didn't want to have this conversation where everyone could hear. A perfect excuse to get out of this room for a while. She'd been inside way too long anyway. Since this whole debacle had started, running outside had been impossible. Running on a treadmill wasn't the same. She needed sunlight. Fresh air. To enjoy the beauty of an Alaskan summer.

"I'm going outside for a few minutes." She pushed back from the table.

Carrie glanced up from her computer and nodded. "Just stay alert while you're out there. Don't stray too far from the building."

Tracie gave her a thumbs-up and grabbed her phone. Shoving it into her back pocket, she walked the now familiar path from the conference room at the back of the squad room, through the locked glass doors, and into the lobby. She gave Rob, the officer on guard, a wave.

"Are you leaving for the day, Miss Tracie?" He opened the door for her. His southern charm always made her smile.

"No, just need some natural vitamin D."

Rob glanced up at the cloudless blue sky. "It's a beautiful day for that."

Tracie thanked him and made her way down the wide walkway. The sun instantly warmed her, taking away the chill of air-conditioning that lingered on her skin. She found a small bench nestled among a cluster of evergreen trees that lined one side of the sidewalk, and sat down.

Rob wasn't lying. The day was practically perfect. Seventy degrees. The sky a soft blue with tiny, fluffy clouds drifting by. The scent of pine wafting on the breeze. It reminded her of home. That little parcel of land that had been her haven before everything came crashing down.

She closed her eyes, lifted her face to the sun, and relished its bright rays. Already she felt ten times better than five minutes ago. Maybe if she promised to run without earbuds, Mac would agree to let her exercise on a public path until she went home.

Mac.

How much had changed in the last seven months! Who knew when he'd rolled into her operating room, on the verge of death, that a friendship would bloom between them. And that his group of friends would welcome her into their circle with such kindness.

It was as if the Lord used one of the darkest moments of her life to draw her into a community willing to walk alongside her. How had she thought she could survive without the gift of friendship and camaraderie? Her conversation with Carrie from a couple days ago came to mind.

Pride. That's how. Relying on herself. Not handing over her burdens to the Lord. In her quest to do the very best she could, she'd sequestered herself from anyone else. She didn't want to ever let someone down again. To do that, she had to remain in control and keep everyone at arm's length.

Something else that needed to change.

Lord, I'm definitely going to need Your help overcoming my pride and desire to do everything on my own. Please, Lord . . . She exhaled a long breath.

She let her mind wander back to Mac. He was the first person she'd allowed in for a while. Probably because she'd forced her way into his life to get him to heal. Still, had it not been for Jason and Scott, Mac would probably be dead on the side of the road somewhere.

Her heart clenched. She cared more about David McPherson than she let on. It was more than his just being her patient. More than just a friend.

Somehow that big bear of a man had opened up her heart.

She glanced back at the building and could envision the team huddled in the squad room. It would be nice to be a part of something like this. Was there even a chance of that up in Fairbanks? Jason and his wife lived up there. But where would Mac land?

He'd probably come back here. Cyber Solutions was his firm, wasn't it?

She shook her head and banished the thoughts. She'd have to start fresh on her own. Once all this blew over, she'd make an effort to develop some real relationships. Maybe it was time for her to get more involved at church.

If she was going to start over, she needed to call her boss and get back to work. Plain and simple. Slipping in her earbuds, she pulled up his contact information and hit Call.

It rang twice. "Tracie. This is a surprise." His voice was light, unguarded.

She immediately relaxed. That was a good sign. She used as much lightheartedness as she could. "Hey there. I just wanted to check in and see how things are going."

"Fine, fine. We are definitely missing your skills and presence in the operating room."

She couldn't keep the grin from her face. "Well, I definitely miss being there." She cleared her throat. Was it too soon after the news had died down? She'd risk it. "That's actually why I'm calling. I had a conversation with the detectives out in DC this morning."

"Oh really?"

"Yes, and they've let me know that there is no evidence, concrete or circumstantial, that links me as an accomplice to that cold case. The only evidence is the log-in information that was released online. And that can't be substantiated in any way. The videos have all been proven to be fake. So they won't be pressing any charges." She left off the fact that the detective had said *at this time*. A positive outlook was her best bet to get her job back.

"That's excellent news. I will be sure to let the board know the progress on that front." Now he sounded distracted. Of course, as hospital administrator, he was always juggling twenty different things at once.

"Thank you so much. I really appreciate that. Do you . . ." She hesitated, then plunged forward. "With this news and the lack of press coverage . . . would the board allow me to come back early?"

Silence stretched between them.

"I'm sorry, Tracie." He sighed. "The board is adamant that you take all six weeks of the administrative leave. Just to be sure this dies down and goes away for good. Then there's also the fact that you haven't taken any vacation in a long time. This is for the best."

Disappointment rippled through her. "Oh. I see."

"It's nothing personal, Tracie. And quite frankly, despite the unfortunate circumstances, I think the break is good for you. I can't have my best surgeon breaking down due to lack of time off. Your hours have become too many in the last year. Getting away from this place and the stress is healthy for you."

Tracie fought the prick of tears. That stung. She wasn't on the verge of burnout. Why didn't anyone understand that helping people was what the Lord had called her to do? That she needed to work, to be available for her patients.

"Tracie?"

"Hmm? Oh. Sorry. I appreciate your candor. And your willingness to let the board know what the status of this situation is."

"I'm glad to do it. And don't be upset about what I said earlier. I think all the surgeons at the hospital should rotate on sabbatical. The amount of pressure you're all under is heavy and extreme. A long break and the chance to get away are good things. The next several weeks will fly by. Come August, we'll be waiting for your return with open arms."

Tracie bit her lip. She knew he meant well and was doing what he thought was best for her and her career. And she really didn't have much choice, did she. "Thank you. I will see you then."

They exchanged goodbyes, and Tracie yanked out her earbuds. She dropped her head in her hands. Frustration clawed at her, begging for release. She'd never been one for throwing things, but she was tempted to throw her phone against a brick wall.

"Excuse me?"

A high-pitched voice interrupted her thoughts.

Tracie opened her eyes and looked up. A young woman stood just to her left, brown hair piled on top of her head in a messy bun. She wore jeans and a black-and-white-striped shirt with a black blazer over it. A lanyard with a large, laminated pass reading PRESS hung around her neck.

"Are you Dr. Tracie Hunter?" the young woman asked, pushing a pair of large black glasses up the bridge of her nose.

"Yes." She drew out the word. "And you are?"

"Hailey Thomas, from the *Daily Alaskan*." The reporter held out her hand.

Tracie shook it hesitantly. "What can I do for you? Are you supposed to be here?"

Hailey scooted around Tracie and sat at the other end of the bench. "I'm part of the press pool here at the ABI. And I've been following your story the last few weeks. It's crazy what's been posted, and . . . well . . . I think it's wrong. You've been treated unfairly by some of my colleagues."

Tracie blinked. "Oh?" Maybe all press weren't bad.

Hailey nodded. "Everyone wants to be the first to have the big break on a major story. But not everyone cares about the facts. It's just a rush to get the biggest, craziest headline up before anyone else."

"It does seem like a cutthroat industry." Tracie smoothed her hands over her knees. "I appreciate your recognizing that the story hasn't been reported fairly."

"It's not what we're taught in school." Hailey brushed her wispy bangs out of her eyes. "We're supposed to be neutral, not picking a side. And, man, they are treating this Typhon Killer almost like he's a hero!"

Tracie's eyes went wide. "Yes! That's so frustrating. It's almost like he's being glamorized in the press for all his brilliance and planning."

Hailey leaned forward. "I can only imagine how hard it is. Especially when someone has the kind of storied career you do. I did some reading about your history as a surgeon. Very impressive. So many of your patients sing your praises."

The compliment warmed her. The fact that so many people were willing to stand up for her, to vouch for her character meant the world. "Thank you."

"It must have taken time to build such a good reputation." Hailey tipped her head to one side. "I mean, it's hard to care for people in any profession for a long time."

"Oh, surgery is incredibly rewarding. Being able to bring order out of chaos, literally fixing what's wrong in someone's body so they can heal . . ." Tracie smiled. "There's nothing like it."

Hailey straightened. "Interesting that you would use the phrase 'order out of chaos.' It's a phrase that's similar to things the Typhon Killer has said."

Tracie furrowed her brow. "What?"

"Chaos is his thing. Or haven't you been reading the news?" The reporter leaned forward. "Just this morning he sent in a statement. Creating chaos and then trying to bend the will of people through fear to what he wants."

The hair on the back of her neck prickled. "I'm sorry, but what are you getting at?"

Hailey arched an eyebrow at her. "In studying you, Dr. Hunter, I've noticed several language similarities between you and the Typhon Killer."

Anger and shock shot through Tracie. "I think you need to leave." She stood.

Hailey stood with her and blocked her way back toward the ABI building. "How do you explain the fact that you were in Fairbanks the day of the 26 Below attack and *conveniently* left before the power went out? Were you helping him set up his targets, then getting out while you still could?" She shoved a recorder into Tracie's face.

This was not happening. Her chest tightened. She couldn't breathe. How? Why? What was this woman saying?

"And you were in Anchorage the day Peter Chandler was killed. Did you kill him, Dr. Hunter? To cover your own tracks?" The reporter continued to shove the digital recorder in Tracie's direction.

She could see the bright-red Record button pulsating, the timer flicking numbers across the screen.

She'd been recording the whole time they'd been talking. Tracie's stomach rolled.

"You okay out here, Miss Tracie?"

The deep rumble of Rob's voice nearly buckled her knees. "This reporter has been asked to leave," she croaked. "And refuses to."

Rob turned his dark gaze to Hailey Thomas. He glanced at her press badge and then back to her face. "The press pool has been dismissed for the day. And I believe Dr. Hunter has asked you to leave."

The young woman clenched her jaw and stuffed the recorder in her pocket. "Fine. But mark my words—I know there is a story here. And you won't get away with your lies." She stormed down the walkway to the parking lot.

Tracie looked at Rob. "You are a lifesaver."

The big man came and stood beside her, offering her his arm. "Let me help you inside. We'll tell Alan and Carrie what happened. They need to know the press is poking around again."

Tracie nodded and slipped her arm in the crook of the agent's arm. What would have happened had he not stepped in to help her? And where on earth was Hailey Thomas getting her information? Tracie let out a breath as the cool air-conditioning enveloped her. Suddenly, she couldn't wait to be back in that conference room.

It was the only place she was safe.

✦ ✦ ✦

53 Days Until Final Judgment
18 Members Left

July 10—2:58 p.m.
Latitude: 61.1802913° N, Longitude: 149.7792549° W
Alaska Bureau of Investigation

Obviously, the hungry little reporter had taken his anonymous tip.

Perfect.

Now to see what she would do with it.

Griz watched Dr. Hunter rush inside the building. She wouldn't stay there. Couldn't. Not with the weight of this pressing down on her. The question was, would she tell the team inside or be a martyr and run away to deal with her pain by herself?

This was better than reality TV. He leaned forward over the steering wheel so he could watch. Then glanced down at the clock on the dash. How long would it take for her to come dashing right back out?

If she did, he knew exactly where she would go.

The collar around his neck itched his skin, and he undid the top button and rubbed at it.

There. Just as he'd predicted.

Dr. Hunter exited the building as if it were on fire and headed toward a vehicle. It took her only a matter of seconds to peel out of the parking lot.

Griz followed. "Will she or won't she . . ."

Two turns, and he grinned. "She will."

He parked right beside her and waited a few moments before walking inside the coffee shop. The bell jangled as he entered. He hated bells. They made him twitch.

He walked up to get in line behind the doctor. Six people stood in front of her. Just enough time. Oh, now only five.

"You and I"—he leaned close and spoke in a low voice—"are a lot alike."

She whipped around, and her already pale face went almost white. She froze.

Four ahead now.

"Our struggles. Wanting to help people. I even understand how strong the pull of alcohol can be." Putting on his best sympathetic face, he plowed ahead to his captive audience. "I like control too. I like order out of chaos. In fact, many of my peers call me a perfectionist." He released a dramatic sigh.

Three in front of her now. A group of teen girls giggled and rushed to the counter to make their orders.

She held her hands up—one holding her phone, the other her keys—and waved them at him. "We are *nothing* alike. Nothing." The fire in her eyes was back as color filled her cheeks. But then her hands shook as her head wagged back and forth. "Leave me alone." She ran out of the coffee shop, her fear unmistakable.

He shoved his hands into his pockets and nodded at the barista as the pimply-faced teen boy waved him forward. It was his turn now to order. "Chai tea, please." He laid a hefty tip on the counter. "Thank you for your hard work."

The kid grinned and showed off his braces. "Thank you, sir. I'll get that for you."

In less than two minutes, Griz strode out of the shop with his tea and put on his sunglasses. His plane was waiting.

CHAPTER TWELVE

Eight Years, One Month, Eight Days Sober
July 10—3:21 p.m.
Latitude: 61.1802913° N, Longitude: 149.7792549° W
Alaska Bureau of Investigation

ROB SAW HER COMING AND opened the secure doors for her. "You all right, Miss Tracie?"

Afraid that putting words to her emotions would lead to her melting down before she made it inside, she shook her head and moved as fast as her trembling legs could carry her. Back through the squad room to the conference room and the team.

Mac glanced up first. As soon as he saw her, he dashed around the table and put a strong arm around her waist just as she collapsed. He barely caught her before she hit the floor.

"Tracie! What is it?"

Jason scrambled over with a chair. Scott poured a cup of water.

Once she was seated on the chair, her limbs shook. "I saw him." She choked out the words.

Instead of blowing a gasket like she expected, Mac knelt in front of her and laid a hand on her leg. He kept it there. Firm. Steady. His lips tight, his jaw clenched.

Carrie morphed into full-on agent mode. Her steps to Tracie were swift. "What happened? Tell me everything."

Tracie kept her eyes on Mac. His gaze bored into hers, and she could feel his heartache, anger, and worry—they were so clear in his eyes. Taking a steadying gulp of air, she nodded and closed her eyes. "I was overwhelmed with that reporter who ambushed me, so I raced out for coffee. I needed something to steady me. In line, the man behind me spoke in a low voice. He said, 'You and I are a lot alike.'"

Repeating that evil man's words made the shaking start all over again. She'd never dealt with anything like this. Not ever. She opened her eyes and stared at Mac, willing for some of his strength to ooze through the connection and help her. Because she couldn't deal with this right now. She couldn't.

He squeezed her leg, but she didn't miss the clenching and unclenching of his jaw. Without shifting her gaze from his, she relayed the rest. Carrie asked if she saw him leave and what kind of car he drove. Or if she'd gotten a license plate.

Tracie shook her head and then lifted her phone. "But I tried to get a picture. I haven't looked to see if it came out, but all I wanted was to get away from him as fast as possible."

"That's understandable." Carrie's voice soothed. "Unlock your phone and let me check?"

Tracie did, then handed the phone over.

"It's a tad blurry, but it's our guy." Carrie handed the phone to Alan. "See what you can do with that and send it to everyone. And I mean *everyone*."

"On it." Alan took the phone, typed for a few seconds, and then handed it back to Tracie. "I sent it to myself because I'm sure you'll need this."

Tracie hated the pity in his gaze. Irritation prickled her skin. If she didn't get some time alone, she was going to snap. The day had been horrid enough without alienating her new friends. "I need to go back to my hotel. Please."

"I'll take you." Mac stood and moved his hand from her leg to her shoulder.

Carrie stuck her head out to the squad room. "I want a detail attached to Dr. Hunter's hotel."

Tracie shook her head. "No. That's not necessary."

"Yes, it is." The edge to her new friend's voice brooked no argument. She dipped her chin in acknowledgment. "Can I go now?"

"Yes." Carrie's features softened. She walked back to Tracie and hugged her tight.

Tracie clenched her jaw as warmth enveloped her. She would *not* break down here.

Pulling back, Carrie went into agent mode again. "Promise me you'll stay put and stay securely bolted in your room. That you won't go off on your own again."

Tracie nodded again. "I promise."

As Mac drove her rental car to the hotel, she sat with her hands clasped and tucked between her knees so he wouldn't notice the shaking. To his credit, he didn't say a word and gave her space.

A few blocks from the hotel, her phone buzzed in her pocket. She pulled it out. Her mother. "Hey, Mom—"

"Those media people trampled my prized roses. Seriously, does no one have respect for privacy anymore?" Her mom's laughter filled the line, but there was a strained edge to it.

The sound grated against Tracie's already frazzled nerves. "I can't deal with this right now, Mom." The words were snippier than she'd ever spoken to her mother as an adult.

"I'm so sorry, honey. I was just teasing. I didn't mean—"

"I can't talk, Mom, okay? I'm sorry I snapped. I'll call you tomorrow." She hung up before the tears overwhelmed and Mom decided to fly to Alaska on the next flight.

Mac parked in front of the hotel and glanced in the rearview mirror. "Your security detail is here. Let me get you inside." He exited the driver's side and came around to her door.

By the time he had it open, she was bawling. Great sobs racked her, and she couldn't do a blasted thing about it.

Mac squatted outside the car and simply pulled her into his arms. "It's been a rough day. Let me get you inside, where you have some privacy."

Everything in her shook, so she had no idea if her nod was even perceptible against the onslaught. Strong arms lifted her from the passenger seat. He must have kicked the door closed, because the sound reverberated in her ears.

Thankfully, her room wasn't far. But she could hear voices all around her, so she squeezed her eyes as tight as she could and buried her face in his shoulder.

Several moments later he whispered, "I need your key card."

She sniffed and worked to calm the sobbing that seemed to control her.

"Can you stand?"

"Probably." She gulped.

He gently set her down. Her legs felt like overcooked pasta, limp and rubbery. She reached into her jeans for the key card and waved it over the lock.

Mac went in first and searched the room. When he turned back toward her, he led her to the bed and made her sit down, which wasn't a difficult feat.

He went to the bathroom and came back with a wet washcloth. "Here. This will probably help your eyes and head feel better." He knelt in front of her again, grasping her free hand. "I'd like to go back to the ABI. With a fresh lead like this, we might be able to nab him. But I don't want to leave you if you need me to stay."

More than anything she longed to beg him not to leave. But if they could catch this guy, she might get her life back. They might save a lot of people's lives. She gave his fingers a squeeze. "Go ahead. I just want to cry myself to sleep."

"Are you sure?" His voice was softer now.

"Yeah. I'm sure."

Mac studied her for a moment, then nodded. He let go of her hand and stood. "We'll come here in the morning for breakfast then. If anything happens before then, I'll text you."

She bit the corner of her lip. "Okay."

He pointed his thumb at the door. "I'm going to leave, but I want you to follow and make sure you use the deadbolt and chain. Then I'll talk to the guys here to protect you."

A nod was all she managed as she stood on her wobbly legs.

Mac left.

She bolted the door.

Then she leaned her back against it and stared into the empty room.

Great big tears puddled in her eyes, but at least the sobbing had stopped.

Memories of the day bombarded her mind, and she couldn't shut out all the noise.

So she walked over to the minibar and opened it up.

✦ ✦ ✦

52 Days Until Final Judgment
18 Members Left
July 11—1:34 p.m.
Latitude: 70.193385° N, Longitude: 148.444766° W
Griz's Small Compound

All the news stations and newspapers were talking about him. And not just in Alaska—throughout the entire country. Warmth spread through him all the way to the tips of his fingers and toes. He grinned wide.

This. This was exactly what he loved. What he wanted.

Oh, another report was starting. This time on one of those popular news talk shows. He turned up the volume.

"The Typhon Killer has made headlines again. More than one hundred people are still hospitalized after the water hack in Juneau, where lye was increased to a lethal amount. Mark, what are we hearing from the sources on the ground?"

The frame went from the host on the set to a man standing outside the capitol building in Juneau. "Fifty-seven people have now died from this deadly attack . . ."

The microwave beeped, and Griz went to get his food. This was going to be good. He grabbed his plate, a fork, and a napkin and headed back to sit in front of the TV.

"But some are saying that our killer is losing his edge. Juneau was simply a copycat of the attempt on Tampa years ago—"

"Imbeciles. They stopped that one before it did anything. No one died." He shoveled food into his mouth and tuned out the bland reporter. Even though he hadn't set it off, it was *his* malware that did the trick here. And he'd usurped the Members in the process. These news chumps had no idea who they were dealing with.

Griz flipped the channel. If they wanted creativity, he'd give them creativity. They were already connecting the dots from the explosion of that small aircraft. Just wait until they confirmed who was on it.

"We have an exclusive to share with you tonight. Does the Typhon Killer have an accomplice?"

It made him laugh. An accomplice. He shook his head. But he sat back and listened while he ate.

"People are clamoring to know more about the world's craziest terrorist."

Wait a second. Did that reporter really just say "craziest"? They weren't supposed to use words like that.

He. Wasn't. Crazy.

"Many believe he couldn't pull all this off on his own and there must be a secret accomplice—a mastermind—behind the man craving attention."

This wasn't news! What was this?

Griz threw his plate against the TV. When that didn't do any damage, he picked up the lamp and threw it. Then screamed profanity at the walls and overturned every piece of furniture in the place. "*I* am the mastermind. Me. It's only me!"

CHAPTER THIRTEEN

Eight Hours and Thirty Minutes Sober
July 11—4:00 a.m.
Latitude: 61.174133° N, Longitude: 149.887813° W
Hyatt House Hotel

HER MOMENT OF WEAKNESS HAD turned into twenty minutes of
drowning out the world with two tiny bottles. Self-loathing and hatred quickly followed, then crying and screaming into her pillow
for another half hour. Finally, she sat up, wiped her face, then furiously emptied the contents of every bottle from the minibar down
the drain.

All the logic and reasoning in the world, everything she knew
as a physician, and even the resources she'd learned in AA couldn't
take away the cravings. Couldn't fix what was happening in her life.
Couldn't make her feel better.

She understood that deep inside. But she'd been too proud to let go
of her hurt and anger. She longed for control.

It wasn't hers to claim.

To make matters worse, what she'd drunk had tasted awful, and
she'd thrown up several times before crashing onto the bed for a
three-hour midnight nap.

When sleep no longer quelled the pounding in her head, she gave
up the fight. "I can't do this on my own. I can't. I'm so sorry!" She

lowered onto her knees and cried out to God in humility and re-pentance. She'd had control for eight years. And in her mind, she'd proudly thought that the accomplishment was because of her own determination. Her own wisdom. Her own willpower.

Oh, how wrong she'd been. She wasn't capable of anything in her own strength. Not one blessed thing.

"Why do I always yank the reins out of Your hands?" She stared up at the ceiling. "You've given me gifts to use, and I've wanted to take credit for that. The last eight years of sobriety were relatively easy . . . until the world came crashing down around me. Until I lost control. Again." She ducked her chin to her chest, and memories flashed through her mind.

Drinking had started as a way to control her emotions. To soften the blows she'd inflicted upon herself for failing.

And it had led to loss of control too.

Even as what she would consider a "strong believer," she'd strug-gled and watched so many do the same.

Just because she'd made the decision to stop eight years ago didn't mean she wouldn't fail again. She *knew* that. And yet, in her arro-gance, she'd thought she could master it.

Perfectionism was a horrid mindset to overcome. It led to the very failure she feared.

Her parents had even confronted her lovingly about that. Saying that she'd run away from her family and all she knew because she was a perfectionist. That her expectations couldn't possibly be met by anyone. Including herself.

At the time she'd brushed their words aside.

But now . . . she owed them an apology as well.

"Lord, I need Your help to keep my focus on You. I know I'll still fail. I know I'm not perfect—even though I would really like to be. But I can't keep trying to seize control. I can't conquer this on my own." She opened her eyes and glanced toward the minibar. Her stomach rolled at the thought of ingesting any more alcohol, and yet at the back of her mind, the little voice, the cravings, the urges, the temptation—they were all still there. "You are the only way out. Keep me on that narrow path, Lord. Keep me from my own stupid self."

She was forgiven. No doubt about that. What Christ did on the cross paid the price. Past. Present. Future. But she still felt like scum. Disgusted with herself for another failure.

She glanced at the clock. Four thirty-two. Maybe a shower would help. It had to. Mac had texted that the team was coming to her hotel for breakfast this morning.

An hour later, she sat on the edge of her bed. Clean. Dressed. Makeup on. But there were still forty minutes before they would arrive at 6:15. Her eyes darted to her bag, and she went over and grabbed her Bible.

When the time finally arrived, Tracie felt better—at least inside—than she had in a long while. Physically, she was exhausted, but she could power through that. She left her room and walked down the hall toward the breakfast area. The team was already there, deep in discussion, so she filled her plate and sat in the empty seat next to Mac. He was talking in some sort of cyber-gibberish computer code to Jason, but he reached over, grabbed her hand, and gave it a squeeze.

It warmed her in a way she wasn't expecting, and she squeezed his hand back. A deep conviction filled her heart. She needed to tell him about her alcoholism. Especially after last night. As the guys continued their conversation, she determined that at some point today, she'd speak with him alone. Her stomach growled, and she listened to the guys while she ate.

The hostess in the breakfast area headed toward them with a remote and turned up the volume on the TV behind them.

"And now a bombshell report from investigative reporter Hailey Thomas from the *Daily Alaskan*. Last night we hinted there was an accomplice to the Typhon Killer. New details have emerged showing a connection between Dr. Tracie Hunter and the TK. Hailey is with us from Anchorage now. What can you tell us, Hailey?"

Tracie's eyes were drawn to the television screen. The eggs she'd just eaten lay like concrete in her stomach. Her worst nightmare was coming true in front of the whole nation.

"Thank you, Janet. The *Daily Alaskan* has uncovered several connections between Dr. Hunter and the Typhon Killer. As we reported on our website earlier this morning, Dr. Hunter was spotted in Fairbanks the day of the infamous 26 Below attack, leaving just before power was cut off. We can also confirm that she was here in Anchorage the day that Peter Chandler was killed after the FBI and ABI raided the hospital to stop the 8 DOWN killer. A source within the FBI provided a quote from TK during his reign, where he said that as a serial killer, 'Creating order out of chaos is my specialty.' When I confronted her about the similarities in their beliefs, Dr. Hunter had this to say."

"Being able to bring order out of chaos . . ." Tracie's voice filled the airwaves. ". . . there's nothing like it."

"That was not my response!" Her fork clattered on her plate.

Scott hopped up and turned off the TV.

The whole room was silent, tense.

Black spots danced before her eyes. She squeezed them shut and pressed her fists into them. No. She was not going to faint. *Oh, God, why? Why aren't You stopping this? Please help me!*

A hand gently gripped her shoulder. "I'm so sorry, Tracie." Mac's voice was strong yet gentle. "We will do everything we can to—"

Tracie whipped her head up and glared at the man beside her. "To what? What is there to do with this psychopath? With the media? They want a scapegoat. They want a face to put with that monster. They have one, but the authorities refuse to release it." The words flew from her lips like daggers. "So guess whose face everyone is going to equate with the Typhon Killer? Mine." She pushed away from the table. "I get your rage now, Mac." And she did. It coursed through her, tightening her muscles. Clouding her mind.

"I know you feel powerless right now. I *know* that." Mac locked eyes with her. "But I also now know the error of that way of thinking. And the destruction."

Destruction. Yes. That was exactly what was needed. She inhaled sharply. "I know you know what I'm going through. And I know I haven't lost anyone." She swiped at the angry tears slipping down her cheeks. "But my whole livelihood is being destroyed by this man's manipulation. And it's all I have. Helping people is *all I have*, and he's ripping it from me."

Tracie wanted to scream. Punch a wall. Something to relieve the intensity of emotion welling within her. "I'm not going to the ABI with you guys. I need some time to process this on my own."

Jason and Mac exchanged a glance. Carrie kept her gaze trained on Tracie, her expression thoughtful. Scott looked at Tracie, then his two friends.

"Is that wise?" Mac finally spoke up. "I think—"

Tracie stood and threw her napkin on the plate. "Forgive me, Mac. But I don't care what you think right now. I'm going to my room. Please just leave me alone." She stomped out of the room and heard chairs slide from the table.

"No, guys." Carrie's voice floated into the hallway. "Let her go. She's got protection. Give her space."

Tracie released a breath. Good. At least someone listened. She stalked to her room. With jerky movements, she waved her key over the lock, opened the door, and then tried to slam it. But it was on a hydraulic hinge and robbed her of the satisfaction of a loud bang.

Frustration bubbled up, and she let out a loud growl. The peace that had filled her just an hour before was gone.

Her life was a black hole. She was Alice, always falling, never finding Wonderland, no relief from the despair. And the anger was almost suffocating. Never before had she felt such rage. Adrenaline pumped through her body. How she wanted to go for a run. At this rate she could run ten miles without stopping.

She could go for a run in Griffin Park. Maybe the monster was there at this very minute, staking out his next victim. And then she could take some of her own revenge. Man. If that jerk showed his face right now, she knew she was fully capable of throttling him.

"'Vengeance is mine, I will repay,' says the Lord."

The verse cracked through the haze of emotions. Shock replaced the rage boiling in her belly.

Had she really just thought she was capable of taking a human life?

Tracie looked at her hands, hands that had fixed so many things wrong in so many bodies. Her hands had been used to heal, not hurt. *Father, forgive me!*

"Do not be overcome by evil, but overcome evil with good."

Tracie sat on the edge of her bed. Waves of remorse doused the flames of revenge. Huge sobs racked her shoulders. The rage, the anger—that's what this killer wanted. He wanted her to be just like him. Seeking his demise at her own hands, giving in to her desire to take the law in her own hands.

No one had known when Hailey Thomas would go public with her suspicions. And now they were out.

"I can't do this alone," Tracie cried again. "Lord, God . . . help! I feel like I have nothing left. Forgive me for my anger and hatred."

She lay on the bed until her tears dried. Stress and fear still haunted her, but that horrible anger was gone. Exhaustion took over instead. Her limbs felt like hundred-pound weights. Perhaps a nap would help shake off the events of the morning and last night.

She texted Mac, Jason, and Scott.

> Please tell everyone I'm sorry for my outburst. I appreciate how much you guys care about me and have supported me. I'm going to lie down for a while.

She changed back into her favorite pajamas and slid between the cool sheets, praying sleep would come quickly.

"You can't escape me. I'm everywhere. You are in my clutches, and I will destroy you!"

The voice echoed through her. A large face with glowing red eyes and a long black beard loomed over her.

"You are mine!" he roared.

Tracie scrambled backward. Where was she? How could she fight this monster? What weapon did she have to slay the beast?

He closed in, and she screamed. "No. No!"

"No!" Tracie jolted up, her eyes scanning the space. Thank the Lord she was safe in her hotel room. She flopped backward onto the pillows. Just what she needed. A new nightmare.

Why had she ever looked up pictures in Greek mythology of Typhon?

Stupid, that's what that was.

She'd done this to herself. She was shaking and couldn't stop. Sweat soaked her pajama top. Her watch was alerting her that her heart rate was high. Tracie tapped the screen and went to the Stopwatch feature. Technology was nice, but she was going to check her vitals for herself.

Besides, it would give her something to do.

She pressed two fingers to her neck, right on her carotid artery. Lifting her left hand, she watched the seconds tick by. One hundred beats per minute. She dropped her hands and sucked in a deep breath through her nose. *One. Two. Three. Four. Five.* And then released it slowly through her pursed lips. *Six. Seven. Eight. Nine. Ten.*

The cinched feeling in her chest relaxed, and her heart slowed its pace. But for how long? Was this her life now? Living in the shadows, waiting for another lie, another catastrophe to collapse on her? She couldn't pick up and find another vocation. Not when her face had been plastered across the nation as a fake. An accomplice. To murder.

Shaking off the thoughts, she headed back to the shower. Another good scrubbing with some hot water was the only cure she could think of right now.

Twenty minutes later Tracie donned a fresh pair of leggings and a

University of Alaska sweatshirt. She padded back into the bathroom and swiped her hand over the steamy mirror. Pulling the towel off her head, she grabbed her wide-toothed comb and studied her reflection. Two months ago—the time of her last haircut—she'd had no idea what was coming down the road. Now as she looked at the unkempt strands, she didn't want to even think about what horrors might still be coming. With quick motions she swiped the comb through and worked out the tangles. She had to get her mind off all the negative.

Grabbing her skin-care bag, she pulled out the moisturizer and applied a soothing layer.

The ritual brought some normalcy to her frayed heart. Sure, she still resembled a raccoon with the massive circles under her eyes. And she'd lost weight. She could see it in her face. But here in this tiny hotel bathroom, she almost felt like herself.

A knock broke through her thoughts.

Tracie frowned and made her way to the door, looking through the peephole.

Mac.

She bit her lip. She'd been so horrible to him.

"Come on, Tracie. I know you're in there." Mac's gruff voice was muffled, but she heard the concern loud and clear.

She gripped the flat handle, turned it, and pulled the door open. She leaned against the jamb. "Hi."

Mac's eyes swept from her head to her toes, his eyes and smile warm. "You look much better—well, more rested anyway—than a few hours ago."

"Wow. Thanks." Sarcasm dripped from her voice.

He rolled his eyes. "You know what I mean. You look . . . You know what? I'm going to stop there. I'm just digging farther into what I am guessing is an already deep hole."

Tracie chuckled. "I thought I was the one in the hole. I'm really sorry for earlier, Mac. I shouldn't have lashed out like that."

Mac took one more step toward her, and she could smell the spicy scent of his aftershave or cologne. Goodness, he was handsome. The thought sent a flush up her neck. Nope. No. Nuh-uh. She could not afford to have feelings for anyone. Especially not Mac. Not when the memory of his wife and daughter were still so fresh with him.

"Did you hear what I said?" Mac tapped her on the arm.

She startled. "Huh? Oh. No. I'm so sorry. I spaced out for a minute."

Mac gave her a sympathetic look. "I said there's nothing to forgive. The Lord knows I took my anger out on you more times than I care to admit. We're good." He shifted and leaned against the wall in the hallway. "I know it's been a lot. But if you're willing to come with me, there's someone waiting in one of the hotel conference rooms who would like to talk to you. And I think they can help us clean up this mess."

Tracie's heart rate picked up again, but this time with hope. "Really? Then let's go."

Mac held up a hand. "As adorable as you look, you might want to change into something more . . . better for the public."

She blinked. Did he just say "more better"? And had he called her adorable? Her cheeks burned with the compliment. It was getting difficult to tamp down her warm feelings for this man. With a grin, she teased, "More better?"

"Leave me alone. I'm a tech head, not an English professor." He chuckled. "Just change. I'll wait out here for you."

Tracie nodded and slipped back into her room. She changed into a pair of jeans and a dark-pink button-up shirt. She threw on a black cardigan and shoved her feet into a pair of black boots. Glancing in the mirror, she winced. Maybe putting on some makeup was in order so she didn't scare off whoever had come to visit. She walked into the bathroom and applied concealer, blush, and mascara. Her hair was almost dry, framing her face in soft waves. And there was a sparkle in her eyes that hadn't been there fifteen minutes ago.

Please let this be something amazing, Jesus. I could really use good news right about now.

She met Mac in the hallway and fisted a hand on her hip. "Is this more better?"

Wait. Was she flirting? With Mac? She needed to rein it in. They had a maniac to catch and her career to save. She had no time for a relationship anyway.

His laughter echoed down the hallway. "Yes. Perfect. Let's go." They made their way down the hallway, past the lobby, and to a conference room with the shades drawn. Two men in black suits with curlicue earpieces in their ears stood outside the door. Tracie's brow furrowed. What on earth was going on?

Mac paused outside and turned to her. "You ready?"

"I guess . . . You still haven't told me what this is about."

"Trust me," he whispered and opened the door. He gestured for Tracie to walk in ahead of him.

She entered the room and spotted a woman on the opposite side of the large table. Her blood ran cold.

Congresswoman Louise Sanderson. The mother of the young man from Tracie's cold case. Tracie turned a glare on Mac, her hands trembling. "What is—"

"Dr. Hunter," the congresswoman interjected. "It is good to see you again." Her voice was calm. Confident. Kind.

Good to see her? The last time they'd seen each other, this woman had screamed all sorts of horrible things at her. Not that Tracie blamed her. Her son's murder had been horrific for everyone involved. She couldn't imagine the depth of grief when it came to losing a child. To have hope that the killer had been caught and then have that hope so cruelly ripped from them must have been agonizing.

She licked her lips and took Congresswoman Sanderson's outstretched hand. "It is good to see you as well."

The older woman smiled, and Tracie couldn't help but notice the years had been kind to her. Despite the heartbreak. The three of them took their seats.

"I'm sure you're wondering why I'm here. I'll get straight to the point." Congresswoman Sanderson folded her hands on the tabletop. "This media maelstrom has been particularly distressing to our family, and I'm sure to you as well."

Tracie nodded. "This has dredged up all sorts of horrible memories, Congresswoman Sanderson. But I promise you, I had no part in covering anything up. I was young and foolish to make that promise to you, but I wasn't in the wrong. I only wanted to help."

The woman held up a hand. "First, please call me Louise. Congresswoman Sanderson is too much of a mouthful. Besides, we've known each other a long time. You were there for my family in the darkest of times, and that is still greatly appreciated."

Her kindness caught Tracie off guard. But she was thankful for it all the same.

"Second, I know you are innocent of what you've been accused. May I call you Tracie?"

"Of course."

Louise pulled a slim tablet out of the briefcase next to her and tapped the screen a few times. Then she slid the device across the table to Tracie and Mac. Images and notes were arranged on some sort of digital whiteboard. In the center was a photograph. She picked up the tablet and zoomed in. She knew this man. She looked back at the congresswoman. "Is that Detective Young?"

"It is. You see, when this all blew up again last week, I hired a private detective. I've had plenty of threats over the years, being a public figure. But this time, to be honest, something just didn't add up. I remembered you, Tracie." She leaned forward. "Were you naïve? Yes. But a manipulative, crazy accomplice to the person who murdered my son?" Louise shook her head. "No."

Wait. What? Tracie blinked. "I'm sorry—what are you saying?"

The congresswoman gestured to the tablet in her grasp. "What you are looking at is the culmination of my private investigator's work. We've discovered that Detective Young"—she cleared her throat and put a hand to the pearls around her neck—"Detective Young murdered my son."

The revelation ripped through the room like a tidal wave. Tracie stared at the face of the detective, now a good deal older. He'd lost most of his hair, and there was a coldness in his blue eyes Tracie didn't remember being there when they'd worked together.

"How? Why?" she stuttered, handing the tablet back to Louise.

The congresswoman put it to sleep before sliding it back into her briefcase. "It turns out Detective Young was on the payroll of a crime lord with deep roots in DC. My son got in over his head and owed this crime boss money. We had no idea."

Tears pooled in the older woman's green eyes. She pressed her lips together for a moment, clearly trying to gather her emotions. "When Michael didn't pay, this guy tapped Young to take care of him. Apparently Young owed him and this was the way he could pay him back."

Tracie leaned back in her chair, shocked. "I don't know what to say."

Louise nodded and smoothed her hands back and forth over the table. "My PI found that Young hid the evidence you brought forward from the autopsy. That evidence has now been recovered." She glanced down at her watch. "The former detective was arrested an hour ago, and I am prepared to do a press conference tomorrow with the district attorney in DC, exonerating you from any involvement in this matter. With your permission, of course. I don't want to cause any more upheaval for you. That's why I flew up here as soon as I knew the authorities had everything they needed."

Mac began typing on his phone. Probably to tell everyone the good news.

Joy and relief slipped over Tracie like a beam of sunlight. She closed her eyes. It was over! *Thank You, Lord.* She was free. Her name would be cleared!

"Yes please. Shout it from the rooftops; do whatever you have to do to get the truth out there. Thank you so much. I'm so sorry that I failed you and that you've had to live with this for all these years, but I'm forever grateful to you for finding the truth."

The congresswoman nodded. "You must accept my apology for the nasty things I said to you all those years ago."

"You were grieving, ma'am." Tracie couldn't contain a couple of joy-filled tears. "It's completely understandable."

"Nevertheless, I'm sorry. Thank you for all the work you did back then."

"You're welcome." The smile that lifted her cheeks felt like the first genuine one she'd had in a long time.

Mac let out an audible sigh, and they turned to eye him. He was staring at his phone. He lifted his face. "This is incredible, Congresswoman Sanderson, but—"

His voice sounded so heavy. Why? Tracie narrowed her eyes and stared at him. How could he not rejoice with her?

He straightened. "I'm afraid we can't accept your generous offer right now."

The words ripped through Tracie like a bullet. "*What?*"

CHAPTER FOURTEEN

943 Days After
Latitude: 61.174133° N, Longitude: 149.887813° W
July 11—11:57 a.m.
Hyatt House Hotel

"IT'S JUST NOT A GOOD idea," Mac blurted. The look on Tracie's face stabbed him in the heart.

"What do you mean?" Her piercing eyes drilled into his. "How is it not a good idea to clear my name?"

"I'm sorry. I know this is torture, but I texted Carrie to let her know as soon as Congresswoman Sanderson told us her plan. She discussed it with the ABI director and the head of the investigation with the FBI. They all agreed." He shook his head. "We need this guy to think he's winning. It's the only way we have the upper hand. He obviously instigated this. He did it out of spite. And he wanted to keep us distracted. So let's let him think he's accomplished that. He needs to think he's knocked you off your feet and defeated you. And he also needs to think we will be so worried trying to help *you* that we're not completely paying attention to what he's doing."

The congresswoman stood. "You know, Dr. Hunter . . ." She paused and bit her lip. "I think your friend might be correct. Speaking on behalf of the US government, who has had to watch these events very carefully, I think it might be good to keep this to ourselves for a while longer."

Utter betrayal and hurt clouded Tracie's features. "I can't believe you're saying this. I thought . . . I thought you were my friend, Mac." She put a hand to her forehead. "This is my career—my life—and my reputation that we're talking about here."

"How about this." Congresswoman Sanderson stepped closer. "I call your hospital administrator in Fairbanks and explain what is happening. That way he—and the board—can know that you have been cleared. Then I will call the assistant district attorney handling the case in DC and ask her to keep things as quiet as she can. It won't go to trial for weeks, and the suspect is already in custody. There wasn't any media coverage of the arrest. They quietly picked up Young outside his gym. I received confirmation before I came to the hotel."

"I hate this." Tracie stood with her hands fisted at her sides. The glare she sent Mac's way made it clear that was just the tip of the iceberg as far as her feelings went. "This is *my* life that's being ruined."

"I know. I'm sorry." He shook his head. "But I have to agree with the guys in charge—it's a smart move, and we really don't see any other choice."

"Oh, there's another choice. They just don't like it because it doesn't fit into their plan to catch this guy." She wrapped her arms around her middle and glared at him like she was trying to protect herself. From him. Like *he* was the bad guy.

He did not like that feeling. He opened his mouth. But no words came out. He didn't have a great explanation, nor words of comfort.

Congresswoman Sanderson stepped over and wrapped her arms around Tracie. "This is a huge sacrifice on your behalf. And I can't thank you enough for all you have done for my family. But I have to ask the tough question, my dear." The older woman's voice had turned soft and motherly. Gone was the politician, the well-put-together, wealthy socialite.

Tracie sniffed and stood stiff.

"You've always cared about people first. You've gone above and beyond in the field of medicine for close to twenty years now. Don't you think it's worth it—even though it's awful for you right now—to suffer for a little while longer so that in the long run, a multitude of lives can be saved?"

✦ ✦ ✦

One Day, Twelve Hours, Fifty-Three Minutes Sober
July 12—8:23 a.m.
Latitude: 61.707777° N, Longitude: 148.911882° W
A Remote Cabin—Sutton-Alpine, Alaska

How. *Dare*. He.

Tracie gripped her coffee cup between her hands so tightly she was afraid it would break. She needed to relax. It wasn't the mug's fault Mac was a jerk.

Deep down she knew he was just the messenger, but it was easier to be angry at him because she could control that. Her life, on the other hand? Yeah, not a lick of control there.

She didn't care that it was the right decision for everyone involved. What she'd wanted was for Mac to stand up for her.

And he didn't.

She hadn't slept a wink last night because she'd been so fired up.

She took a sip of the black liquid and let the warmth seep through her. Leaning her hip against the log railing, Tracie looked out at the peaceful scenery. Tall pines stretched up toward the expansive blue sky, their fresh scent filling the air. Squirrels darted from branch to branch, chattering at one another, making her wish she understood their communication.

Yes, coming out to this cabin had been exactly what she needed. So what if it looked like she was running? Anyone in her position would do the same thing. Escape reality. Get some space. Take stock of life.

Even if that life was unraveling.

Tracie frowned. She'd been so careful to do the right thing. Live the right way. Love her neighbor. Treat others how she wanted to be treated. Take care of people. So why was this happening to *her*?

And why, just when freedom was offered to her, would Mac, of all people, snatch it from her grasp? He knew what Louise Sanderson's offer meant to her. How much going back to work was necessary to her well-being. And he thought he could play God?

Oh sure, she knew the FBI and ABI were in charge. Of course they couldn't let Mr. Typhon know they'd figured out the truth. But—

Tracie rolled her eyes and pushed off from the railing, making her way inside. She dumped the rest of her coffee down the drain and put the mug in the dishwasher. It was one thing to vent in her mind about all the wrongs done to her, another thing entirely to put the case in jeopardy.

That didn't stop her from exhausting every avenue to get it out of her system. This was the best way.

The cabin she'd rented was cozy and about fifty miles outside Anchorage. Only Carrie and Darcie knew exactly where she was—well, other than her security guys. And the women promised not to tell Mac unless it was absolutely necessary. It would take her a good while to get over his lack of defense for her.

Tracie plopped down onto the couch. Every muscle in her body was ready for battle, but what she wanted was a really good cry. Again. Goodness, she hadn't cried this much ever in her life.

She leaned her head back on the overstuffed, comfy cushion and willed the tears to come. Exhaustion took over instead, and she practically melted into the piece of furniture.

She closed her eyes and willfully unclenched her fists. Holding on to the anger—having someone to blame—it was her last bit of control. But what good did it do?

Oh, God. I'm doing it again. But as much as she knew it was the right thing, she refused to let go.

What was wrong with her?

It wasn't like she had anything else to lose. Her life lay in shambles.

She was being irrational. She knew it. And probably putting her new friends in a difficult place. But if she didn't hide from Mac, he would invade her space with his stupid, handsome face and twinkling eyes and caring and . . . and practicality. He'd make her feel safe and like part of a team.

And what was wrong with that?

Quite frankly, she was terrified. Without the safety net and security blanket of her job, who was she?

These new feelings for Mac scared her almost as much as the monster turning her life upside down. She couldn't afford to care for Mac and risk losing her heart. Could she?

Tracie pulled a pretty blue afghan from the back of the couch and draped it over her legs.

It wasn't like he felt the same about her anyway. They were friends. That was it. And she was happy with that. Why would anyone want to be with her? The internet had a memory that didn't die. All it would take was a few keystrokes and this whole debacle would come right back to haunt her.

She rested her head on the plush cushion of the couch again. What a mess.

"The Army Song," with its snare drums and horns, cut through the silence of the cabin, startling her. Tracie lifted her head as she pulled her phone out of her pocket. A picture of her with Dad at Denali National Park filled her screen. She swiped to answer.

"Hey, Dad."

"Hey, Tracie." Dad's voice wafted over the line, and she fought the lump in her throat.

"It's so good to hear your voice." She sniffed. *Now* the tears were willing to come.

"Well, I've been praying for you. How are you holding up?"

She chewed her lip. How did she answer that without making Dad worry? "Oh, okay. It's been rough. But I'm pushing through, I guess."

"Hmm." Dad grunted. "That's not real convincing."

She sighed. "Probably because I'm not real convinced of it myself."

Dad let out a chuckle. "Lay it on me, honey."

With a deep breath, she launched into the events of the last few days. Every last detail. From being ambushed by that horrible reporter and the national news picking up the fake "bombshell" to being offered the chance of exoneration and Mac delivering the hammerblow that they needed to wait to spill the news.

"So I've rented a cabin for a few days. I just needed to get away from it all. I couldn't get a spare moment to hear myself think."

It was so quiet on the other end of the phone, Tracie pulled it away from her ear to make sure the call was still connected. It was. "You still there?"

"Well, my girl." Dad cleared his throat. "I know it's been a lot. And I can't imagine how hard all this has been on you. It's a lot to take in all at once."

"Yeah," she whispered. It felt good to have her frustration validated.

"But I think you need to get out of your own head."

Tracie frowned. "What? What is that supposed to mean?"

"Don't get defensive. I'm your dad. I know you. You are overthinking and wallowing in how this is absolutely ripping apart all your dreams. You don't have control. Look, honey. You're driven and ambitious. It's why you're an excellent surgeon. But I think that the Lord is using this situation to help you understand that your value doesn't come from what you do."

Logically she knew that. But if she wasn't a surgeon, who was she?

Leave it to Dad to cut straight to the heart of the matter. She could hear the kindness and concern in his voice, but that didn't take the sting out of his words. "Being a surgeon is all I know. If it's taken away from me, I don't know . . . I don't . . ." The admission of her deepest fear was stuck in her throat. Finally she whispered, "I don't know who I am without it."

"I know, honey, I know." He sighed. "We are alike in that way. My career in the Army, my ambition to climb ranks, almost destroyed me. Your mother and the Lord had to help me see, through a series of particularly difficult failures, that my identity is not in a job. It isn't even in being a husband or a father. Who I am at my core has to be rooted in Jesus. Or all of those other things become idols."

She leaned forward, the truth of what Dad said ringing true in her spirit. With her forehead in her hand, she let it sink in. She was such an idiot. So blind. The line was silent for several moments. "How did I get here, Dad? How could I stray so far from what is most important?"

"We all do it, Tracie. But thank God He gives us people in our lives who have made the same mistakes, who can help us see where we are straying from Him and get us back on the right path. I know it's not easy, but I think you should take some time and ask the Lord to help you release your career to Him. Hand it over and ask Him to do with it what He wants. That means your reputation too. Your hopes and dreams. You've got to let go of that tight grip you've held for so long. God will take care of it."

Tracie ran her free hand through her hair. "You're right." And he was. Oh, but it was so difficult to let this go. She could hear the defeat in her own voice.

"I'm not trying to hurt you when you're down." Dad's voice was rough, as if he were fighting his own tears. "I'm so proud of you. So is your mother. And we have been praying for you. In praying for you, I have a feeling the Lord is going to use this in a powerful way in your life."

"If only it didn't have to hurt so much." She sniffed and wiped her face. "Will you tell Mom I love her?"

"Of course, honey. I'll check in with you in a few days, okay? I love you so much."

"I love you too, Dad."

They hung up, and she leaned her head back again, letting his encouragement and gentle correction settle inside. *Lord, I hear You. And I need You. Please give me the grace to let this go and follow You. To find my identity in You alone.*

Dad was right. She needed to pick herself up and move forward.

No more pity parties. No more clinging to her job as if it were the only thing that gave her purpose.

Opening her Bible app, Tracie scrolled to Romans 12, where the verses that had convicted her yesterday were located. She pored over the Word of God, asking the Holy Spirit to transform her and renew her mind for the battle that was ahead.

Half an hour later, her phone buzzed with a text.

> Sorry to be the bearer of the news, but my sister, Susan, passed away two weeks ago. Our family has really struggled with the loss, and we apologize for not telling you sooner. We appreciate the prayers during this difficult time.

Her heart sank. Susan was dead?

Did Griz have anything to do with it? Would he do that just because of their connection from her past?

Of course he would. He didn't care who he hurt.

A chill went up her arms. "When fear and despair try to take me down, Lord," she whispered, "help me to remember Your Word."

She typed a reply and hit Send.

> I'm so sorry for your loss. Please know that I am praying for your family during this difficult time. Susan was one of the best people I've ever known.

The words were lacking, but it was all she had to give.

She stood and stretched, doing her best to shake off the fear and anxiety. At the kitchen counter, she grabbed the to-do list she'd started earlier and added *send flowers, find new sponsor.*

She filled a glass with water and drank the whole thing. Nothing like hydration to clear the mind.

A thought about another kind of hydration wiggled its way in. No. No! She wasn't going to go there. Maybe being by herself without a lot to keep her busy wasn't the smartest idea.

She filled the glass with water again and headed out to the back deck with her list and phone. She settled into a comfy chair and scrolled through her email.

A subject line caught her eye: "Return Date." From the hospital director.

Tracie clicked it and scanned the email. The board wanted to know when she could start again. Her job was back within her grasp. With trembling fingers, she pulled up the admin's contact information and hit Call.

"I see you read my email." He chuckled.

"I did." Doing her best to keep her voice calm, she waited to hear what he would say next.

"We had a phone call from a certain congresswoman." He cleared his throat. "While we are under a strict media embargo, we know that you are completely cleared of all the charges. I will say that I think it prudent to still wait a few weeks to start again. But we can definitely explore options."

"Thank you so much." Tracie mulled his suggestion over. "I think you're right. Just know that I am open to any date after my administrative leave is up to start again."

"Excellent. Please hear me say, we are all thrilled with this outcome, Tracie. The board included. Your reputation as a skilled surgeon is unmatched, and we can't wait to have our star doctor back again."

"Thank you for the compliment, sir. I look forward to serving our community again soon."

They exchanged pleasantries, and Tracie ended the call, tapping her phone to her chin, deep in thought. How strange would it be to go back to work after all this? Would everyone believe her innocence? What kind of reception would she get?

A bald eagle dove down into the large yard, his powerful wings fully outstretched. Gliding in the breeze, the majestic bird swooped down to the deck and perched on the large log railing. Tracie's breath caught. The eagle bobbed back and forth, his golden eyes examining her. She stilled, hoping he would stay awhile. She studied his rich white and dark-brown feathers. The beautiful yellow of his curved beak. The piercing clarity in his sharp gaze.

He puffed and fluffed. Then as suddenly as he'd landed, he was in the air again, soaring back into the alpine forest with a screech.

Tracie pressed a hand to her chest. The majesty of God's creation never failed to evoke awe in her. Her spirits lifted by the brief nature encounter, she padded back inside.

She needed a break from the heaviness of her life. Even though she was feeling much better, the temptation to wallow was still strong. Maybe there was a new season of *The Great British Baking Show*. Watching people create delicious pastries was a great way to pass the afternoon.

Her phone buzzed with a text message, and she tapped the screen.

Praying for you today. Hope
you're well.

Her irritation with Mac from earlier melted away. He was being a good friend, trying to encourage her. The decision to keep her innocence under wraps for a while longer was the right one.

Tracie tapped out a quick response.

Doing good. See you in a
couple days.

She put her phone on silent and flipped it over. The draw of her favorite cooking show called. Maybe she'd even go to the store later and buy the necessary ingredients to bake something herself. That was always time consuming and helped her feel better.

She turned on the TV, surprised to see it on a local news channel. Wait. Was that . . . No. It couldn't be.

Tracie groaned. It was.

"We have with us Courtney Oliver, who used to work with Dr. Tracie Hunter. What can you tell us about her?"

Courtney flipped her hair over her shoulder. "There was always something a little off about Dr. Hunter. She was almost . . . too perfect. You know what I mean? No one was ever as good as her or worked to her standards. And when the news broke about her being an accomplice to murder, I knew I had to speak up. Because suddenly it all made sense."

"What made sense?"

Courtney looked into the camera, her gaze unflinching. "That she could be a murderer."

Tracie closed her eyes. Out of the frying pan and into the fire.

Any minute now the board would renege on their invitation to come back—she just knew it.

CHAPTER FIFTEEN

49 Days Until Final Judgment
18 Members Left
July 14—2:00 p.m.
Latitude: 64.83156° N, Longitude: 147.73836° W
Fairbanks Memorial Hospital

GRIZ STRAIGHTENED HIS CUFF LINKS and walked into the hospital.

Time for another board meeting. He'd missed the last one, and today's promised to be a good one.

He adjusted the shoulder holster under his suit jacket and allowed a smirk.

The suppressor made his FNX-45 heavier, but it was a necessary weight to bear.

The board met in a spacious room at the top of the building. Plush and cushy. Just what all the highfalutin snobs liked.

The Members had infiltrated boardrooms all over the state. An impressive piece of their overall plan that Griz had particularly liked and implemented himself. He'd enjoyed pretending to be one of the powerful, hoity-toity know-it-alls. It had been a fun side gig. And it kept him informed.

But today . . . change was about to happen.

He'd already gotten rid of their best surgeon, at least for a while. That was a nice distraction. But this was so much more fun.

He enjoyed playing a part.

As the elevator dinged at his floor, he smoothed his neatly trimmed beard and exited.

"They've just started, Mr. Linden. Go on in. Would you like me to bring you something to drink?" The secretary for their meetings always asked the same question.

"I'll take a coffee."

"Black?"

"Yes." He took purposeful strides into the room and fully put on the persona of Mr. Linden, prestigious hospital board member.

The first half of the meeting was always boring. This time they raved about new ventilators for the NICU. Yay for the babies. Whatever.

Then the hospital administrator turned to personnel issues. "I have some good news to share. But this must be kept completely confidential."

Everyone in the room nodded. Including the secretary. She typed with great speed on her laptop.

The administrator continued. "After a phone call from Congresswoman Sanderson and our brief meeting and vote, Dr. Hunter has been cleared of all wrongdoing. The specifics of the case are being withheld at the moment, and nothing will go out to the press yet, because the authorities are hoping this will help them stay a step ahead of the Typhon Killer."

What? This was new. He stifled a sigh. He shouldn't have missed that meeting.

"Ahem." Mrs. Wright didn't appear impressed. Her lips were in a tight line. "I was unavailable for the so-called brief meeting and vote. Are you telling me all of this was a charade? I don't appreciate being lied to."

The administrator held his hands up, as if in surrender. "No. That is not what happened here." He cleared his throat. "I wasn't sure how much I should say, but it appears this *psychopath* focused in on Dr. Hunter because of a patient she saved here. The criminal went after her to distract the authorities. I'm told they are very close to catching him."

Oh really. So the mouse wanted to play the part of the cat. And they thought they were close to catching him? They had no idea. He willed his lips from turning up in a smug sneer.

"Well then. Kudos to them, and we get our best surgeon back." A stuffy man at the end of the table held up his thousand-dollar pen. "I wasn't looking forward to the work it would take us to replace her."

As if he carried the burden of it all. Griz wanted to voice his derision but kept himself in check. The time was coming for these power jockeys to get over themselves.

"This brings me to the next order of business. After Marshall's retirement, we had a seat that needed to be filled. We've completed an intense vetting process, and Dr. Windsor will be filling the seat." The administrator nodded to the secretary, and she opened the door.

The moment Griz had been waiting for.

"Allow me to introduce to you our newest board member—Dr. Vincent Windsor."

Windsor walked into the room and shook hands with the administrator. As his gaze traveled the room, he connected with each board member and offered a brief nod. The split second he saw Griz, a flash passed across his features, but the man covered it well.

Griz gave the man a few moments to ponder the depth of their situation.

Dr. Windsor adjusted his tie, his gaze stern and leveled at Griz. He opened his mouth.

But Griz was fast. He pulled out his weapon and opened fire on the room.

It was over in less than twenty seconds.

He holstered his weapon and put on a pair of latex gloves. He wiped down his chair, the china coffee cup, and the table. He slid a piece of paper to the center, and then he strode to the door and out to the elevators.

With his phone, he sent the code to delete the surveillance feed from the boardroom, then replaced it with a loop of the feed from the first few seconds of the meeting. Video without him in his chair.

✦ ✦ ✦

946 Days After
July 14—6:41 p.m.
Latitude: 61.707777° N, Longitude: 148.911882° W
A Remote Cabin—Sutton-Alpine

He knocked on the cabin door, hoping and praying Tracie would let him in. Praying, too, that she wouldn't be angry at Carrie for giving up Tracie's location. But this couldn't wait.

She opened it a crack and eyed him. "Hey, Mac."

"Hey." He held up two brown paper bags. "Peace offering?" Did he look too eager? Would she kick him to the curb?

Her lips twitched as she studied him for a moment. Then she stepped back and opened the door all the way. "Come on in."

His heart did a slight shift at the softness in her tone. What was it about her that made him want to be a human being again? To live. Actually live.

"I brought food."

"You said. I can smell it." Her grin widened, but the lines around her eyes showed the mess she'd been going through. "Have a seat at the table. I'll grab some plates."

"Okay." At least it was something. And hey, she'd opened the door and let him in. That was a good start. "Your security guys say it's been quiet."

When she joined him, she handed him a plate and napkin. "Yeah. It's been nice."

He opened the sacks and pulled out burgers and sweet potato fries. "Hope that's okay. I noticed you ate them at the hospital a couple times."

"Yeah. They're my favorite junk-food snacks." She filled her plate and then shoved her hands in her lap. "Would you pray?"

"Sure." He said a quick blessing over their meal and their time together. Hoping and praying that she would be willing to hear him out. And forgive him. Again.

They ate in an awkward silence. She kept her head down, staring at her food most of the time.

His skills with women had been buried with Sarah and Beth. But he had to do something. He finished scarfing his food and took a deep breath. "I'm sorry." There. It was out.

She shook her head.

Great. She wasn't going to forgive him, was she?

"It was the right call to make, Mac. I know that. I mean, look at what great things my last surgical nurse just said about me. It wouldn't have mattered if Congresswoman Sanderson cleared my name. Courtney's interview yesterday would have dredged it all up again." She looked defeated and wiped out. "I'm just waiting for the call from the hospital administrator saying they've decided to let me go." Pulling her knees up to her chest, she rested her feet on the edge of her chair.

How did women do that? He doubted he could even bend his knees that far. Especially after all the knee surgeries he'd had over the years. Too much basketball had ruined them.

"Tracie." He loved how her name sounded.

She lifted her gaze.

"You haven't seen any more of the news, have you?"

"I haven't watched a single thing since Courtney's interview. I couldn't take it."

How was the best way to approach it? "Two other news outlets interviewed some of the other people who've worked with you. Every one of them talked about what an incredible surgeon you are. They didn't believe for one minute that you could be involved. Said you cared too much about your patients to do something like that." He watched her carefully as his words sank in.

Tears pooled in her already red-rimmed eyes. "Really?"

He nodded. "I don't think you're going to have to worry about your reputation as a physician. Lots of people have your back, and once word gets out about what happened to you? Getting doxed and the real killer being caught? Well, I think you'll have even more people rallying around you."

She reached across the table and gripped his hand. A couple of tears trickled down her cheeks. "Thanks for letting me know. I've been doing a really good job of feeling sorry for myself. My dad even called and basically told me to suck it up. Well, he was nicer than that"—she laughed, an actual, real laugh—"but he was straight with me. I thought I'd turned a corner in my pity party until I saw Courtney's interview. And then I tanked. Yet again."

"It's understandable."

She let go of his hand and grabbed a couple fries, slathered them in ketchup, and popped them into her mouth. After a moment she let out a sigh. "I didn't realize how much of my own self-worth rests in what people think of me. That's not how it should be. I should be focused on God's approval and that's it."

He leaned back and laughed. "Yeah. Keep telling yourself that. No matter how hard I try, it always comes back to pride for me."

Her eyes snapped to his, and she rapped the tabletop with a knuckle. "Me too! Ugh. I hate it. Wish I could throw my pride out the window. It was bad in medical school—you're constantly told you have to have all the answers and fix everything. Talk about instilling god complexes. It runs rampant in the medical field."

"I can imagine. But it's just as prevalent in the cyber world. Information is power." His thoughts turned toward Griz. "I wonder if that's what first made him go down this path?"

"Blech. You're talking about my least favorite person right now, aren't you?" She rose and cleared the dishes from the table.

Cringing, he squinted at her through one eye. "Sorry?"

She came back and perched on the edge of her seat, elbows on the table. "I need to tell you something."

Why didn't he like the sound of that? "Okay."

"You might hate me after this, but it's time I come clean with you. You're my friend . . ." She bit her lip and squirmed in the chair.

What he wanted right now was to be more than friends. But how could he tell her that when he didn't even understand it himself? Plus, they were in the middle of chasing down a mass murderer. "I could never hate you, Tracie."

Licking her lips, she stared at him, as if measuring if his words were true. She squared her shoulders. "Okay." Her tone was flat. "I'm an alcoholic."

He leaned back in his chair and raised his eyebrows. No need to tell her that Griz had already spilled the beans on that one. "All right . . . Well, do you need help? Rehab? Counseling? What do you need me to do?"

Tracie shook her head slowly. "This isn't something for you to fix, Mac, as hard as that is to believe." She patted the table with her hand. "Up until a few days ago, I'd been sober for over eight years."

"A few days ago?"

"After my little sobbing exhibition and you tucked me away in my hotel room." She sat up straighter, eyes clear, palms down on the table. "It's the first and only time I've ever slipped since admitting that I had a drinking problem. And don't give me an excuse and say it was understandable. People in my AA circles told me it was understandable that I fell into drinking in the first place because of what happened with the Sanderson case all those years ago. I don't need excuses or understanding. What I need is to tell you the truth."

Silence hung between them for a moment. He wished he knew how to express the admiration he had for her courage and honesty. Instead, he'd keep it simple. "Okay. You told me the truth."

Disbelief covered her face. "What? You don't have a problem with this? You're not shocked and disappointed to find out that your surgeon is an alcoholic?"

"Not at all." Mac shrugged. "Lady, you've seen me at my very worst. Most people would have run far and fast from that man. But you stuck by me. We're all messed up, Tracie. Every single one of us. We're all sinners. We all need grace in unmeasurable amounts every day."

All she did was blink. Just stared at him and blinked those wide brown eyes.

"The doc is speechless. I'm not quite sure what to do with this."

Her laughter broke her silence, and she shook her head at him. "You really don't feel anything different toward me now that you know?"

"Nope."

"Huh." Her fingers drummed the table. "Well, I need to go to a meeting later."

"I'll take you."

She bit her lip again. "My sponsor died, so I need someone else to hold me accountable until I find another one."

"I'll be happy to be here for you. But I'm not going to ask you about it. You have to come to me if you need anything." He had no desire to smother her about her issue. Several of his friends were recovering alcoholics, and he'd walked with them on their journeys.

"Thank you." Her eyes shimmered. "I wasn't expecting such a positive response."

"Obviously. You literally thought I would hate you?" It wasn't even fathomable.

One shoulder lifted. "I haven't even told my family, because I guess . . . I guess I just thought everyone would think less of me."

"You can't scare me away, Tracie." Reaching across the table, he took her hand again and held on.

For several moments they simply gazed at each other. He wondered what she was thinking. She probably was doing the same.

The tension built, and he had no desire for today to go sideways. He wasn't about to hurt their tenuous relationship. A change of subject was in order. "The only person I hate is . . . Well, you know who it is."

The connection between them broke, and she took a sip of water.

"I had an awful thought that he could have been behind Susan's death. Susan was my sponsor. You don't think—" She looked away.

"I'll pass the info along, but you can't blame yourself for this. This is *all* him."

"You're right. Now that we've brought him up, why don't you explain to me how you guys are trying to track him." She stood and then puttered around the kitchen and paused at the coffeepot. "Want some?"

"Sure. I'd love some." Even though this wasn't her place, the homey atmosphere helped him relax. "Explaining is going to take some time. What do you know about malware?"

"Absolutely nothing. Sorry." She brought two cups of coffee back to the table.

"This guy is good. I'll give him that. But we do have his malware from Juneau. That's a huge help."

"See? Right there. I'm completely confused already. How did he do that?" She sipped her coffee and tucked her feet up under her.

Mac wasn't sure how to explain it to someone who didn't live in the cyber world like he did. "He used a Stuxnet variant to get his program onto an air-gapped network. Upon infecting a machine, the malware would identify whether that machine was part of the target network. If not, it would go dormant, waiting for a USB drive to be plugged into the infected machine, whereupon it would infect the thumb drive and so on and so forth until it found its target. Once it made it to the water system, it did its thing."

"Oh." She blinked several times. "Sure. Yeah. I guess that makes sense."

He laughed at the comical look on her face. "Hey, next time I ask you to explain a complicated surgery to me, I'll make sure to use that same expression."

"Good. Let's agree that you shouldn't be in possession of a scalpel, and I won't touch"—she waved her hand in a circle toward the laptop on the table—"any of this other than to check my email and the weather."

Laughing together was incredibly healing. Mac didn't realize how heavy his heart had become until the shared laughter made it lighter.

"Go on." She sat up a little straighter, feeling her toes tingling. Untucking her feet, she rotated them a couple of times to get the blood flowing again. "What's next? I'm pretty sure you've got a plan in that brain of yours."

"Yeah, well, the guys have analyzed the malware for his digital fingerprint. Which we now have. What we still have to do is track one of his traps. Yes, that means setting it off. Reverse engineer it. But reverse engineering is a painful, bleed-through-the-eyeballs process. It's long and laborious. But it's our best bet. He's smart, so he's used many different things and is all over the map. He's not predictable. He's switched gears so many times, we're not really sure what he's after now, other than the fact that he seems determined to create chaos. Which brings attention. Which makes him powerful? I don't know." He shook his head. "I don't want to get into his head that much. But we've got to find him."

"How? Is there even a way? If he's that smart?" She took another long sip of her coffee.

Mac reached for his own cup and wrapped his hands around it, the warmth feeling good on his hands. "We need to know the target before he hits it. If he uses a remote trigger, it has to be accessible from some public-facing IP address because he has to be able to communicate with the implant from another location."

Her eyebrows furrowed, and she blew over the top of her mug. "Yeah. Uh-huh. That makes sense."

The expression on her face made him laugh, and she joined in again. "Did you understand any of that?"

"Um . . . IP address? I think I have one of those." She crossed her legs and leaned over the table. "But keep talking. I'm a pretty quick learner."

"Without getting into all the technicalities, the key is to find his remote trigger and track the data packets going to and from. We'd have to trace from device to device to device until we ultimately find him at the source. But that's the kicker. He's told us if we get too close, he'll set off a trap. So I'm pretty sure if we start getting close, bad things are going to happen."

"Even worse than what's already happened?" She scrunched up her face.

The responsibility of trying to fix this sat heavy on his shoulders. "Maybe. Probably. That's the thing. None of us knows what he's got planned."

"And?" she prodded. "I can see there's more . . ."

"He went silent for more than two years, Tracie. Stayed underground. To me that means he's been planning something big. Bigger than what he's already done."

"Not good."

"Yeah." He took a sip of his coffee and hated the thought of more people dying because he couldn't stop this guy. His phone buzzed in his pocket. A text from an unknown number:

I left you a little present. You're
welcome.

A chill went up his spine. "Great. It's from him."

His cell buzzed again, this time a phone call. "It's Darcie up in Fairbanks. I'll show you the text in a minute." He then answered. "Hey, Darc. What's up?"

"We've got a problem. Can you hop on an encrypted video chat?"

"Yeah, I'm at Tracie's cabin."

Darcie released a sigh. "I'm glad you're there. This is going to be hard for her."

And things were going so well. His stomach sank. "But she's allowed to listen in?"

The phone muffled and then cleared. "Yes. How long do you need before you can be on?"

"Let me grab my laptop. Just a minute or two as soon as you send me the link."

"Headed your way now."

The call ended, and Mac ran out to grab his computer from the truck. He came back in and eyed Tracie. "It sounds like this isn't going to be pleasant."

"I can handle it." She pulled her chair closer to where he'd set up.

Once connected, Mac surveyed the screen. Jason, Scott, and Carrie were in the conference room at the ABI in Anchorage, Darcie was at the EOC in Fairbanks, and the other three guys he didn't recognize.

Darcie spoke first. "Let me introduce you to Trooper Mitchell, Agent Spirelli from the FBI, and the head of the ABI, Heath Kingston." Each man raised a hand as they were introduced.

Mac nodded along with the other heads on the screen.

Mr. Kingston shared his screen. "I apologize to each one of you for this—especially you, Dr. Hunter. This is going to be disturbing, so prepare yourselves." He cleared his throat. "This afternoon during a hospital board meeting at Fairbanks Memorial Hospital, someone infiltrated the building, the conference room, and then killed every member. The surveillance video shows an empty chair, and we don't know who should have been there, but it's under investigation. Every board member listed on the hospital's website was present."

He played the surveillance video. It went from everyone around the table talking, to people slumped over the table or on the floor, dead.

"Obviously the footage has been altered for us to see what the killer wanted us to see." The screen changed and focused on a piece of paper with letters in red calligraphy. *For Mac and Tracie.* "We're pretty certain this is the work of the same guy they're calling the Typhon Killer. Now, I don't have to tell you that I—"

"Sir." Mac cleared his throat. "I apologize for interrupting, but you need to see something." He pulled up the text on his phone and held it up to the camera.

Tracie gasped and put a hand over her mouth.

He turned, hating that he hadn't been able to prepare her. "Sorry."

Then he looked back at the screen. "This came in seconds before Darcie called."

Kingston shook his head. "We'll put a team on tracing it—not that I expect anything will come of it."

Tracie nudged Mac's elbow and leaned toward the computer. "There *is* a board member missing, sir. I can't place him at the moment, but I will . . ." She dipped her head and shook it. "His name is on the tip of my tongue . . . started with an *l*?"

"There's no record of that." Kingston looked over his shoulder, off-screen. "Dr. Hunter, are you one hundred percent positive?"

"Yes, sir." She bit her lip. "Linden! That was his name. He's the only one I'd never met, but he was talked about a lot because everyone liked him so much. Every staff member wanted to meet the guy."

The head of the ABI nodded to his team around him and paused.

The room was quiet as they waited for a response.

Kingston turned back to the camera, and his jaw tensed. "If this guy wasn't already our number one priority, he would be now. There is absolutely no record of a Mr. Linden ever being on the board at the hospital. Mr. McPherson, we're hoping your team can add that to your list to check into—can you determine if facts have been erased?" His eyes narrowed to slits. "Threats are coming in from all over. There's a lot of chatter. I don't know if he's planting it all or if others are in on it or even if it's legit. But we've had reports all over the state of massive doxing happening to innocent bystanders. Government employees have had their identities stolen and credit hacked. There've been weird power surges in Juneau, at hospitals, and at the airport. Two planes almost collided this afternoon." He took a breath. "But the worst terror chatter we've heard is that the pipeline is going to be hit and it will be worse than Exxon Valdez, Deepwater Horizon, and the next top-ten oil disasters combined."

Mac clenched his jaw. "What do you need us to do, sir? My company is at your service."

"Darcie told me as much." He leaned closer. "I need all of you in Fairbanks as soon as possible. Can you do that?"

Everyone nodded.

"This is also not public knowledge. Agent Spirelli?"

The FBI man nodded at the attendees. "We've decided that our UNSUB enjoys the notoriety too much. As much as we tried to keep this out of the press to starve his appetite for attention, that's no longer a viable option. We can't stop it. It's everywhere."

Mac wasn't sure that was the best plan. "Sir, if I might interject."

Spirelli lifted an eyebrow. "I'm listening."

"I've seen this guy up close and personal. I have pictures of him that I shared with Carrie from the ABI. If you can no longer stop the spread of the story online or in the media, why not use that to our advantage? If we circulate the pictures, don't you think we'd be able to drive him out of hiding?"

The agent stared at him through the screen. "Mr. McPherson, we are all aware of what this case means to you, and we are sorry for your loss. While we appreciate your expertise in the cyber world, we need you to take a step back. Rest assured, the picture of our UNSUB has been circulated to all local and federal authorities. We are already dealing with mass panic. We need him caught, not blasted across social media. Let us do our job, and we'll appreciate your cyber team's help."

It took everything Mac had to swallow the words he wanted to unleash and keep his emotion from showing on his face. *Help me keep my cool, Lord.* He looked down and shut out the conversation around him. These guys knew what they were doing. He simply had to trust.

With a deep breath, he looked back up at the screen. Instructions were shared, and everyone signed off. He closed the laptop and turned to Tracie.

Her shoulders were shaking. "He's horrible."

He'd been so angry at Griz that he hadn't taken time to process the fact that she probably knew everyone around that table. "I'm so sorry."

Completely helpless, he pulled her into his arms and held her as she cried.

CHAPTER SIXTEEN

Four Days, Thirteen Hours, Forty-Five Minutes Sober
July 15—9:15 a.m.
In the Air over Alaska

THE PLANE RIDE TO FAIRBANKS so far hadn't been bad, especially since she had Mac beside her. With Scott flying the plane, Carrie in the copilot seat, and Jason behind her and Mac, Tracie felt safe and secure. But the thought of going back to the hospital made her stomach churn.

Everyone must be in shock. And mourning.

For the first hour, Mac tried to explain the deep web. She'd heard of the dark web or deep web, but she'd always thought it was just a place for criminals to do black-market dealings. Boy, had she been wrong.

Apparently the deep web was the part of the World Wide Web that wasn't indexed and couldn't be found on search engines. Okay, she understood that much. On the deep web were the dark-net websites—what most people thought of as the dark web—which could only be accessed with specific software or special authorization. She'd never tried to go there, so she really had no idea, but at least she could make sense of it now.

But when Mac started talking about Tor, Riffle, Freenet, I2P, and other popular networks that were encrypted friend-to-friend networks that allowed everyone to be anonymous and for nothing to be traced, she told him she'd had enough. That was not the kind of thing she wanted to know about. Granted, that was probably like hiding her head in the sand, but it was all too much for her. Sure, she could understand that people didn't want to be traced. They valued their privacy. Theirs was a country of rights and free speech.

But to know that there were evil people out there hiding who knew what on these encrypted dark-web places made her want to throw out her computer, iPad, iPhone, and Apple Watch.

"Sorry. I didn't mean to make you uncomfortable." Mac put his arm around her shoulders. "I forget how unnerving it is to find out this is out there. It's not a bad thing. But evil people do lots of harm with it."

"This whole onion-routing thing makes sense, that it's layer-by-layer encrypted, but shouldn't things like this be illegal? Especially if everyone knows it's the place for bad people to do bad things?"

Mac squeezed her shoulder. "Like I said, it's not a bad thing to protect your privacy, but you're right—there are a lot of evil people in the world using it for horrible things."

Maybe she was too naïve, but she didn't like knowing it was there. Accessible. And secretive.

Then again, she understood how important it was for people to have the right to privacy. Especially since hers had been completely snatched away. But wasn't that different?

Who could be trusted to make the rules anyway?

So she'd done her best to talk about happy things the rest of the trip. But the closer they flew to Fairbanks, the harder that became.

As soon as the wheels touched down, she turned Airplane Mode off on her phone. Then realized what a hypocrite she was. It was such a habit to check her email and social media.

She shoved her phone into her back pocket. But when they exited the plane, her phone buzzed.

Oh good. Sherry.

Mac took her bag so she could answer and juggle her coffee cup.

"Hello?"

"Dr. Hunter, it's Sherry." She sounded out of breath. "I'm so glad I caught you."

"What's wrong?"

"Can you come out to Anaktuvuk Pass? It's an emergency."

"What's going on?" It was so easy to switch into doctor mode. And it felt good to be needed.

The phone muffled for a moment and then Sherry continued. "One of the village elders refused to be flown out, and his gallbladder is in bad shape. He needs surgery right away."

"I'm at the airport now. Let me see what I can arrange."

"In Fairbanks?" Her voice lifted.

"Yes. Just arrived."

"Oh, well, that's an answer to prayer. The pilot that left here after he delivered supplies said he would wait at the airport in case I found a doctor who could come out."

"Tell me the plane's tail number, and I'll hunt him down. Would he be here by now?"

"Possibly." Sherry mumbled something to someone else. "I don't remember what time he left. I've got all the medical supplies you need at the clinic. I'll prep the patient and the room for surgery. You just get here."

"Thanks, Sherry. I'm on my way." For the first time since she was put on administrative leave, she felt like herself again. Useful. Surely the board couldn't say anything about her going to help save some-one's life. She'd been cleared, after all.

Mac waited for her inside the airport. "I'm guessing you need to leave?" He handed her the rolling carry-on she'd brought with her.

"Yeah." She stared into his eyes. So much had happened since they'd met, and yet she felt like they were just getting to really know each other. After she'd cried her eyes out on his shoulder, they'd had a heart-to-heart. He'd shared his anger, grief, and fears. She'd shared hers. And now she felt connected to him in a way she'd never felt to a man. Good grief, she was thirty-eight years old. It wasn't like she had a teenage crush on the man, but she hated the thought of not seeing him for a day or two.

"I hate to leave you guys in the middle of all this mess, but I need to perform a surgery."

"Go." He leaned down and kissed her forehead. "We'll have plenty of time once all this is over." He offered the handle of her bag to her.

"But will it ever be over?" She shook her head. After everything he'd shared with her on the plane, she felt like she needed a technology bath.

"Have a little faith in me . . . I'm determined." He placed his hands on her shoulders and gave her a little push. "Go on."

She nodded and then took off to find someone who could help her find a plane that had just returned from the bush.

✦ ✦ ✦

Four Days, Nineteen Hours, Forty Minutes Sober
July 15—3:10 p.m.
Latitude: 68.143245° N, Longitude: 151.733673° W
Clinic—Anaktuvuk Pass, Alaska

As Tracie stitched up the patient on the table, she looked at Sherry. "I couldn't have done this without you."

"I couldn't have done this without *you*, Dr. Hunter."

"Please call me Tracie. It's just the two of us." She finished up the stitches, and Sherry cut the surgical thread. "It was touch and go for a bit there—I thought we might lose him. But I'm thankful he'll be here to share his wisdom with his grandchildren." Before putting him under, she'd asked him about his family. It was always good to get them thinking about what they had to look forward to rather than the pain and thought of dying.

"Me too." Sherry cleaned up the instruments. "We don't have a recovery room, so this will have to do."

"I'll go talk to the family. I'm sure they are worried." As Tracie pulled off her gloves and outer scrubs, she turned back to Sherry. "Thank you for calling me. I needed to feel useful again." As hard as she tried, the tears still welled in her eyes. She did her best to blink them away but wasn't successful.

"I would hug you, Tracie, but I don't want to get you messy." Sherry's grin was wide. "You are a wonderful doctor and an even better human being. I don't know many people who would've dropped everything to come out here to save this man's life."

Tracie nodded her thanks and scurried out before the tears got the best of her.

In the front of the clinic, several members of the man's family sat. As soon as they saw her, they all dashed to their feet.

"He's resting comfortably. The surgery was a success."

Hugs and a cacophony of voices thanking her filled her senses.

An hour later, she went back to check on her patient. The family wanted to know everything, and one of them had slipped out to gather more of the villagers. Before she knew it, she'd been surrounded by people thanking her for coming.

As she entered the surgery room that had been turned into the patient's recovery room, she smiled at Sherry.

The nurse was scribbling notes, glancing from the machine hooked to the man and back to her chart. "All his vitals are good. He should be waking up anytime now."

She looked down at the man and then took the chart Sherry offered to her. Her eyebrows arched. It was incredibly thorough. Sherry had even taken the time to write comprehensive notes about the surgery.

Tracie added a few things here and there, but she was impressed with Sherry's attention to detail.

The man moaned, and she lifted her gaze. His eyelids fluttered.

She stood over him. "I'm Dr. Hunter. Your surgery went well. You'll need to take it easy for a while, but you should make a full recovery."

The deep wrinkles on the old man's face relaxed as he nodded. But it was the gratitude in his eyes that meant the world to her.

Thank You, Lord.

✦ ✦ ✦

947 Days After
July 15—3:30 p.m.
Latitude: 64.841130° N, Longitude: 147.716869° W
Emergency Operations Center—Fairbanks

Since the Emergency Operations Center had the best space and Jason's equipment was already installed, the team had set up shop here. Mac surveyed the room. A lot of computers humming with a ton of wires protruding were set up around the main space. They'd tried to keep the tripping hazards to a minimum, but he'd reminded everyone to be vigilant and watch their step.

Two cyber specialists from the FBI were with them, along with Carrie and Alan from the ABI, Scott, Jason, Darcie, and himself.

As they gathered every piece of potential evidence, they were actively trying to get on whatever network Griz used. They needed one of the end points, but they didn't have it yet. If only they could get a glimpse of his infrastructure.

Jason wasn't convinced that Griz would trust Tor's anonymous services, so he'd been deep on the dark web looking for another network Griz would find worthy.

Reports came in regularly of small hacks and outages. Each one made Mac cringe. He hadn't heard of any people in serious danger, but would the team hear right away?

So far it didn't seem like they'd set off any of Griz's traps. Unless that's what he wanted them to think. It relieved Mac in a way and discouraged him in another. Were they even getting close?

Kingston, along with Spirelli from the FBI, was determined to continue on in his pursuit. Tripping some booby traps along the way couldn't be as bad as whatever Griz had planned for his endgame.

They'd seen his handiwork.

Too many people had died already. Time was of the essence.

Mac scanned each of the specialized traces he had going. There was only so much that could be done undetected. And Griz knew they were looking for him. He'd basically dared them to. Once they were close, they could set off a trigger for an implant. Which was probably exactly what Griz *wanted.*

Oh, this was interesting. "Hey, Jas!" he called across the room.

Jason jogged over. "Whatcha got?"

"Take a look." Mac was so bleary-eyed that he wanted to double-check.

"Yep, that's how he controlled the surveillance video." Jason shook his head and jotted down the numbers. "How much do you wanna bet he triggered it to delete and had a fresh video ready to replace."

"At the hospital." Mac shook his head. "But it disappeared. He cleaned up after himself and deleted the logs. We have *got* to find his next target in advance."

"He must have been using a VPN. Then flipped it out for a few seconds to set the trigger."

Mac's mind whirled with the possibilities. They had one instance of a digital footprint from Juneau. Now they had this. Every tiny window they caught a glimpse through would help them to stop him. It had to.

✦ ✦ ✦

48 Days Until Final Judgment
17 Members Left
July 15—4:35 p.m.
Latitude: 64.83156° N, Longitude: 147.73836° W
Fairbanks Memorial Hospital

The nurse flipped her hair over her shoulder and headed for her car.

Griz caught up with her and shoved his gun into her side. "Hush, or I pull the trigger."

Her eyes widened, and she nodded.

"Good. Now let's get into your vehicle." He opened the driver's side door and waited for her to be seated. Then he opened the door behind her and climbed in. "Nice and easy. Hands on the wheel."

Her body shook as she did what he said. "Please. Don't hurt me."

"Have you been enjoying your fifteen minutes of fame, my dear?"

Her brow creased as she stared at him in the rearview mirror. "I . . . I don't know what you mean."

"Let's not play games, Courtney. I've been watching you."

She swallowed and blinked, her arms trembling even harder now.

"You were useful for a few minutes, and for that I'm appreciative."

Tears streamed down her face. "Please . . ."

"Don't worry. It won't hurt one bit. I promise." He pulled a syringe out of his pocket. "You've been a beautiful pawn in my game of chess."

She shook her head and screamed.

He reached forward and covered her mouth with one gloved hand, then gently injected his concoction into her neck with the other. "There now. All done."

He exited the back seat and opened the driver's door again. Her badge was in her left front pocket. Once he had it, he shut the car doors and walked away.

Whistling as he went.

CHAPTER SEVENTEEN

15 Fellow Members Remain
July 16—10:00 a.m.
Latitude: 61.302290° N, Longitude: 149.470746° W
Eagle River

Two more found dead this morning.

The two extras she'd had on Griz's tail. Or so she'd thought. Now there was no one close enough to get a signal from the tracker. Other than the man they hadn't heard from in sixth months. Which meant he must be dead too.

He'd reduced their number by more than half. Unacceptable. She refused to live in fear of the man but had to face facts. If she didn't stop him soon, she wouldn't see her next birthday in three weeks' time.

Every single one of the Members was taking precautions. Preparing for the worst. Leaving instructions for their most trusted colleagues, friends, and family.

She glanced up from her notebook to Kirk Myers. "I had really hoped that it wouldn't play out this way, but it's time for our contingency plan, Mr. Myers."

"You've got it."

She pushed an envelope of cash across the desk. "This should be sufficient for the first part of our agreement. The remaining payment will be made once the job is completed."

"Yes, ma'am."

"If you're killed along the way, I'll have your remains sent to your family with the letter."

He blinked several times, then gave her a single nod. "I understand. Thank you."

She hated having to stoop to Griz's level, but that's what it had come to. Breaking the rules of the Members was the only way to stop him now. "You'll need to dispose of any phone or tablet you've used in the past."

"Already done. Believe me. I understand him."

"And he has no idea you're aligned with us?"

"No. None. He's become a lone wolf for the most part but still reaches out when he needs me sooner than our scheduled meetings."

Excellent. That was all the information she needed.

"There's already one in the books?"

"Yes." His gaze was unflinching as he studied her.

That would play perfectly into their plan. As long as she could keep everyone else alive long enough to put it into action. "I'm trusting you with a great deal, Mr. Myers."

"I won't let you down."

✦ ✦ ✦

47 Days Until Final Judgment
15 Members Left
July 16—10:14 p.m.
Latitude: 70.193385° N, Longitude: 148.444766° W
Griz's Small Compound

Someone new was following him.

He hadn't seen them, but he could *feel* them.

No matter what Griz tried, he couldn't shake them. Since noon the hair on the back of his neck kept standing up.

He wasn't one to get spooked. Not ever. He was in control.

Popping his last pill for the day, he went to the safe to unlock his stash. A couple more wouldn't hurt. He needed focus. Clarity. Calm.

Not this ludicrous idea that he was now the prey.

He wasn't. He refused to be.

After washing two more pills down with a glass of water, he lifted his chin.

Fine. He could outsmart whoever it was. They might have won a single volley, but he would win the game, set, match.

To be honest, this was just what he needed. If they wanted to play, he would play.

His plan was perfect.

The press might be refusing to talk about him today, but tomorrow? Once he moved up the timeline and crushed their spirits, he'd be the top story again.

His neck burned and itched, and he clawed at it with his hand. "Forget forty-seven days." It made him laugh. "How about . . . sixteen?"

That would work.

Just wait.

✦ ✦ ✦

949 Days After
July 17—9:25 a.m.
Latitude: 64.841130° N, Longitude: 147.716869° W
Emergency Operations Center

The large main room of the EOC buzzed with activity. Not only did they have twenty massive computers now running, but they were constantly sharing information back and forth with every law enforcement agency that had any piece of evidence, fact-finding mission, or trace they had in place. Mac was impressed with how much they'd accomplished so far, compiling more information than he'd thought possible on this guy, but still their quest was like finding a single snowflake in a blizzard. Especially since they didn't know what Griz had planned. There were so many possibilities of what he could do—and what he had already done was bad enough—how could they predict him?

They couldn't.

And that's what Mac wrestled with the most. The unknown.

The source from the Members had been mysteriously silent. Mac's team had determined that the numbers the source had given them last time could mean or stand for several different things—but their best guess was a low-frequency, passive RFID transmitter. Which meant someone would need to be within a few feet of it to scan it and find out if it was even transmitting. How could that be helpful?

So they'd focused on the insight they *did* have.

Everything with Griz was well planned. The trigger he'd used at the hospital to delete and alter the surveillance video had proved to be telling. But he always cleaned up after himself. No logs. No fingerprints. No digital fingerprint other than the single blip the second he triggered it, then disappeared.

In addition to all of that, he was apparently off the grid most of the time. Either that or he was in complete control of a network. Like he owned it.

They needed him online to be able to find him.

Jason hopped up from his seat and removed his headphones. "Mac!" He waved frantically.

Mac ran over to his friend's desk. "Whatcha got?"

"I followed a random data packet from when he was at the hospital and found this." He pointed to the screen.

"It leads us to another device used in that boardroom." Mac leaned forward and studied the data packet. "Cell phone?"

"Yep." Jason clicked to another screen. "Belonging to a Dr. Windsor."

"He was killed along with everyone else in the room. What's the tie?" Mac shifted and sat on the edge of the desk.

"I'm thinking that Windsor was a Member. Just a thought, but Griz would have no trouble playing off one of his old partners and eliminating him all in one fell swoop."

Mac mulled it over for several seconds. "Maybe we need to look into this Dr. Windsor and his history. See if there's anything else that can lead us back to Griz and what he's got planned."

"On it. I think I'll ask Carrie and Darc to help with this." He leaned closer. "They're better at dealing with the FBI. Their excuse that they can't share what they know about the Members because it's national security spooks me. Maybe we can connect Windsor to other Members as well. I know it's a shot in the dark, but it's worth a try. We just need one of them to work with us."

Mac grunted. "Shots in the dark are about all we've got at this point. Do it."

Jason nodded back. "On it. Let's see what the good Dr. Windsor can lead us to."

Agent Spirelli from the FBI strode over. "Anything new?"

Mac filled him in on the other device in the boardroom. If only these guys could share what they knew rather than keeping everything compartmentalized. If the left hand would help the right hand do its job, it sure would be nice. And sure, he understood that the government had to protect people and all, but still. He'd rather just get the job done than have to jump through hoops or navigate all the red tape.

"Sounds like a solid lead if he can—"

An alarm went off over their heads. Unfamiliar with the procedures of the EOC, Mac searched for Darcie. Her eyes were wide as she raced out of her office. "Explosion at Northern Lights Elementary School."

✦ ✦ ✦

Six Days, Fourteen Hours, Thirty-Three Minutes Sober
July 17—10:03 a.m.
In the Air Somewhere Between Anaktuvuk Pass and Fairbanks

Tracie stared out the window of the small twin-engine plane and watched the low clouds thin and break enough for her to see the rolling landscape outside of Fairbanks as Sherry snored softly in the seat next to her. Her friend had taken the news of what had happened to the hospital board pretty hard, and Tracie had convinced her nurse to take a few weeks off to visit her family.

If only she could promise that by the time Sherry returned, the bad guy would be caught. Tracie shook off the thoughts and stared down at a large herd of caribou running along a stream.

She never tired of living in Alaska. The sheer vastness of the state had overwhelmed her at first because she'd wanted to see it all. But that would take a lifetime.

The Alaska Range was by far her favorite mountain range. With Denali in the center, surrounded by many other majestic peaks, she could spend weeks hiking in the national park. That was, if she'd ever take the time off.

Even so, the national park—while bigger than many states back east all by itself—was only one of the many wonders she'd seen.

Glaciers would have to be second on her list. She'd only seen a few, but the idea of seeing all the accessible ones in Alaska was on her bucket list.

Another dream that would take a lot of time.

Something she didn't give herself. She could pretend that one day she would . . .

So many of the other doctors were missing out by not volunteering their time for the remote villages. Not only did they pass up the opportunity to help people, but they didn't get to experience the culture, the extraordinary views, and the chance to visit places few outsiders had ever been.

The Native cultures in Alaska were many and varied. Yes, there were issues with smoking, alcohol, and drugs, which seemed to be what most outsiders equated with Native villages, but there was so much to gain by getting to know the people and learning about their history and traditions. They were proud people. Noble people. And so very grateful for the care she offered. Care that otherwise they would go without.

Perhaps she should increase her own volunteer hours. Maybe even start a ministry with other believers who were physicians throughout the state.

She liked that idea. It would also help her break down her own walls and get to know people better. Another venture worth investing her time.

Working with the guys from Cyber Solutions had opened her eyes to so much.

And her heart too.

Ever since she'd said goodbye to Mac at the airport, she'd had a hard time getting him off her mind. Granted, they'd come together during life-threatening circumstances, but that didn't doom their budding relationship, did it?

She'd gotten the distinct impression that he was healing in more ways than one and cared about her. When he'd kissed her forehead and said they would have plenty of time once it was all over . . . it gave her hope that he felt the tug toward her like she felt for him.

It had been a long time since she'd even allowed herself to look at a man and appreciate his good looks.

Not since . . . well, not since the Sanderson case.

Back in college, she'd admired several men. Even went out on a few dates with guys she'd met in Bible studies. But once she hit medical school and then residency, there was barely enough time to sleep, much less have a social life. When she'd taken the ME position, her parents had encouraged her to think about settling down. And she'd attended the singles' group at church with that intention.

Life had been simpler back then. Full of dreams and happy thoughts of the future.

All that changed when the events of the Sanderson case sent her spiraling. Back to medical school. Years and years of training, residency, and fellowships had taken all her time and energy.

It had been her survival mode. Even if she was only surviving, it was an okay life. She was content with pouring everything she had into her patients.

But then Mac had come along.

She wanted more now. Once she'd cracked open the door to her heart, she wanted to swing it wide open.

Her phone buzzed multiple times in her lap. They must be back in a serviceable area. There hadn't been a signal back in Anaktuvuk Pass. She spoke into the microphone on her headset. "Will this mess up your controls? I forgot to switch it to Airplane Mode."

The pilot grinned at her, and his voice sounded tinny through the headset. "Nah. But when we get ready to land, it's safer to switch it off. We've got a good bit of time, so if you need to catch up on correspondence, go ahead. I'll let you know when we're close to arrival."

"Thanks." She scrolled through her email and found one from Mac. The only one she wanted to open. Everything else could wait.

Hey Tracie,

The gang all says hi. We're praying for you and the much-needed work you are doing out in the bush. It's been a tough couple days here. Then again, I don't see it letting up until we've caught this guy. But that's not why I wanted to email.

First, you are missed. Second, I'm way out of practice for this and will completely understand if you say no. Especially since I haven't been the nicest person to you in the past. Forgive me for that, please?

Anyway, I'd like to ask you out for a cup of coffee or even dinner if you think you could put up with me for that long. I was going to put it off until the crazy time we're in is over and the maniac is behind bars in a high-security prison somewhere, but Jason and Scott gave me a stern talking-to last night and told me waiting is stupid.

Oh—and before you give me the excuse that relationships that begin in crisis rarely survive, let me remind
you that those two guys met their wives in the middle of
disasters caused by this lunatic. With God on our side,
we might actually have a chance at making a go of this.
Gotta run,
Mac

Wow. Her heart ached with what that email must have cost him.
To open up and place the ball firmly in her court. She would not take
this lightly. She needed to pray about how to respect a man's heart
who'd lost his wife and daughter.

Still, Tracie couldn't keep the grin off her face as she reread his
words, her heart skipping a beat, like she was back in high school
with a crush on the star football player.

After her third read-through, she noticed another email in the
chain. Her stomach did a little flip. Just seeing his name made her
happy. Oh, she was ridiculous. It was a good thing she hadn't allowed
herself time for this when she was younger. How goofy would she
have been then? She scrolled to the next message and thought about
her response to him.

Tracie,
A lot has happened since I sent that last email to you.
I don't want to end on a sad note, but it's important that
you know what has transpired. It's best for me to just
be blunt.
Griz killed Courtney. I'm so sorry to have to share
that with you, but I hope you read this before you listen
to the radio or see the news. The city has been rocked
the last few days.
Our UNSUB—the FBI guys must be rubbing off on me,
because that's what I'm calling him now—has taken a

lot of lives here. I know how difficult it is . . . losing so
many people you knew and worked with. If there's anything I can do, tell me. I'm here. I can't fix it, but I've
got a strong shoulder.

See you soon,

Mac

His words sank in. *Courtney?* She closed her eyes against the burning and swallowed back the bile that threatened to rise up her throat.

Then it really hit. Courtney was dead. With a gasp, she put a hand
to her mouth.

"You okay?" The pilot's voice broke through the hurricane in her
mind.

She took a huge gulp of air and tried to calm herself. "Not really."

CHAPTER EIGHTEEN

949 Days After
July 17—10:26 a.m.
Latitude: 64.841130° N, Longitude: 147.716869° W
Emergency Operations Center

THEY'D SET OFF A TRAP. The monster had warned them. And it happened.

All those children.

At an elementary school.

Oh, God . . . please help those kids be all right!

Every bit of grief that had hit Mac when the explosion at the pipeline overlook had killed his wife and daughter now rushed to the surface and threatened to overwhelm him. Like massive waves crashing over him, the emotions dragged him down until all he could see was dark. He put a hand on the desk next to him and closed his eyes.

Not again.

Red seared his eyelids, and for a moment he considered allowing the anger to take over. He clenched his jaw and his fists.

A hand landed on his left shoulder. Then another one on his right.

Strength and peace seemed to vibrate through those hands. Mac forced his mind to think on truth. The only Truth. In the seconds that followed, he knew without a shadow of a doubt that his brothers were praying for him.

It was the only explanation—God's supernatural work through His people.

Mac relaxed the muscles in his face and then his arms. But when he opened his eyes, his legs threatened to buckle.

Someone shoved a chair under his rear end at just the right time. Otherwise he might have hit the floor. But the hands stayed on his shoulders.

Mac took deep breaths and scanned the room.

No one said a word or even moved as Darcie made a call and stepped to the central smart whiteboard for disaster response.

He blinked several times to clear his vision.

Darcie hung up and put her hands on her hips, looking shaken. "We're still waiting on confirmation, but I think we just had a miracle." She cleared her throat. "Northern Lights Elementary had a scheduled fire drill this morning. The entire school was well outside the building when the explosion was triggered. There are some injuries from flying debris, but they haven't found anyone in critical condition."

Applause sounded throughout the room.

"All right, everyone." Spirelli held his hands up as he walked to Darcie. "We've got to stop this guy, and now. We can't afford any more—"

Mac's phone buzzed. Rescued. He couldn't take it to listen to that FBI guy give them the charge back into battle.

At what cost?

Minutes—possibly even seconds—had separated them from mass casualties.

Granted, a few weeks ago he would have led that charge. He still wanted to. But the thought of innocent children dying while the team hunted their prey was too much.

It opened his eyes to the reality of his revenge.

Yes, he wanted the guy caught.

But not with the sacrifice of more lives.

He left the EOC's main level and went out to the staircase. Taking a seat on the top step, he tamped down his hateful thoughts toward the man behind all this.

Once his breathing was steady and normal, he unlocked his phone.

Another text from an unknown number. Wishful thinking that it was the source, but he'd already seen the first sentence.

> You got lucky this time. Better
> stop while you're ahead. You
> know by now that I don't give
> empty threats.

Sweat prickled across Mac's back. His heart pounded so hard it felt like it was coming out of his chest. When would this madness stop? Responsibility to catch this guy hung like a millstone around his neck. They couldn't stop hunting him—who knew how many lives would be in danger? But the thought of helping in a pursuit in which his actions could cause casualties shook him to his core.

The door opened behind him.

He turned and spied Scott. "I need to tell everyone—just got a text."

"Spirelli is really fired up." His friend sounded resigned and sat next to him on the step.

"Yeah. I bet."

"What did the text say?"

Mac showed him his phone, unable to keep his hand from shaking.

Scott cringed and closed his eyes briefly. "I'm really beginning to hate this guy."

"I'm already there, and I've been asking God to help me with that." His shoulders slumped. "The situation is impossible, and the thought of putting more people at risk sickens me."

"Me too." Scott gripped Mac's shoulder and stood. "But maybe there's something we can do. Let's go ask Agent Spirelli if you can text him back. If Griz responds, there's a minuscule chance we can get a location on him."

It was the best option so far. Mac stood and braced himself. "Let's go tell the team."

Entering the EOC, Mac felt a rush of cold air. They'd had to crank the AC down as low as it would go to keep not only themselves but their computers as cool as possible. He stepped to Spirelli. "I just received this text. Scott thinks that if I respond, Griz might text back. If I get him worked up enough, maybe he'll make a misstep and we can have a brief window to trace him."

The FBI agent read the screen, then waved at Mac to follow him as they walked back to his two other agents working on their laptops. After filling them in, he turned back to Mac and nodded. "You have permission to rile him up, McPherson. See if you can get him to respond. My guys will do what they can to trace it."

Riling the guy up would be easy. Mac typed on his phone and showed it to Scott and Spirelli.

> It wasn't luck. You failed. Won't
> be long now until we have you
> in our sights.

"That should do it." The FBI agent's face was hard as stone. Mac hit Send.

It was only a matter of seconds before a response buzzed.

> You're dumber than I thought,
> Mac. How about a taste to
> show you just how weak you
> are up against me?

Spirelli stood over his guys and watched the screens. "Well? Did you get him?"

One of the younger agents frowned and leaned in closer to his computer. He typed frantically. "No," he growled.

"What's happened?" Mac walked behind the computers.

Several lines in Darcie's office rang.

That couldn't be good.

"Internet seems to be down, sir." The other young agent gave a look to their boss.

Mac went to other computers around the room. No signal.

Jason shook his head and jogged across the room. "I'll check the server."

Then Darcie exited her office, a serious dip in her brow. She stood in the doorway and held up a hand. "Looks like our guy has shut down the internet across the city, Fort Wainwright, and the surrounding areas. Alaska Communications, GCI, Fastwyre, Borealis Broadband, Microcom, the remote providers—they're all down."

✦ ✦ ✦

Six Days, Fifteen Hours, Forty-Eight Minutes Sober
July 17—11:18 a.m.
Latitude: 64.8455° N, Longitude: 147.5338° W
Along Columbia Creek

Tracie's keys jingled as she dropped them on her kitchen table. It was strange to be home again after being away and with everything that happened. It felt like a year had passed. And yet seeing her things, smelling the lingering scent of vanilla and cinnamon from the automatic air freshener, sitting on her couch . . . were exactly what she needed in this moment.

Especially after the last thirty-six hours.

She tossed her overnight bag on the bed. A hot shower would be just the thing to wash it all away. The memory of the blood from the surgery. The grateful tears on the villagers' faces. The horror she'd felt at the news about Courtney. The board members. Her beloved boss. She'd hardly had time to digest it.

It had been one thing for Mac to tell her, but when the radio station paused its uplifting music to give an update, she'd had to pull over on the side of the road until her hands had stopped shaking.

Courtney.

Grief overwhelmed her. Guilt quickly followed. Their last conversation lingered in her memory. Every bad thought Tracie had allowed to fill her mind after Courtney's interview chased her down. She had so many regrets. Things she would change. She could have been a better witness. A better boss. Kinder. The list just kept growing. How could she process *this* death? Her own surgical nurse. Murdered. By that monster.

Tracie rubbed her face. How many more people had to die? At this point, the man would be remembered as the worst serial killer in the history of America. And that was saying something.

Leaning against the wall in the bathroom, she slid down and crouched on the floor. What was their world coming to?

She shook her head. If she stayed in this spiral, she would never leave the house again. Her old vice would claim her. Anxiety and self-pity and grief would cripple her, and she wasn't about to let that happen. She needed to shower. Then she would call Mac. See where they were, find out what she could do to help and keep busy. Make a plan.

Thirty minutes later, Tracie plucked her phone off the wireless charger, glad it was almost at full battery power. She slipped an earbud into her ear and hit Call on Mac's contact.

"Hey, are you back?" His voice sounded weary. But it was sweet that he'd at least tried to sound upbeat.

Her shoulders relaxed at the sound of his voice. "Hey. Got in a little while ago. Had to make myself feel human again after everything."

Mac grunted. "I bet. Surgery in the middle of nowhere sounds like a real test of skills."

"I've definitely experienced new appreciation for how surgeons worked in the old days, over the last few years, that's for sure." She took a deep breath. "I read your emails and then heard the news about Courtney on the radio too. Have you heard if it's this maniac for sure?"

"I'm so sorry, Tracie." Mac let out a breath. "Yeah. Carrie and her team got a communication from Mr. Typhon himself earlier claiming he did it. Along with the same old taunt that we'll never catch him. We've obviously struck a nerve, though, because we're getting close. We set off a trap—" His voice cracked. He cleared it. "Thank God no one was in the school building when the explosion occurred."

"School building?" Her voice caught. As Mac filled in the details, she wanted to get in this guy's face and give him a piece of her mind. Then she'd see how he liked meeting her scalpel without any pain-killers. How on earth could this guy think it was all right to hurt children? "Oh my goodness, that's awful. I can't believe he would set a bomb at a school!"

"Believe it." Mac's voice took on a hard edge. "You should see the text he sent me. For a second, the FBI thought for sure we would be able to trace him if I taunted him back. But instead, all the internet across the city seems to be down. We haven't even begun to investigate how he pulled off such a stunt, but nothing really surprises us anymore when it comes to this guy. One thing that gave me a smidge of satisfaction?"

"Yeah? What's that?"

"We're pretty sure I ticked him off. I doubt I wiped the smug look off his face for long, but it's nice to think that maybe I accomplished that feat for a brief moment."

"Without any internet, how are you going to track him?" Maybe the question showed her ignorance, but Tracie couldn't fathom how the Cyber Solutions guys would be able to do what they did best without being connected to the internet.

"He's definitely tied our hands behind our backs, that's for sure. But we're working on the backup satellite link for the EOC. We've got to make sure it hasn't been compromised as well. Cell phone hot spots are temporarily giving us a little bit of help, but they can't handle the load or scope of what we need to do. And of course, it's not secure." The breath he released gave her a bit more insight into his frustration than his tone of voice had. "It'll take time, but we'll get there. Especially since this stunt riled up our forces too. As we speak, the FBI is securing a warrant to ask for the data logs from VPN servers. Only problem is, it'll be as intense as searching for a needle in the proverbial haystack. But we have a timestamp. A two-second window. We've got enough guys to go through the logs and hopefully find the packet that triggered either the explosion at the school or the internet. If—and that's a really big *if*—we can identify the packet transmission, then we will see the to and from. The latter being the most important."

"Oh." She had no understanding of how that worked, but at least they had a plan. "Anything I can do to help? Do you guys need coffee? Food? Just tell me, and I'll bring you whatever you want."

"Food sounds amazing. Tell you what—I'll ask the team what they want and then text you our order in the next ten minutes."

"Perfect. See you soon." Tracie hung up and put her earbud back in its charging case. She slipped it into her purse along with her phone and grabbed her car keys. No matter what the team wanted, she was getting coffee. Otherwise she wouldn't be much use to them.

✦ ✦ ✦

949 Days After
July 17—12:01 p.m.
Latitude: 64.841130° N, Longitude: 147.716869° W
Emergency Operations Center

The phone lines in the EOC had rung nonstop. Cell towers were beyond capacity. Not only were the citizens of Fairbanks in an uproar about the bomb at the school and that the lack of internet was keeping them from getting vital information, but the EOC was having trouble connecting to the backup satellite relay. Which meant all the emergency services were also flying blind.

Again.

Mac and his team had tried to help Darcie come up with every scenario possible. So far . . . no luck. They'd asked all the radio stations to broadcast the need for people to reserve the use of their cell phones for emergencies only, but were they listening? No. Every person with a cell phone was probably glued to the screen, trying to find out what was going on.

Griz was probably sitting somewhere laughing. People were ridiculous when it came to losing the internet. They were cut off. And to the younger generation? Taking away their internet was worse than taking away their electricity.

The last half hour had passed as if in slow motion. If they couldn't get things up and running soon, they'd have a riot on their hands.

His phone buzzed in his pocket. Mac didn't recognize the number. "Hello?"

"I've got another clue for you. Meet me at the southeast corner of Sixth and Noble in five minutes. Bring Jason but no one else."

Three beeps indicated the call was gone.

Mac searched the room for Jason. He wasn't going to miss this chance.

His friend was in Darcie's office. He jogged over and tapped on the door just as Darcie hung up the phone.

She waved him in. "Well, the governor is furious this is happening again. Says everyone is asking why we haven't stopped the madman. He was about to call Agent Spirelli, so stay away for a while if you don't want to get blowback." She shook her head and sat back in her chair.

Mac stepped closer and darted a glance at her husband. "Mind if I steal Jason for a while?"

His friend's eyes questioned, but he stayed silent.

Mac looked back to Darcie.

"Sure." The phone rang again. "I'll be on the phone, putting out fires."

"Thanks." Mac left the room in a quick stride.

Jason caught up to him as they exited the EOC and headed down the stairs. "What's going on?"

"The source called me. Asked us to meet with him in a few minutes because he had something for us. Southeast corner of Sixth and Noble."

Jason tugged on his arm. "That's a funeral home."

"Great." Mac checked his watch. "Let's go. I don't want to miss him." He took off at a steady jog. It was only a block away.

When they crossed the street and reached their destination, a man facing the funeral home turned around.

Mac stopped and waited for the man to talk.

But Jason surged ahead, grabbed the man by the shoulders, and shoved him back. "What are *you* doing here? We thought you were dead! How could you put Mom and Dad through that? Besides that, you should be in jail after all you pulled." He shoved the man again.

Mac got between them and held Jason at arm's length. "Hold up. What's going on here?" He glanced at the other guy. "Are you the one who called me?"

"Yep." The man stared him down.

"And you are?" His tone sounded harsh to his own ears, but Mac was tired of playing nice.

"You gonna tell him, Jason?" The guy smirked.

"I thought you were dead." Jason shook his head. "All this time." The words were mumbled. But then he relaxed against Mac's hold and straightened. "Mac, meet my brother . . . Kirk. Who should be in jail."

Realization hit Mac. "The one who mysteriously disappeared from prison and is dead, according to to the FBI?"

Kirk laughed. "As much as I'd love to stay for a nice family reunion, I'm here for a purpose." He held out a piece of paper and handed it to Mac. "With this, you've got everything you need to stop him."

"Are you *working with him*?" Jason lunged forward. "Have you been a part of all this?"

Mac stopped him before he could tackle his brother.

Kirk held up his hands. "No. I'm part of the Members. We want Griz stopped as much as you do." He stepped back. "I hate to tell you this, Mac, but your source is dead. Or is about to be. We're not certain which of our tails Griz has eliminated, but we've lost contact with all of them. Which doesn't bode well. That's why you got me. We've gotten word that Griz has shortened his timeline, so you'd better hurry." He turned and walked a few steps, then a dark Mercedes sped to a stop beside him. Kirk climbed in, and the vehicle raced away.

Still holding his friend's arm, Mac tried to get a look at the paper Kirk had given him.

Jason jerked out his grasp and stomped a few feet away, then returned. "I can't believe he's alive." He raked a hand through his hair. "I've got to call my parents."

"Go ahead. I'm taking this back to the EOC." He read the paper and furrowed his brow. Huh. What did it mean? He looked up at his friend again. "You okay?"

Jason looked shell-shocked. "Yeah. Just have to figure out what to say."

"I'll let Darcie know."

Jason nodded.

"Promise me you'll be back in just a few?"

"Yep."

Mac would have to take his word. He ran back to the EOC, entered the building, and took the steps two at a time. When he made it to the top, he almost plowed over Agent Spirelli. "Take a look at this." He shoved the paper toward the agent.

"'Memorial Hospital is his next target. Follow the signal. 70 north.'" The man read it aloud and then looked at Mac. "Any idea what the signal is?"

CHAPTER NINETEEN

Six Days, Seventeen Hours, Thirty-Two Minutes Sober
July 17—1:02 p.m.
Latitude: 64.841130° N, Longitude: 147.716869° W
Emergency Operations Center

Tracie walked into the Emergency Operations Center an hour later carrying a large box. The scents of onions, cheeseburgers, and fries wafted from the bags, making her mouth water. It had taken some time to pick up the food. Most restaurants had closed, unable to process payments, as their credit card systems were crippled. And many places weren't equipped to take cash.

Fortunately, her favorite burger joint was a cash-only operation, and she'd had enough on her to cover the order.

She gave the security guard her name and ID. He glanced over it, then radioed her name to some location. Once the affirmative came through to let her in, he handed her ID back and held the large glass door open. He even pushed the button for the fourth floor and held back the steel doors when they tried to close too soon.

"Thank you," she called and let out a breath. There was still kindness in the world. She stepped off the elevator and followed the carpeted hallway to yet another nondescript conference room. She briefly wondered if there was some sort of mail-order conference room catalog all these office buildings ordered from. They all looked the same to her.

Shaking the absurd thought away, Tracie pressed the handle down and bumped the door open with her hip. "Lunch has arrived!"

Heads swiveled her way, smiles on each face.

Carrie jumped up from her seat. "Let me take that from you." She grabbed the box and took a deep breath. "You are my new best friend." She plucked a few fries from the bag and shoved them into her mouth. "Seriously. I'm starving."

"Well, if I'd known all it would take was a cheeseburger, I would have bought you one as soon as we met." It felt good to laugh in the midst of such an awful time.

"I could have told you that." Scott stepped up beside his wife. "A cheeseburger or pizza is the way to this woman's heart."

Carrie rolled her eyes as she pulled out the cartons of fries to be passed around the table. "You make me sound like a teenage boy."

Scott shrugged. "Not my fault you have the diet of one."

"Oh, go sit down." She shoved him away.

Darcie was next, and she gave Tracie's shoulder a squeeze. "Glad you could make it. Thank you for bringing lunch."

Even with all the stress around them, the group felt like a family. "You're welcome. How are you doing?"

Darcie let out a breath, blowing her corkscrew curls off her forehead. "Oh, you know. Just trying to save Alaska. Again." She sobered. "But seriously, this is about as bad as I've seen it. And I lived through the nightmare of the 26 Below attack. It's crazy just how deeply being online is integrated into every facet of life." She shook her head. "The guys are working with the ABI and the FBI and several other agencies to get the connection restored. I'm just trying to manage a city turned on its head."

"I can't imagine that level of responsibility, Darcie." The enormity of the woman's role as the head of emergency operations for Fairbanks made Tracie's head spin. The director of the EOC clearly had a gift for managing all the politics that came with her job. "This city is lucky to have you."

This time Darcie laughed, and her face relaxed. "Would you call the mayor and the governor and let them know that? It would be a huge help."

"I'm all over it. Text me their numbers."

"Hey, Darc," Scott interrupted. "I need you to come take a look at this screen for me."

"Duty calls." Darcie sighed. "Thanks again for the lunch."

Mac came up and slid an arm around Tracie's shoulders in a gentle side hug. "Hey. How's my favorite doc?"

She couldn't help it. She leaned into him, relishing the strength of his friendly embrace. "Surviving. How's my most ornery patient? Have you fixed the internet yet?"

Mac groaned. "No. And don't ask. You holding up?"

Tracie bit her lip and pulled away from him. She plucked a Mountain Dew from the box and took a long drink. "I'll be better once I'm fed and caffeinated."

Jason stepped over. "Now you're speaking my language. Thanks for bringing food. Glad to hear that the surgery was successful." He paused. "And also incredibly sorry to hear about your friend. Especially after the boardroom attack."

Friend . . . Courtney and Tracie were about as opposite that word as possible. But she still gave Jason a nod, not bothering to correct him. "Thank you."

"Hey, Mac, come take a look at this." Alan beckoned him toward the back of the room with a wave of his hand.

Tracie watched him jog over to the ABI agent, feeling lost. She walked to Carrie and sat down. "What can I do to help?"

"Well, that is a good question." Carrie typed a note in the open document on her laptop, then turned toward Tracie. The other woman studied her. "You okay?"

"If I say no, will you tattle on me to Mac?"

Carrie chuckled. "The best way to deal with our emotions in the middle of a crisis is to hash it out. At least, that's true for women. Jason just found out his brother—who he thought was dead—is still very much alive. And still mixed up with the Members. But look at him—he's a guy. He vented, and now he's turned his attention back here." Carrie bit her lip. "Doesn't work the same for us, does it?"

Tracie blinked at the tears pooling in her eyes without permission.

"Let's find a quiet place to talk."

She grabbed her drink, and Carrie tucked a legal pad under her arm. The two women made their way to a smaller office, and Carrie shut the door. The walls closed in, and Tracie felt claustrophobic.

She paced the room, her heart rate picking up. "Mind if I open the window?"

"Not at all." Carrie watched her. "I'm not going to interrogate you." Her tone was soothing. "I mean, I'm sure any information you have would be helpful. But you looked like you were about to break down in there. This is just two friends having a chat. You can't keep all of this bottled up."

Tracie walked the length of the office, turned on her heel, and retraced her steps. "Right now I don't feel anything. I mean, I do, but I don't. I don't know how to feel, really."

Carrie nodded. "That's a very normal reaction to something like this."

"Well at least something is normal around here." Tracie plopped into a chair. She massaged her scalp, trying to get the racing thoughts under control. "I just feel so guilty," she whispered after a long stretch of silence.

"About what?"

Tracie pulled her fingers free from a tangle of hair. "Courtney. I . . . We parted on awful terms. Said horrible things to each other. I wasn't kind to her the day she quit."

"Would it help to talk about it?" Carrie shifted in her chair, folding her arms on the table.

The thought was both enticing and terrifying. Lately all she felt like she did was talk. And cry. About everything. Her fears and sorrows. Her frustrations. About this stupid maniac who was ruining the lives of hundreds of thousands of people.

She was sick to death of the sound of her own voice and said as much to her friend.

"I get that." Carrie tucked her hair behind her ear. "I really do. It seems like when you have something traumatic happen, everyone is always asking you questions. Trying to get in your head. It can be exhausting."

Tracie nodded, the guilt still eating at her.

"But I also think, in this situation, it can be helpful. What if you told me one good memory you have about Courtney. Instead of processing all the bad things, give me one good memory about working with her."

Tracie sat with Carrie's request for a moment. To her surprise, several memories came to mind. Most of them in the operating room. The way Courtney could anticipate what tool Tracie would need or when suction was necessary. Her confidence with patients who were nervous. She'd had a way with people who were scared of surgery—somehow, her boldness transferred to them and made them feel brave. Even silly things like racing other nurses down the hallway, wanting to be the first one to swipe her badge to the operating room or—

She sat up straight and looked at Carrie. "Her badge!"

Confusion drew Carrie's brows together. "Her badge is a good memory?"

"No." Tracie waved her hand. "No. When they found Courtney's body, did they find her hospital badge on her uniform? Or in her purse?"

Carrie shot out of her chair. "Come on, let's go talk to Alan. He'll know."

They raced back to the conference room, bursting through the door.

"Alan, do you have the evidence log from Courtney's crime scene?"

Alan shuffled through a few folders, then plucked a bright yellow one from the pile. "It's right here. Why?"

Scott looked at his wife. "Are you guys okay? What's going on?"

Adrenaline coursed through Tracie as Carrie opened the file and slid her index finger down the item log.

"It's not on the list," Carrie muttered. "There was no badge at the scene."

"Then there's only one place it could be." Tracie prayed she was wrong. But somehow she knew she wasn't. "The Typhon Killer has it. He was Mr. Linden on the board. If he erased his identity, then his badge wouldn't work. That's why he . . ." She swallowed the lump growing in her throat. "That's why he killed Courtney. He's got something planned for Fairbanks Memorial."

"And that corroborates the note Kirk gave me." Mac's face hardened.

"All right. What's the play?" Jason's hands were fisted on his hips. "We wanted a way to reverse engineer his next target, but to do that, we have to allow the attack to happen. I'm not sure we want to put lives on the line like that."

Scott crossed his arms over his chest. "We don't have any other choice, do we? If he's shortened his timeline? This might be the only chance we have."

"Scott's right." Mac's jaw clenched, and he glanced at Tracie. "You know the hospital better than we do. Can you get us into the server room? We'll need access to anything that's run by a computer."

Her eyebrows shot up. "That's pretty much everything."

"I know." He shook his head. "And we don't have time to waste. Let's fill in the big dogs and scarf down some food. I hope everyone is well rested, because we're going to need everyone to work around the clock."

✦ ✦ ✦

14 Days Until Final Judgment
15 Members Left
July 18—8:58 a.m.

Latitude: 70.193385° N, Longitude: 148.444766° W
Griz's Small Compound

Griz slammed the laptop closed. He'd found the leak. The spy. The one who'd made his skin crawl. The one who'd betrayed him. The one who'd made him feel hunted. How the guy had evaded him only made his anger burn hotter.

He strode outside, climbed into his SUV, and barreled down the dirt road toward the coordinates. He threw the vehicle into park when he reached the destination.

The door of the small building swung open. Sam.

As soon as his fellow Member exited the tiny building and spotted him, the lanky man raced toward his own vehicle.

Griz pulled out his pistol and suppressor. Then he lunged out of his vehicle and charged toward Sam. His fury burned hot, and his legs ate up the ground beneath him.

Sam fumbled with his keys, but they fell to the ground.

Griz lifted his pistol, but his arm shook. He gritted his teeth and tried again, fighting through the shaking. He pulled the trigger and shot Sam in the leg.

His victim yelled out in pain and tumbled to the ground beside his keys.

"So . . ." Griz laughed as he closed the distance, scratching at his neck with his free hand. "You're the one who tipped off Mac. Or was that your predecessor? Doesn't matter, because he's already dead."

Sam dragged himself to the wheel and leaned up against it. Blood gushed out of his thigh. It appeared as if he would say something, but then he clamped his lips shut.

"You better do something about that." Griz pointed to his leg. "Wouldn't want you to bleed out."

Sam moaned and pressed his hand against the wound. "The Members will stop you."

"Like they've ever had the power to do that."

"Well, that cyber team is all fired up—thanks to you and your lunatic plan. I bet . . . I bet they can stop you if the Members don't."

"No one can stop me."

"You're wrong. And too arrogant to see it." Sam gave a wry laugh, his face paling with the loss of blood.

Griz studied him for a moment. "You were there, weren't you? When I shot Mac?"

Sam nodded. "Yep. Several of us have followed you . . ."

"They sent you to track me." Now, that wasn't a pleasant thought, that they'd actually succeeded. The ramifications trickled through his mind. No. He was lying. Griz had killed everyone on his tail.

"And . . . they're watching every . . . move you make." Sam's smile stayed, but the light in his eyes dimmed.

The second and third shots were unnecessary. But Griz wanted him to shut up.

He walked back to his SUV and ground his teeth. Why wouldn't this infernal itching stop?

Sam's last words weren't true. Otherwise, the Members would have had the power to stop him before now.

Unless . . . she . . .

No. No one could stop him. Besides, soon, there wouldn't be any of them left.

Only fourteen remained.

CHAPTER TWENTY

950 Days After
July 18—3:24 p.m.
Latitude: 64.841130° N, Longitude: 147.716869° W
Emergency Operations Center

"I DON'T HAVE TIME FOR this." Mac tried to be nice. He really did. But Darcie was asking too much.

She narrowed her eyes as she stepped closer to him. "We don't have any other choice, Mac. The satellite feed is up. If you don't get in there"—she pointed to the secure conference room—"with the director of the ABI and speak with the director of the FBI, the governor of Alaska, and some guy from the Pentagon, you won't be cleared to actually do the plan to stop this guy. Don't you get it? You're wasting more time by arguing with me than it would take to explain it."

He grunted at her as he turned back to the room. "If only it were that simple. But I'll do it. Only to take Griz down once and for all." He yanked on the door too forcefully, and it crashed into the bumper on the wall. "Let's hope someone in here understands computers, because I'm going to have to explain fast." Everything except the idea that had hatched in the middle of the night. For now, he, Jason, and Scott were the only ones in on it.

Introductions were swift and to the point. Mac walked up to the wall of screens and nodded, a little intimidated by the power behind the other cameras. Best to just dive in.

But Darcie beat him to it. "All right, gentlemen. Our objective is simple. To stop the terrorist Griz before he unleashes whatever his final showdown might be. All intel I've been given is that his planned attacks could devastate our country for decades. With recent breaks in the case, the guys from Cyber Solutions believe they have a plan."

She moved to the side so Mac could step forward. "Your turn," she whispered.

Mac cleared his throat. "It's pretty simple. At least in theory. In practice it's intense and time consuming. We need to identify the next target, which we believe we've done. After that, we'll have to find the malware, reverse engineer it—or at least the command trigger—and identify what the data portion of the command packet looks like that would trigger the malware. Then we'll set a firewall rule to capture and block any packets with that command data.

"Once we have the packet, it's just a matter of pulling on that thread—tracking it from source to source—until we find the ultimate source, namely Griz's network and computer."

The governor didn't look convinced. "If you know the intended target, can't you simply quarantine the device? My assistant told me that was the standard practice for an infected device. Wouldn't that stop him without having to allow him to set off whatever he's got planted?"

Mac swiped a hand down his face. *Lord, help me explain this with language they can grasp.* "It's a little more complicated than an infected device, sir. Yes, standard practice once an infected device is found is to quarantine it. Then get a forensic image of it. Then wipe it, reload it with clean software, and put it back into operation."

The governor opened his mouth to say something, but Mac pushed forward, praying the powerful men before him would understand the magnitude of what they were facing.

"This malware is different. It communicates with a command-and-control node. Griz knows what's still in place. If we wipe the malware from the infected systems, those packets will not come back up, and he will know.

"If he knows the malware is gone, he won't send the command packet. If he doesn't send the command packet, we won't get the first breadcrumb. If we don't get the first breadcrumb, we won't get the rest of the breadcrumbs. We don't find him. We don't stop him. We don't catch him. And he has the ability to carry out his brand of terrorism."

The governor muted his mic and spoke with his advisers. The director of the FBI did the same.

But the general from the Pentagon spoke up. "Seems clear to me. We have to leave the malware in place and pray that you find it and reverse engineer it. Yes, it's a big gamble. But it's not like we're playing games with people's lives like this guy is. Do it. You have full approval from the Pentagon."

Relief rippled through Mac. He looked at the governor and FBI director, holding his breath.

"From here as well," the governor said.

The director of the FBI scowled. "Let's take this guy down."

✦ ✦ ✦

13 Days Until Final Judgment
14 Members Left
July 19—9:15 a.m.
Latitude: 64.83156° N, Longitude: 147.73836° W
Fairbanks Memorial Hospital

Everything flickered in the server room. Well, would you look at that. Mac and his boys had gotten the internet back up and running. Perfect timing.

Griz studied the layout, determining which data center connected to which area. Not too hard. Everything was rebooting, which would give him exactly the slip he needed.

Fifteen minutes later he shuffled back around the server room, checking his work. He would wreak havoc in every area of the hospital, which would create the distractions needed to pull off the next part. And wouldn't they all panic when they found out what he'd done.

No one would expect him to go after babies.

Well, they were calling him the father of all monsters, weren't they? He had to live up to his name.

He reached into his pocket and pulled out the little Tic Tac container. Popping two more pills, he swallowed them and adjusted the sleeves of his jacket.

Man, this was fun.

But the curly wig on his head made his scalp itch. Which made his neck itch. He kicked the wall, wishing he could douse himself with a bucket of cold water.

The itching intensified. What he wouldn't give to just rip off his skin right n—

He closed his eyes against the urges. *Breathe.* No one could pull this off but him.

No one.

Maybe if he had just one more pill.

No. He needed to cut back anyway. Power was calming. Control was calming. Chaos was calming.

With a deep breath, he opened his eyes and willed away any other thoughts.

Maybe he was making this too challenging for Mac and his crew. After all, they had no idea what he'd planned the past two years. At this point they were just trying to catch him. Stop him before he killed more people.

He might as well leave them a little hint. It would keep them distracted for a while, and he could focus on the beginning of his grand finale for Alaska. Then he could focus on the world.

✦ ✦ ✦

951 Days After
July 19—10:43 a.m.

Latitude: 64.83156° N, Longitude: 147.73836° W
Fairbanks Memorial Hospital

Most of the telecommunications companies had restored their internet, thanks to the team. But now, as they raced toward Fairbanks Memorial Hospital, Mac's stomach felt like someone had yanked it out, tied it in knots, and then slashed it to shreds.

It wasn't a good feeling.

The past couple of days had passed in a blur of implementing every section of their plan and reverse engineering the malware they'd discovered on the ventilators in the ICU. It had taken five members of his company to do the impossible feat in a mere forty hours. Scott had gone from machine to machine throughout the entire hospital, checking and rechecking. It was the only place they'd found it. Mac hoped and prayed that was a good thing.

Before they'd brought the internet back online, they'd made sure to set a trap of their own for Griz in the server room. About ten minutes ago, it tripped, sending everyone into action.

Once again surveillance cameras had been hacked and changed. Which meant he'd been there. Somewhere among them. The FBI was convinced he was a master of disguises. Mac didn't want to think the man was a master of anything.

While worry gnawed at him, Tracie looked focused. Composed.

It had been a stroke of genius that she'd thought of Courtney's hospital badge two days ago. It had given them the advantage they needed—and the time. Now they were ready for him. All they could do was go to the hospital and wait. A rotating schedule for naps was in place, which the whole team looked forward to, since no one had slept much the past two days.

Courtney's badge gave Griz access to just about anywhere in the hospital. He'd been in possession of it for several days, so they'd been tracking everywhere it had been swiped. Which was the parking garage entrance and the cafeteria. What good did those locations do him?

Darcie navigated the streets like a seasoned pro, and Mac found himself holding on to the handle above his head with a death grip. He sneaked another glance at Tracie. "How are you so calm?"

She tucked her hands between her knees. "This is my arena, Mac. Emergency situations involving the sick. I know everything about that hospital. I know how things work. I've been disoriented since he stole my job—I never knew how to help you and the others. But this is my territory. I know I'll be able to help."

He placed a hand on her arm. "You're an amazing doctor, Tracie Hunter."

"Thank you." She raised an eyebrow at him. "You're awfully good at what you do as well."

"Let's save the compliments until this is over, all right?" Darcie snipped. "He wants your admiration. You want his. We get it."

Mac laughed. "Remind me not to get on your bad side, Mrs. Myers."

"Sorry." She tossed him a sideways grin, but her eyes looked weary. "I'm *so* ready for this to be over."

"You and me both."

They reached the hospital, and Darcie parked in a special area for law enforcement in the garage. "All right, let's do this."

"Which way?" Mac asked Tracie.

"You want the server room, right?"

"Yep. Jason and Scott should be there already."

She tipped her head to the left. "Let's go."

He followed after her. Obviously she'd had plenty of experience dashing up and down these halls. She stopped at an office and leaned in the door. "I need you with me, now!"

Whoever the guy was, he was on the chubby side and had a hard time keeping up with Tracie, but they made it to the server room.

"Chris—there's no time for introductions or explanations—but these guys are going to fill you in on what you need to do."

"Hey, Chris, I'm Mac, and this is my team. Before we restored the internet, my guys here planted some little guys we call spiders to trace our bad guy. We need you here to make sure no one but us comes in or out, all right?"

Chris didn't balk. "Yes, sir. Should I call for backup?" The security guard put a hand to the radio on his shoulder.

"That's not a bad idea."

Mac, Jason, and Scott split up to divide and conquer, plugging into terminals and scanning them. The server room was huge and covered the ICU, the CICU, Labor and Delivery, the ER, the NICU, and then the different wings of other patient rooms.

Every one they plugged into, they found Griz's handiwork.

The cooling system in one area. The refrigerators in another.

But there had to be more than just that. Those weren't enough of a distraction for their guy. Even though they knew he was going to hit the ICU . . . there had to be something else.

"Got a data-replay implant over here!" Jason raised a finger. "Basically like a CCTV loop. In this case it's looping healthy data so that if you're not in the room, no one would be the wiser."

"One here too," Scott said.

They switched terminals. Same thing happened.

They finished scanning their tracers, but Mac wasn't satisfied. "You two stay here and run it again. I'm going to head up to my little hiding place in the ICU. I want to be there to capture it as soon as possible so I can—prayerfully—get them back online." He turned to Tracie. "There's extra staff every shift, right?"

Her chin bobbed up and down, making her ponytail move too. "The acting hospital administrator offered triple pay in that ward so we could do this."

"Good. Come find me if you need me. I'm turning my phone off. Don't want to take any chances." Ever since the Members had cloned his phone, he had a feeling Griz always knew where he was.

✦ ✦ ✦

One Week and One Day Sober
July 19—11:04 a.m.

Latitude: 64.83156° N, Longitude: 147.73836° W
Fairbanks Memorial Hospital

Tracie watched Mac stride out of the room. *Lord, watch over him, please. We need Your help to catch this guy.*

She turned back to the guys to see if they needed anything else, but over her shoulder something caught her attention. What was that?

She surged toward it and picked it up off the floor.

A pacifier? In the server room? Her eyes widened.

"No! The NICU!" She took off out of the room at an all-out run. She didn't even know how to pray anymore. *Help. Please, Father. Help.* The phrases rolled through her mind nonstop. Every drop of grace the Lord was willing to give, she would take.

The level of depravity it took to attack the Neonatal Intensive Care Unit of a hospital was unfathomable to her. Innocent babies. Little lungs and hearts struggling to keep them afloat so they could finally know what it was to be held in the loving arms of their parents.

Precious, beautiful children worthy of life.

God, help us.

She raced up the two flights of stairs to the NICU. She swiped her badge, thankful to have access in her hospital again. Thankful to be of use.

Guide us, Jesus.

There were nurses everywhere. Running back and forth from the supply room, arms full of Ambu bags, the self-inflating resuscitators.

"What's happened?" Tracie caught one nurse running past her.

The brunette stopped for a moment and glanced at Tracie's name badge. Her eyes widened a fraction. "The ventilators have gone down. We have to manually bag these babies."

Tracie's heart sank.

Griz had followed through. Was it happening in the ICU as well?

She shook off the defeat that tried to settle around her. "Where can I help?"

The nurse glanced around, then nodded at the left corner of the room, without staff. "We've got four more babies over there who need bagged stat."

Without hesitation Tracie grabbed a pair of gloves from a dispenser on the wall and ran to the supply closet. She grabbed four Ambu bags and raced to the incubators. Tears pricked her eyes as she watched these small lives fight for breath. Hopefully more staff were on their way to help.

"Dr. Hunter!" Sherry jogged across the room. "I wasn't expecting to see you when I got the call for the alarms on the ventilators, but, boy, am I glad you're here!"

Tracie gave Sherry a nod. "It's good to see you too. Bag the twins right next to me. I've got these two here."

Sherry needed no further prompting. Two more nurses approached, both doing a double take when they spotted Tracie.

"Aubrey, come with me," Sherry directed the blonde. "Charlotte, with Dr. Hunter. Let's go."

The redhead grabbed the last bag and rushed to the other incubator. With practiced movements the four women bagged the remaining infants. Relief filled Tracie as her training kicked in with each step, even though this was something she didn't do on a regular basis. Once the masks were secured on the babies' faces, the counting between each breath began.

Tracie ensured she wasn't placing too much pressure on the baby's mouth and began the sequence. One. Two. Three. Slight squeeze. Again and again. Each squeeze was gentle and measured to ensure she didn't oversaturate the infant's lungs. The last thing this little one needed was air getting trapped in her abdomen or, worse, rupturing the delicate alveoli sacs, the tiny balloon-shaped sacs at the end of the bronchioles in the lungs.

The slow, deliberate movements needed to help these precious babies breathe slowed Tracie's heart rate as well. As she counted, she glanced around the room. Doctors and nurses were at every incubator, with every baby, manually pumping air into the tiny lives. More staff poured into the room so that each baby had a team of two. The care and concern was palpable as each team communicated vital signs and other important information to each other. It was like watching a well-choreographed dance—beautiful and synchronized. But instead of a grand orchestra, their music was the rhythmic whooshing of air.

This was why she'd wanted to become a doctor. No life was too small to care for. No life was too insignificant to save.

She looked down at the little girl in her care. Fine lashes curled against translucent brown skin. One tiny fist was tucked by her cheek, and the other clutched the light blanket covering her. Tracie glanced at the chart hanging above the incubator. Baby Girl Martin, born nine weeks early. But according to the notes, she was hitting every growth mark.

Looking back at the infant, her heart swelled. What a fighter this little one was. "You're doing so well, Miss Martin," she whispered. "Nice, even breaths. That's it."

The doors to the NICU slid open, and someone ran in. "The systems are rebooting—we've just got to restart each one!"

Tracie glanced at her nurse and nodded. "Flip it on. I'll keep bagging our girl here."

Charlotte rebooted the ventilator. The seconds seemed to move backward.

Then beeps and alerts echoed through the room. Tracie felt the relief that moved through the staff as they began the delicate process of getting their precious patients back on their ventilators.

"I'm ready to transfer to automatic ventilation, Dr. Hunter." Charlotte nodded at her.

Tracie lifted the bag from the infant's face. She watched as the nurse expertly connected the ventilator back to the tube in the little girl's nose. She adjusted a few dials, and then the familiar rapid bumping rippled over the baby's chest.

Tracie let out the breath she didn't know she'd been holding. *Thank You, Lord.* "Well done, Miss Martin." She brushed her fingers over the fine hair, the little girl never stirring except for the beautiful rise and fall of her chest. Tracie looked up and found Charlotte watching her. "Wonderful job," she complimented the nurse. "Thank you for helping me."

Charlotte tucked a curl of red hair behind her ear, a wide grin on her face. "I have to say, Dr. Hunter, I was surprised to see you here. In a good way." She rushed on. "And relieved. The hospital hasn't been the same without you around."

Heat filled Tracie's face. "That's kind of you to say."

"Charlotte's right," Sherry piped up. "We've all missed you, Dr. Hunter. And your patients miss you too. Any word on when you're officially back?"

"Soon. I've been with the team that's trying to stop this madman."

A few more nurses joined their small circle, and Tracie looked around at their faces. There was no hostility. No reservation in their gazes. She saw only welcome and acceptance. Gratitude welled within her. "I'm so thankful I had the chance to help you all today." She bit her lip and took time to look each coworker directly in the eye. "I've had to deal with a lot in the last several weeks. I struggled a lot with doubt, whether or not I would be welcomed back here . . . if I was even fit to continue on as a surgeon." Tears clogged her throat. Oh gosh. Was she going to bawl like one of their infants right here?

Several nurses nodded at her, some with tears in their eyes. Others with genuine smiles encouraged her to keep going.

Tracie sniffed. "But what we did today, this is what matters. I hope we never forget the work we did here. When technology failed us and evil tried to triumph and destroy the most vulnerable among us, we dug in and we fought. And we won."

As the nurses clapped, the doors to the NICU swished open again.

Mac! Tracie's heart sped up, and she broke through the crowd and ran to him. "The babies are okay, Mac." She lowered her voice. "Did it work?"

The smile that broke through on his handsome face melted her heart. "It did. He tried to crash the entire ICU, CICU, and the NICU

. . . but I think we've got him. I'm going back to the EOC to work with the guys on what we have. We're close, Tracie. Really close."

"I'm going to stay here and help with the aftermath. I'll be there as soon as I'm done." She rubbed her temples. "I can't wait for this to be over."

"Me too. Because then we get to talk." He slipped his arm around her shoulders, gave her a brief squeeze, kissed her forehead, and jogged away.

CHAPTER TWENTY-ONE

13 Days Until Final Judgment
5 Members Left
July 19—12:00 p.m.
Latitude: 70.193385° N, Longitude: 148.444766° W
Griz's Small Compound

"You and me, kid." Griz had an arm around his son's shoulders as they watched the beautiful mansion explode as the clock struck twelve. "Just look at what we can do . . . what I can give you."

The boy shrugged off the arm. "Dude, you're even more whacked than Mom said. And she would know because she's pretty crazy." He stalked to the corner and slumped into a chair.

But Griz didn't miss the fear in his son's eyes. "Your mother shouldn't have said such ugly things about me all these years. We made a great team."

The twelve-year-old before him rolled his eyes in oh-so-typical preteen fashion. "For the psych ward," the kid mumbled.

Griz whipped out the Glock from his waistband and pointed it at the boy's head. "*What* did you just say?" A slight tremor began in his arm, but he willed it to go away. His body didn't listen as well as it used to.

His son's face had gone white, but his eyes darkened. "You heard me, old man." He crossed his scrawny arms over his chest. "You don't scare me. I live with Mom, remember?"

The snarled words made Griz laugh.

He lowered the weapon, tucked it back in the holster, and then flexed his fingers. "Your mother used to scare me. When I first met her."

Silence stretched between them.

"Why did you just kill all those people? I knew them." Insolence and anger radiated off him.

Griz scratched his neck. "They double-crossed me. It's best not to get too attached to people."

Something flickered across the preteen's face. It looked a lot like hatred. "Has Mom crossed you too?"

"We shall see."

"But that's why you kidnapped me." The kid knew how to push.

"It's not kidnapping when it's your own child."

His son looked at him as if he'd lost his mind. "Uh, *yeah it is*, especially when legally you have no right to me whatsoever."

"*Legally*"—he spat the word inches from his son's face—"I can do whatever I want. I make the rules now."

His son stood and got in his face. "Yeah, like mutilate your own kid"—he held up his bandaged arm, where Griz had dug out the RFID tracker—"or hold them hostage!" He pointed to the ankle monitor Griz had installed. "You're pathetic. Why would I want anything to do with you?" He tried to scoot past his father. "You're just a psycho drug addict. Why couldn't I have normal parents?"

Like a cobra going in for the strike, Griz latched on to his son and yanked him back.

✦   ✦   ✦

One Week and One Day Sober
July 19—12:54 p.m.
Latitude: 64.83156° N, Longitude: 147.73836° W
Fairbanks Memorial Hospital

Tracie stared at the mirror above the sink as she washed her face. The ICU was the worst hit, but thanks to the extra staff, things were under control once again.

The CICU was a different story.

Two patients lost their lives today. All because of this one man.

She pressed her hands against the edge of the sink and fought the tears. The families were angry and distraught. She couldn't blame them one bit. Everyone was wrestling with those emotions—how could they not when devastation and death always seemed to be right around the corner?

But after everything else was put to rights, the acting hospital administrator told her to go on home. Did they think she was somehow responsible? Did she make people uncomfortable? Even though the truth had come out?

She splashed another handful of water on her face and forced the negative thoughts back. It was best for her to leave, and once all this was over, she could help again.

Hopefully.

She left the hospital without saying a word to anyone and climbed into the Uber she'd ordered from her app. Leaning her head back against the seat, she prayed the driver would take the hint and not want to chat on the drive to the EOC.

"We've had a lovely summer, haven't we?"

So much for not chatting. "It has been." She lifted her head and studied the woman in the rearview mirror. Might as well be nice. "Have you been driving for Uber long?"

"Not long." The woman glanced quickly to the mirror, and their gazes connected. She looked away as she took the next left turn into an empty parking lot.

"You turned too soon. It's another block or so up the road." Tracie leaned closer to the front seat. She hated being a backseat driver.

When the driver placed the gearshift into park, Tracie's stomach plummeted.

"What do you want? I don't have anything of value on me." She used her calming surgeon voice despite the fear racing through her body.

The woman swiveled toward her. "Dr. Hunter, I don't have a lot of time. I need you to listen and do exactly as I say."

"Or what?"

"Or I will blow up the EOC with everyone in it."

✦ ✦ ✦

951 Days After
July 19—1:28 p.m.
Latitude: 64.841130° N, Longitude: 147.716869° W
Emergency Operations Center

The team was close, he could feel it. From one packet to the next, they followed the trail.

Mac leaned back in his seat and rubbed at his dry eyes. It was a drawback of the job—lots of screen time, lots of eye strain. Especially since he wasn't getting any younger.

He stood and glanced at the clock. Where was Tracie? A couple of hours had passed since he'd left her at the hospital. Prayerfully, they had all the patients stabilized after Griz's attack.

How Griz had gotten himself into the hospital past security and evaded all the cameras for the NICU and CICU were beyond Mac's tired imagination. The malware had to be installed on each device. Each. One. And since Mac had only found it in the ICU yesterday, *when* had Griz installed it?

And why the pacifier? That little taunt was pure evil. Kingston and Spirelli were furious about the whole thing and had tripled their manhunt. The only thing that kept all of them going was the fact they had Griz in their sights.

Jason waved him over. "Mac."

He headed over to Jason's desk. "Do you have him at the source?" He tried to keep the eagerness out of his voice, but it couldn't be helped.

"This is what's problematic." The head of his team here in Fairbanks was the best of the best. So if Jason thought there was a problem, it was a pretty sure bet he was correct.

"Show me." Mac leaned over and studied the screens.

"Every single end source goes straight into the Beaufort Sea."

His gut twisted as he watched each little line plunge into the sea far above the Arctic Circle. "It's got to be a glitch. Try it again."

"That's the thing"—Jason pointed—"this is my seventh attempt. They all show the same thing."

Mac refused to believe they were stuck once again. "What are we missing? This should have worked."

"It did work." Jason showed him the pages and pages of data. "But unless our guy is in a submarine north of the Alaska coast, I don't know what to tell ya."

"Mac!" Darcie yelled from her office and then ran toward him. "Quick, you've got to come with me." She darted out of the EOC and down the many flights of stairs.

He did his best to keep up, the urgency he'd seen in her eyes spurring him on.

When they made it outside, Tracie was there. With a bomb vest strapped to her torso.

✦ ✦ ✦

4 Fellow Members Remain
July 19—1:46 p.m.
Latitude: 61.302290° N, Longitude: 149.470746° W
Eagle River

It hadn't been her intention to threaten the doctor. But Griz had pushed her over the limit this time. Just like he always did.

Throwing things from her desk into another suitcase, she looked up at her security monitors. Griz had breached it once—he could do it again.

But if she knew him, he was long gone. With her son. To a place she couldn't go. Otherwise Griz would kill him.

That's why the doctor was needed. It remained to be seen if she could do what she was told.

Two years ago Muriel would have gone after Griz with both barrels blazing. But now? He was so cranked up on pills that he was completely unpredictable. She'd had to improvise.

It would take time to rebuild the group.

The remaining Members had gone underground. Literally.

To a bunker that no one knew about.

Once she had her son back, she'd head there too.

Because even if she succeeded in getting her son back alive—and she would—Griz was still more than capable of setting off World War III if that was what he had planned. And from what she understood . . . it was close enough.

Life as they'd known it would cease to exist.

Why couldn't he simply have stayed the course? They could have accomplished so much together.

"Ma'am." Gerard, her bodyguard, spoke from the door. "We're ready."

"Good." She zipped up the suitcase and rolled it to him. "Let's go."

✦ ✦ ✦

951 Days After
July 19—2:42 p.m.
Latitude: 64.841130° N, Longitude: 147.716869° W
Emergency Operations Center

The bomb squad had finished their assessment of the vest, and it wasn't good. They couldn't find a way to disarm it without setting it off. As of right now, there was no timer, so that was a good thing. The security camera footage at the EOC had all been checked and—big surprise—had been changed as well.

Mac's heart couldn't take much more of this. Watching her with that vest on made his stomach revolt. He'd already lost Sarah and Beth to an explosion. He couldn't lose Tracie too.

He listened intently as Tracie told them of the woman's threat, and waited while the whole building was searched.

Sure enough, another bomb had been found.

The team was in a tailspin. The FBI didn't want to disarm the bomb in fears that their new opponent might set off others—including the one on Tracie. But there wasn't enough information yet to truly assess the situation.

Darcie and her assistant had scrambled to assemble every available person to move everything to the secured bomb shelter in the basement. The bomb team had padded up the interrogation room so they could keep Tracie there.

Mac stared at Tracie through the thick glass. Along with the rest of the team, he waited.

She paced the room. "Nothing like being stuck in a padded room." Her laugh was light, but he noticed the strain around her eyes. "Any hits on the description I gave? Did you find the vehicle?"

Director Kingston stepped up to the intercom. "Not yet. Dr. Hunter, I'm sorry for these conditions, but we had to scramble. If you could, would you please start back at the beginning and tell us all you know."

Tracie nodded and closed her eyes, appearing to gather her thoughts. After a moment she started recounting the events again. "The woman who picked me up was in the Uber car I ordered. Correct license plate and everything. Not sure what she did with the real driver—but I know that's not our biggest issue. She told me to do exactly as she said or she would blow up the EOC."

"What happened next?" Kingston stood there, his fists resting on his hips.

"She told me to put on the vest. I said I wasn't going to. She lifted a trigger and told me I better or the building would come down." Tracie opened her eyes, sipped some water, and then took a deep breath. "I put the vest on, latched it, and a lock clicked into place. That's when she told me the only way to unlock it was to get within two feet of Griz. The radio transmitter she has implanted in him emits the radio frequency that will unlock it."

Kingston leaned toward the intercom again. "Did she say why she needed you to get close to Griz?"

She shook her head. "Obviously to catch him. But there's more to it than that. I pushed, but she wasn't very forthcoming. She mumbled something about a child, but she was angry and had her teeth clenched."

Kingston turned toward a couple of his agents. "Get on that. Check all the security cameras around the hospital and see if we can get a facial ID on the woman. Then find out if she has a kid. Check all missing children reports." The two agents hurried out of the room.

"Did she say or do anything else? Did you notice anything else unusual in the vehicle that might be a clue?"

Tracie stared at the glass. Right at him. Mac wished, more than anything, that he could go in there and take her in his arms. He hated what he saw in her eyes. The fear and exhaustion. Had she resigned to dying? "When she let me out of the vehicle, she told me that Mac had been given everything he needed to find Griz."

Mac pulled up the info on his laptop. "The first numbers the source gave me were 134.729. We figured that could be a low-frequency transmitter. Can we duplicate it? It could be what she implanted. The source was one of the Members."

"It's worth a shot." Jason went to work on his computer. "Give me a few minutes, and I'll see what I can do."

Spirelli stepped closer to Mac. "All right, what other info was on the note from Kirk?"

Mac had that one memorized. "The first part was that the hospital was Griz's next target—which was true. The next part was more cryptic. 'Follow the signal. 70 north.' The number was written out numerically—not a word."

"Any idea what the signal is?"

Mac clenched and unclenched his jaw several times with a slow shake of his head. "Not unless it's the radio signal of the chip—the 134.729. We don't have anything else that would represent as a signal. But again, it's kilohertz, low frequency, passive. Which would match what our kidnapper lady said—we've got to be within two feet of it. So how could we follow that?"

The FBI agent didn't like that answer. He didn't have to say anything for Mac to deduce that—the look in his eyes was enough. "Okay then, what about 70 north?" He snapped his fingers, getting everyone's attention. "Ideas, people?"

"There's a US Highway 70 and Interstate 70. Both of which travel east to west, but we could look for areas that it says *north*?" One of the cyber guys from the FBI—Mac really should pay attention to names, but he hadn't taken the time—spoke from the corner where he sat on the floor.

Spirelli grunted. "Which brings up a good point—should we focus just on Alaska or no?"

"I don't think we can take that chance, can we?" Kingston unbuttoned his blazer and shoved his hands into his pants pockets. "This guy's crossword puzzle clues were in publications around the country. Not just here. Even though the victims were all here. He doesn't just think outside the box—everything he does is outside the box."

"Good point." Spirelli looked at the corner dweller. "Find everything you can."

Darcie folded her hands in front of her as she walked toward the window. "The paper only said *70 north*, right? So it wasn't *70 degrees north of . . .* something?"

Mac shook his head. "Nope. Just *70 north*."

"Then the simplest and most logical explanation would be the seventieth parallel north. Normally coordinates have a lot more detail, as in 70.4213 degrees or whatever, but what's at 70 north?" Darcie went to her assistant, who was already looking it up.

Mac looked over Misty's shoulder as well. As soon as the map pulled up, Mac's blood went cold. "It's been right there the whole time."

"What do you mean?" Kingston's eyebrows came together.

Everyone else closed in on him, but Mac pushed through the group to get to the glass. "Deadhorse."

Tracie stood in the padded room and bit her lip.

"Deadhorse is at 70 north. That's where we have to go."

She nodded, and the compassion in her eyes just about overwhelmed him. She knew how much it would hurt him to go back there. To experience the trauma all over again. But he would do whatever he had to do—at all costs—to catch Griz once and for all.

"That's where he shot you." Tracie came closer to the glass. So close he could see the condensation her breath was making on the glass. "Will you be all right?"

Did he have a choice? "I have to be."

The room erupted as Spirelli and Kingston issued orders. Plans were made to get several teams up to Deadhorse—a place at the top of the world that wasn't very accessible. All Mac could do was stare at Tracie, looking so vulnerable and alone in that padded room.

When Kingston stepped close, Mac grabbed his arm and looked in the man's eye. "I'm going with Dr. Hunter."

The director frowned. "Mac, we're working on safe transport for her, and I don't know if that's—"

"I said I'm going with her. Nonnegotiable. Make it happen." He stared until Kingston looked toward Tracie.

"All right." Kingston went back to gathering his people and making plans.

While everyone was distracted, Mac left the big room and went straight into the interrogation room where Tracie was. He didn't need to be in the middle of all the chaos. He didn't need a plan. All he needed right now was her.

Without a word he grabbed her hand and sat next to her.

Silent tears streamed down her cheeks, and she squeezed his hand so hard it went numb. When the tears turned into sobs, he gently pulled her into his arms and held her. "I'm here. No matter what. I'm here."

CHAPTER TWENTY-TWO

951 Days After
July 19—5:10 p.m.
In the Air over Dalton Highway

70 NORTH. MAC COULD HAVE smacked himself for not figuring out that Deadhorse, Alaska, was on the seventieth parallel. Prudhoe Bay. The North Slope.

Nothing much was there other than oil and the pipeline. It wasn't exactly a tourist destination. But as soon as the FBI had the tip, they were like a dog with a bone and discovered a man named Paul Chandler had been hired as the resident IT guy. He'd had to be fingerprinted to be working up on the North Slope, and he'd used his real identity. An identity that hadn't been used in decades.

Their FBI pilot kept the plane low and steady. Tracie had a death grip on Mac's arm, and he couldn't blame her. She also hadn't said much. He was fine with that—he could wait until all this was over so they could have a real conversation without a crisis hanging over their heads.

"What I don't understand . . ." Tracie leaned her head on his shoulder. "Chandler. Didn't they know that Peter had a brother?"

Mac nodded. "I heard Spirelli telling Kingston that Paul Chandler had supposedly died thirty years ago. They interviewed people who knew the brothers and everything."

"So why did he shoot you in Deadhorse if he didn't know who you were?"

"He must have thought that I was one of the Members following him. That's why Griz has been killing them off one by one. They ticked him off. But they weren't out to stop him from killing people or blowing up things. He was just an interference they didn't like."

Tracie chewed the corner of her lip, appearing to consider the new information. "And now he's ticked them off enough for whomever this woman is to strap a bomb to me. You don't think she wants me to get close enough to him so that she can just blow us both up . . . do you?"

The thought had crossed his mind, but it wasn't something he wanted to think on for very long. "I'm hopeful that she has plans for him and him alone."

She nodded against his shoulder. "That's what I'm hoping too." She swiped a hand against her cheek. "But more than anything, I want him caught. For good. Have they figured out what he's got planned?"

He released a breath. "I haven't heard everything, but they've gotten intel that he's planted bombs all over the North Slope and in Valdez."

"Striking at the heart of Alaska's economy—oil," she murmured.

"Yep. Then there's also word of bombs in Juneau at the capitol, and Anchorage—downtown and major tourist areas. Airports, hospitals, schools."

She closed her eyes, covering her mouth with her hand. Then lowered it and glanced up at Mac. "That would be devastating."

"I know. That's why we've got to stop him. Before he can trigger anything else."

"How are you going to do that?"

It was the question he'd been asking himself over and over again since the newest chapter in this nightmare began. "That . . . I don't know. He knows what we did to reverse engineer his malware at the hospital, so he's going to be a step ahead. Or at least try. But he also told us that the closer we get, the more traps we will set off. We've seen that in action. Frankly, I'm not sure how much more I can take before my flesh takes over and wants to beat the guy senseless. And before you can say anything, Doc, yeah, I know I shouldn't—I can't—allow that to happen. So here's hoping the FBI guys have a plan. A really, really good one."

Tracie slipped her hand into his and laced her fingers through his. She squeezed them together and stayed silent, letting Mac's confession settle between them. Soon, her breathing evened and her grip slackened.

Mac sent up a prayer of thanks that she could get even a few minutes of rest in the midst of such a harrowing situation.

He stared out the window. For the first time in . . . well, he could hardly remember when . . . he was at a complete loss as to what to do next. His brain was exhausted. His body wasn't in much better shape. And his heart . . .

He rubbed Tracie's knuckles with his thumb, coming to a startling conclusion.

He wanted a future with her more than he wanted to see the killer caught. More than he wanted Griz dead. More than he wanted to see him punished for all that he'd done.

All the thoughts and planned words he'd had in the interrogation room—after he'd insisted on traveling with her—had conveniently flown the coop of his brain once they were in the plane.

The case that involved his nemesis was not at the forefront of his heart and mind anymore. The man that Mac had wanted revenge on more than anything else in the world had taken a back seat to saving the life of the woman next to him and spending the rest of his life with her.

Funny how God had humbled him and worked on his heart through all this.

Well, not really *funny*—it took his getting shot, going through multiple surgeries, and having a massive anxiety attack or two to get his attention. Then it took the patience of a thousand saints on Tracie's behalf. And Jason's. And Scott's. But now Mac wanted to make every moment count.

Tracie stirred and lifted her head, pulling her hand from his. She stretched carefully, clearly trying to avoid disturbing the vest attached to her person. "Ah, there's a welcome smile. What's on your mind? I really need to talk about something other than this bomb vest strapped to my chest."

Mac glanced at the pilot and back at her. It probably wasn't the time or place for this, but he might as well go for it. "What do you say to dinner?"

"As in, a date?" Her eyes widened and then crinkled at the corners as she blushed. "You sure you're ready for that? I've got a lot of my own baggage."

Mac pressed his lips together, fighting a laugh. "You've seen how much I have over the last eight months. And you've seen me at my very worst and still managed to put up with me. I think I can handle it."

"All right. I think we can open the floor for discussion on the topic." She winked at him. "As long as that bear and impossible patient that I stapled together multiple times promises that he will retreat into the past." She raised her eyebrows at him in almost a challenge and held out her hand. "I'm keeping my staple gun handy just in case."

"What? You want to shake on it?" He couldn't stop himself from laughing.

"Yep."

He shook her hand, and she grinned wide.

The plane descended. Mac pulled her close and kissed the top of her head. "It's a date." Mac could feel the heat radiating up his neck, but he didn't care. For the first time in almost three years, he was looking forward to the future.

They landed smoothly, and Tracie grabbed his hand. "No matter what has happened or will happen, God is in control." Her face no longer held joy or the teasing glint in her eyes.

The seriousness of what they were about to walk into sobered him too. He nodded and sent a silent prayer up to his heavenly Father.

Jason waited outside a vehicle just off the airstrip and waved at them. "I convinced them to allow me to try the radio frequency once everyone was gone."

"Let's do it." Mac gripped Tracie's hand.

"Maybe you should stand over there." Tracie tugged at her hand.

He shook his head. "Not a chance." He lifted his chin to Jason. "Do it."

Jason typed something on his laptop.

The vest clicked, but it didn't release.

A cell phone rang.

Tracie pulled her phone out of her pocket. She glanced at Mac. "It's her."

"Put it on speaker."

Tracie answered and tapped the screen for speakerphone.

"Nice try, Dr. Hunter." The woman's voice crackled across the line. "I had a feeling your cyber guys would try something like that. But it's also voice activated. Which means if you're not within two feet and you don't get Griz to say anything, the vest will not unlock."

"How do I know you're not going to blow me up with him?" Tracie's voice broke on the last word.

"I'm not a monster like he is, Dr. Hunter. You have my word that the vest will unlock if you do as you're told."

"That's not good enough." Mac jumped into the conversation.

"Mr. McPherson. You of all people should know better."

He shared a glance with Jason. What? "I'm not sure I know—"

"Because my son is with that monster." Three beeps and the call was gone.

The trio stared at the phone for a moment, then Jason cleared his throat. "Wow. I did *not* see that coming. I guess we should head out."

"Wait." Something didn't add up. Again. Mac paced a few feet around Tracie and Jason. "We've seen that this guy doesn't care about kids. He killed Beth. He planted a bomb at a school. He put malware on all the incubators in the NICU. So why keep *her* kid alive?"

Jason's eyes widened. "Because it's *his* kid too." He yanked out his cell phone and dialed a number. "Agent Spirelli . . ."

They climbed in the SUV as Jason gave their suspicions to the team. A dark pair of aviator sunglasses kept Mac from seeing Jason's eyes but couldn't cover up the tightness of his friend's jaw.

Jason drove away from the airstrip. "They are set up and ready to raid what they believe to be Griz's compound. It's apparently been his base camp for a couple of years. He's used the cover of being an IT guy up here, working seven on and seven off. Apparently everyone loves him and says that he's 'congenial' and always fixes everything." The last words held a good deal of sarcasm.

"Who would call this guy congenial?" Tracie sounded offended.

"I guess he's a good actor." Jason's words were clipped.

"Why haven't they taken him into custody yet?" Mac didn't want to think about Griz being well-liked.

"They were getting ready to surround the place after they checked for bombs."

They drove up behind several other vehicles, and Jason parked and turned off the vehicle. Mac reached over and squeezed Tracie's hand before they climbed out of the SUV. They were silent as they followed Jason behind a small shack.

Agent Spirelli had a radio to his mouth and nodded at Mac. Then he spotted Tracie. "Dr. Hunter, we might need your help."

"Oh?" She inched closer to Mac.

"The dogs picked up the scent of blood and alerted their handlers. We don't know if they're dead or alive, but someone in this compound has lost a lot of blood. If it's our UNSUB and he's got the tiniest bit of life left in him, I need you to keep him alive so we can prosecute him to the fullest extent of the law."

"I don't have anything with me. If it's something major, I might not be able to do what needs to be done." Her voice sounded cool and calm, but Mac noticed her twisting her fingers.

"Just do your best. We've got a small medical bag with us. Doc, stick with me." He turned to his men and spoke into his radio. "Teams one and two, keep that building surrounded. Team three will breach with me. Agent Kintz gets to take the lead since this psycho was hers first." He grinned over at Carrie. Then the agent turned to Mac. "You will not, under any circumstances, follow us in. Is that understood?"

Mac nodded and clenched his fists.

The next few seconds passed in a blur of agents in full gear crossing the distance between him and the building the other teams had surrounded. Carrie was with them. And Tracie too.

He breathed in long and slow and then held it.

✦ ✦ ✦

13 Days Until Final Judgment
4 Members Left
July 19—8:20 p.m.
Latitude: 70.193385° N, Longitude: 148.444766° W
Griz's Small Compound

So they'd found him.

He had one little bomb attached to his left leg. It wouldn't do enough damage to make a difference, and frankly, he wasn't about to take his own life. There was too much to live for.

He looked out the window. He simply needed a different plan. A way to negotiate. There were plenty of ways for him to still win and start again.

He popped a pill and stepped over the body on the floor. Another Member who thought they could outsmart him.

Then an idea struck him. The body. The blood. There it was—his way out.

He moved his computer bag to his back and dipped his hands into the pool of blood. Then he covered his midsection and slouched against the desk in the middle of the room.

Just like he'd predicted, the door burst open.

"Suspect is down."

A radio crackled through the space, and Griz barely contained his grin. How he'd missed the voice of Special Agent Kintz.

The stampede of footsteps into the room as the agents fanned out and searched roared in his ears.

"He's still breathing."

Another woman's voice. Oh, an added bonus. Dr. Hunter. Perfect.

He counted the seconds, listening to the shuffle of feet. Most of them had moved farther into the building.

Except the doc and Agent Kintz were close.

Dr. Hunter, presumably, placed her hands over what appeared to be his wound.

Excellent. He felt her hands lifting the bottom of his shirt.

With the trigger for the bomb in hand, he used one arm to put her in a headlock. Then with his other hand, he pulled a hypodermic needle out of a pocket.

"Don't move, Chandler!" Agent Kintz had her weapon trained on him.

But he dragged the doc to stand with him and used her as a shield. He could see her pulse throbbing in her neck. She was terrified. Something bulky pressed into his chest, and he glanced down. What was strapped across her abdomen? He frowned and ignored it.

Time was of the essence.

He had one final, masterful move.

With his thumb, he flicked the cap off the syringe. He twirled the needle in his hand and placed it against Tracie's throat. Right against that fluttering pulse. The needle pressed into her skin, just a millimeter from piercing it. Perfect.

His neck itched, but he ignored it as he looked at Agent Kintz. "Oh,

I don't think you're in any position to be giving orders. Back up. Nice and slow."

Click. Click. What was that noise? No matter.

"More." He used a soothing voice, his gaze glued on the agents in the room. "More. More! Good. Now shut the door." He directed that at Kintz.

She did as she was told.

He relaxed a hair. But then Tracie wiggled under his arm.

"Where's your son?"

For a second he loosened his grip a tiny bit and stared at the side of the doc's face. "So . . . *she* got to you."

"Let me take this off, please." She sounded on the verge of tears.

With a glance down, he swallowed. Muriel's work?

She didn't wait for permission. It didn't take much movement for her to slip the vest off.

He tightened his grip around her neck. "Who did this?" Not one of them. They wouldn't risk the opportunity to take him alive, and he was pretty sure the feds didn't use bomb vests. No one answered. "Who. Did. This?" This time he screeched.

Tracie tugged at the arm around her neck. "I . . . don't know . . . who she was . . ." She gasped for air.

He released a long, steadying breath. Oh. Well, nice move, Muriel, but it was too late. He loosened his grip a bit so the poor doctor could breathe.

Agent Kintz stepped closer. "Let her go."

"No." Griz shifted, keeping the syringe pressed firmly against Tracie's neck.

"Where's your son?" The agent didn't flinch.

"Somewhere you'll never find him. Now." He looked each person in the room in the eye and grinned. "We're all going to take a deep breath. And you're going to listen. Dr. Hunter here has met the head of the Members, who also happens to be my wife. But alas, she won't take my son from me this time. She will never see him again. And neither will any of you. There's no bargaining chip there, so don't even try."

Something flickered across Agent Kintz's face. "Chandler, let Dr. Hunter go," she barked, her gun still trained on him.

He had to admire her pluck. It took real guts to keep pointing her weapon at him when he had two forms of death pinned to her friend.

"I don't think so." He didn't even blink. How satisfying to see this feisty little agent face-to-face once again. Especially now that she knew who he was. Where she could see the magnitude of his brilliance.

"I can put a bullet in your head right now."

Griz arched a brow. Wow. Her voice was calm. Unwavering. She actually meant it. Such a shame she was on the wrong side of the law. Courage like that, mixed with mercenary tendencies—a rare gift he could have exploited.

Ah well. "You probably could. But you won't. Because if you do that, my final act will be plunging this needle into Tracie's carotid artery. It's filled with my own little concoction I've been working on the last few years. You might have seen my work. I used it on Courtney."

Tracie writhed under his arm. "You despicable—"

"Now, now. We wouldn't want this needle to go into your flesh, would we?" he crooned into her ear. Then he faced Agent Kintz again. "You should probably also know that the trigger I'm holding in this hand"—he wiggled two fingers on the hand around Tracie's neck—"is for a bomb I have strapped to my leg. If you shoot me, I'll kill your friend the doc here, I'll trigger the bomb, and oh, wait! I left out the best part. Everything I have planned will still take place. My final judgment. Without me, you can just watch the world go up in flames."

The agent shifted her weight, faltering for just a moment.

"Seriously. Put it down," he growled.

"No." She locked her gaze on his. And several agents stepped closer. "The whole place is surrounded. You've got nowhere to go."

She stepped an inch closer.

"You're not listening, Carrie." Griz clucked and put his thumb on the flat plunger of the needle. "I don't *need* anywhere to go. At this very moment, I control the fate of the lives of a million people . . . maybe more." The thought made him laugh. Loud and long. They'd never defeat him.

Tracie didn't make a sound.

Agent Kintz stepped back. "All right. What do you want, Chandler?"

That was really the question, wasn't it? Thankfully, he had a list. And a brand-new contingency plan just in case anyone tried to double-cross him.

One more reason he was still smarter than everyone else.

If the Members hadn't gotten in his way, he would have pulled off the whole thing without a hitch.

Well, this would get him what he wanted in the long run anyway.

"Oh, there's plenty that I want. And if you want to stop me from destroying not only your state but the country's economy, not to mention killing lots and lots of people, you'd better listen and listen fast. But before I do, I will say it one more time. Lower. Your. Weapon." He looked back at the blonde. "*Carrie.*"

Her nostrils flared, and anger colored her face. "Lower your weapons," she told the other agents and slipped hers back into its holster.

"Excellent. Now keep your hands up in front of you. All of you." He waited until they complied. "As Special Agent Kintz so helpfully pointed out, your silly little cavalry is surrounding us." He grinned. "However, the only way Tracie lives and the rest of the traps get stopped is if you give me what I want. So I suggest you bring whoever has the power to make that happen *to me.* Now."

✦　✦　✦

951 Days After
July 19—10:17 p.m.
Latitude: 70.193385° N, Longitude: 148.444766° W
Griz's Small Compound

The minutes dragged by. It was a good thing the FBI was on top of everything, because Mac was about to blow his top.

When the door opened and he'd caught a glimpse inside, he almost darted forward at full speed to tackle the creep. But then he'd seen Griz with something stuck in Tracie's throat. A slew of agents exited. Spirelli headed straight for Mac while the door closed again.

They just left her inside with that monster? What were they thinking?

"McPherson." Spirelli marched up to him and Jason. "We need you to drive to the heliport right now and pick up the head of the ABI and our boss with the FBI. They've been waiting to take custody of our perp, but plans have changed. He's holed up in there with a bomb strapped to his leg, a syringe to Tracie's throat, and Carrie as another hostage." He gave them no other details.

Mac had no choice but to do as he was ordered.

Jason held on to the dashboard as Mac drove like a maniac down the unpaved roads. "It's gonna be fine."

"You have to say that."

"I actually don't. Contrary to popular belief, I'm not here to comfort you." His friend grabbed the handle by the window as Mac jerked the vehicle across the road. "I'm saying it because it's true. That's why Carrie's boss's boss and the big man with the FBI are waiting at the heliport pad."

"Yeah, but they don't have a needle stuck in their neck with who knows what kind of poison in it."

"True. But, Mac"—he shifted in the seat—"Carrie is still with Griz to make sure nothing happens to Tracie. You know Scott's gotta be out of his mind too." The inertia from a hard turn sent Jason careening into the door.

"Sorry." Mac gripped the wheel tighter. "I just wish I knew what he was up to. He's still got something planned—he's too cocky. He's proven time and again he doesn't care about anyone. Not even his own brother. He's killed everyone who worked for him except *your* brother. I don't think he's even *capable* of caring." The thought of Tracie in the monster's hands made him want to puke.

Jason didn't argue. "You're right. He's absolutely insane. But you know what is playing in our favor right now?"

Mac glanced at him. "What?"

"Paul Chandler doesn't want to die here. There's no glory in being shot in the head in a small cabin in middle-of-nowhere Alaska. Plus, apparently there's a son in the picture. I can't imagine him being human enough to have a kid, but . . ." He shrugged. "His deep-rooted need for self-preservation is keeping Tracie alive."

Mac mulled over his friend's words. It made sense. Everything had been orchestrated to bring the killer notoriety and glory. If he died in that cabin, the FBI and ABI could wrap up everything covertly, and no one would ever know. Mac snorted. The ego of this guy was beyond comprehension. But that didn't mean Mac felt any better.

"Besides"—Jason tugged at his seat belt—"they've already got a deal in the works. Spirelli said so. They've been planning for his capture. Let's just focus on getting them there."

Like that was comforting. The reality was still that the madman—the monster—had Tracie.

He shook all negative thoughts aside and drove up to the heliport. Thank God it was summer in Alaska. Up here at the North Slope, it still looked like the middle of the day.

They were one step closer to saving her. That's what mattered. And when she was okay? He was going to tell her exactly how he felt. All of it. No holds barred. He had a sneaking suspicion she felt the same way.

The two men in vests climbed into the vehicle with Mac and Jason.

"Ready?" Mac said.

"Yep." One of the men leaned forward. "Fredericks. FBI."

"David McPherson. But everyone calls me Mac." He nodded to the mirror.

Fredericks reached forward and gave Mac's shoulder a pat. "We've been following your company's work. Thank you for all you've done to keep the people of Alaska safe the past few years."

"Welcome." Mac nodded again. At this point, he just wanted *Tracie* safe. Since they'd saved the NICU, he could let someone else worry about the pipeline, the capital, and Valdez.

Even with the bigwigs in the vehicle, Mac continued to drive like an avalanche was chasing them. But he didn't care. Everyone held on for dear life, and that was fine with him.

When they reached Chandler's compound, Fredericks patted the seat from behind before Mac could even turn off the engine. "Let us handle this. We've been trained for situations like this. And we can't let your emotion, no matter how admirable, cloud this situation. It's the only way we can ensure that Dr. Hunter stays safe."

Mac shook his head. They couldn't promise him anything. He knew that. He didn't respond. Just got out of the vehicle.

Jason was beside him in seconds and grabbed his arm in a tight grip. "Stay back, David."

The use of his first name managed to break through his anger. Marginally. Doing his best to hold his temper in check, Mac gave a short nod and allowed the big guys to enter the monster's lair. Once the agents were all in, Mac slipped to the open window and watched.

"Ah, it appears you know the enormity of what you're dealing with." Griz—Chandler, the Typhon Killer—still held Tracie in a tight grip, the needle at her neck and the trigger in his other hand. "Mr. Fredericks, I believe?"

The FBI man didn't flinch. "Mr. Chandler."

"And I presume this is the ever-proper Heath Kingston. Head of our illustrious ABI."

Kingston nodded. "We're here to make a deal, Mr. Chandler. I suggest we get down to business, but the state and the FBI won't acquiesce to any of your requests until you allow your hostages to go."

Chandler laughed.

The sound flooded Mac with anger again. His nostrils flared as he fought to keep it at bay.

"All right, gentlemen. *This* is how it's going to go. Either a helo or a plane is going to have one pilot. Unarmed. They will fly me and Dr. Hunter here to Fairbanks. You can even choose the place for our negotiations. But going to Fairbanks is nonnegotiable. Once we are there, you two will be allowed in the room with Tracie and myself. She stays with me until I have a signed deal. Any attempts to take me down before then will only serve to trip the triggers." He cleared his throat and lifted his chin. "Then and only then will you get the laptop also strapped to me. It controls *all* the triggers."

Dread crawled up Mac's spine. This was an absolute nightmare.

"Why do we need to go to Fairbanks? Let's just take care of the deal here and now." Fredericks inched forward.

"Not any closer." Chandler laughed and looked out the window straight at Mac. "Join us, Mr. McPherson."

Mac waited for the go-ahead from Fredericks, then held up his hands and entered.

"You know . . . don't you?" Griz questioned.

Mac hated to be baited by this guy, but it was best to tell everyone the truth or at least what he suspected. "He's got a fail-safe. Whatever he's got planned to blow the pipeline won't go off if his GPS signal is in the area."

"Bravo, Mac." Griz grinned.

Mac wanted to wipe that arrogant sneer off his face once and for all.

"Good. You can't blow them up while you're here." Kingston huffed. "Let's get down to business."

"You really are a stupid fool, aren't you?" Chandler hissed. "I hate having to explain my brilliance to idiots . . ." He yanked Tracie backward a couple steps and grunted. "You will fly me and my hostage away from here, or she dies and I trigger everything else."

"Everything else?" Fredericks echoed.

The monster had the audacity to roll his eyes. "Don't play dumb with me. I know you know. Maybe not everything. But you have a pretty good idea of what I'm capable of doing." Chandler looked back to Fredericks. "So I'm assuming you don't want pretty Tracie here to die, and you don't want me to blow up, say, oh, a few hospitals, the Valdez Marine Terminal with all the oil stored there, the capitol building, and a few other specially chosen sites." His face hardened into a mask of rage. "Now I'm going to say it *One. More. Time.* You'll fly us to Fairbanks. No negotiations."

The enormity of Griz's demand nearly buckled Mac's knees. He should have known. Paul Chandler had been planning this for two years. There was no way they could know what he'd done unless they broke into his computer. He released a breath and watched as the magnitude of the situation sank into the minds of the men. "Do what he says, please."

The lead FBI agent glanced at Mac and shook his head. "It's too much."

Mac stepped closer to Fredericks. "He's rigged all those places he just mentioned and God only knows what else with bombs. We can't stay here or he'll kill countless people. And you can't kill him. If I'm right, he has a dead man's switch not just on his body but in his computer that would go off when he dies, still killing countless people."

That grin—that awful grin—spread across the murderer's face once again. "Good job, Mr. McPherson. You're smarter than you look." Griz studied him for a moment and tipped his head. "I know . . . I know, you're still bitter that you thought you had me and then you traced me out to the Beaufort Sea."

Mac crossed his arms over his chest and forced his lips to remain clamped. He couldn't give this guy the satisfaction of knowing how riled he was.

"Tell you what, when you guys recover my little toy out of the ocean, you can keep it. Maybe it will help you do better next time."

Everything in Mac wanted to surge forward, but he held his ground.

"I know you want to try it, Mac . . ." His taunting gaze remained locked on Mac's for what felt like an eternity. Then the monster turned to the authorities. "There's no way for you to win, kind sirs. So like I said, *this* is how it's going to go . . ."

✦ ✦ ✦

One Week and One Day Sober
July 19—11:45 p.m.
Latitude: 64.807717° N, Longitude: 147.752629° W
Metro Airfield—Fairbanks

If the last hour of being held in a headlock by that beast in a helicopter wasn't bad enough, she now had to sit next to him on this cold chair as he held a syringe to her throat. Again. As he negotiated his terms.

Terms that the FBI and ABI—and any other sane person who knew the full scope of this man's destructive path—should decline.

Except no one knew for sure what else the man had up his sleeve if they didn't cooperate. She'd paid close attention to Scott's, Jason's, and especially Mac's faces. Most of the time, she was pretty good at reading expressions. And every one of theirs told her they were itching to get their hands on Griz's laptop. It held the key. To fix everything.

Of course, if this guy's history was any indicator, she wouldn't be surprised if he told her that he'd programmed all the nuclear missiles in the world to go off at the same time.

Tracie wiggled to get more comfortable, but it couldn't take away the fact that she had to use the restroom. Not that she even wanted to say that in front of this lunatic. Who knew what his solution would be.

She was a girl who liked her privacy. Plain and simple. She could hold it.

But not for too much longer.

"We'd like to see proof that what you say is true." Mr. Fredericks rested his elbows on the table.

Oh, why couldn't they get on with it?

Her captor tugged at the zipper of the backpack at his feet, managing to pull out his laptop with his free hand. He opened it, and she realized this was her chance to be useful. Just in case he tried to trick them.

She watched as he entered a twelve-digit code at lightning speed, and she said it over and over again in her mind so she wouldn't forget it. At least it took her mind off her need for the restroom. *E9VaLReN6IOt* . . . *E9VaLReN6IOt* . . . *E9VaLReN6IOt* . . .

"As you can see, I don't bluff." Red pins popped up on the digital map. And they continued to display as if they were multiplying as the seconds ticked by.

Tracie's eyes widened. The number of sites he had as targets was incomprehensible.

"Why do you think I've been silent for more than two years? I'm not an idiot. Everything is planned to a T. You can't stop it. You can't stop me. Not even your precious little Cyber Solutions teams can. So you will give me what I want."

He allowed them a whopping ten seconds to survey the screen. Then he closed it. "Time's up, gentlemen. Give me my deal."

CHAPTER TWENTY-THREE

Revelation 9:6
July 20—3:54 a.m.
Latitude: 64.807717° N, Longitude: 147.752629° W
Metro Airfield

MR. KINGSTON OF THE ABI and Mr. Fredericks from the FBI walked into the room. The head of the ABI slid the paperwork onto the table in front of Griz.

He moved forward, dragging Tracie with him. In a show of good faith that they didn't deserve, he slackened the needle a bit.

Apparently she was going to use her new sense of freedom to distract him. She elbowed him in the ribs. He refused to flinch. "Not so tight." She wiggled under the grip his right arm had around her neck.

He ignored her.

"This is it. Everything we agreed upon." Fredericks jabbed his finger in Griz's face. "Let her go."

Both men were intimidating. Mid to late thirties. One was wiry and muscled, the other thick with muscles, like a body builder.

Griz wouldn't want to arm wrestle either of them. He laughed at his own thought.

"What's the problem, Mr. Chandler?" Mr. Fredericks stepped closer.

"Not a thing." He scanned the first page of the deal, noting several things he'd required. There was no reason to think the rest wouldn't be up to his standards. He released Tracie and took a seat at the table.

She scrambled away from him, tripping over her own feet to stand behind the men.

He picked up the papers. After a thorough read-through, he set them down. "Pen, please." He held up his hand.

Fredericks gave him one. How sad he had to sign this document with a subpar ballpoint pen. But it couldn't be helped.

He signed his name. Simple as that. Then slid the papers back.

"We'll need the laptop. Unlocked." The ABI guy was expressionless.

Griz unlocked it and slid it across the table as well.

Fredericks was around the table in a split second, putting cuffs on him. "What's the code?"

Griz raised an eyebrow. "Oh, was that part of the deal?"

"Doesn't matter." Tracie smirked at him. "I know it."

The FBI agent led him out the door while the head of the ABI took the computer and Tracie out another door.

Out in the parking lot, he was ushered to a waiting plane. But out there were three other men. Standing. Watching.

Mac stepped forward, his brow furrowed. But then a slow grin spread across his face as Griz was escorted onto the plane.

✦ ✦ ✦

July 20—4:16 a.m.
Latitude: 64.807717° N, Longitude: 147.752629° W
Metro Airfield

As the plane took off from the runway, Mac could finally inhale a deep breath and let it out. They'd done it. They'd captured the true killer. The mastermind. The man who had plagued them all for close to three years.

"Mac!" Tracie ran toward him from a side exit of the small terminal building.

He opened his arms, and she jumped into them. "You're all right? He didn't hurt you?" He pressed his face into her neck, relishing the feel of her in his arms.

"I've got some sores on my neck from the needle, but the preliminary check by the EMT said I was fine. But I'll probably need to see a good chiropractor." She pulled back and cupped his cheek in her palm for a moment.

What a blessing to see the stress gone from her expression. "That's why it took me a bit to get out here." She tilted her head back as the plane arced over them, then headed south. "Good riddance. That guy was terrifying. He must have taken twelve pills just while I was his hostage."

"Pills?" He brushed her hair from her face, trailing his fingers down her cheek.

Her eyebrows went up as a pretty blush heated her cheeks. "Yep. The guy's a serious addict. Brilliant but way out of control. I'm surprised he's held it together this long. Who knows what horrors he'd be capable of if left unchecked for much longer."

An addict? Mac would have never guessed. "That's why he escalated?"

She shrugged. "Most likely."

He remembered what the guy had looked like down in Healy before Mac had lost him in the wilderness. It hadn't just been a gunshot wound that had given him that haunted, hunted look.

"Mac." Tracie blew out her breath. "There's something I need to tell you."

Uh-oh. That didn't sound good. "What is it?"

"The deal they made with him?" She placed her hands on his shoulders, giving them a tender squeeze.

"Yeah?" He released her and stepped back, hands fisted at his sides.

Jason and Scott stepped closer too.

"He's getting minimum security."

That plane must have blown out his eardrums. "Excuse me?"

Tracie nodded. Her eyes held so much sadness. "They gave him life without parole, but he'll have it cushy. Every single one of his demands, they caved. Once they saw his computer and everything he had in place. Hospitals. Government buildings. Prisons. Power grids. The pipeline. Law enforcement offices. So much more. He had his fingers in everything. Everywhere. Not just in Alaska. We were only the beginning. So they gave him what he wanted."

Mac didn't know what to do with that information. How did he process that in a way he could comprehend that level of leniency? His brain went numb.

Forgive as I have forgiven you.

The words echoed through his mind, and with everything in him, he wanted to shove them away. No. He didn't *want* to forgive. Nor did he want Griz to get off that easy. What about justice? What about punishment?

His heart pounded, and every muscle in his body tensed. No. No. No. No. No.

Forgive as I have forgiven you.

Jason fist-bumped his shoulder. "Hey, at least he's put away, right?"

But was that enough? Now that it was real. In front of him. It didn't seem like that was enough punishment for taking Sarah's and Beth's lives. And there were countless others in addition to theirs.

Mac looked at Jason. "Yeah, he's put away."

But he wasn't. Not yet. The feds just took him away. With his deal, did that mean he just went straight to prison? No trial, no reckoning? No media storm showing the true face of the monster? The mass murderer? Mac turned away from everyone and walked across the parking lot. He passed the vehicles. Kept walking.

His gut churned.

He found a bench and sat. Put his elbows on his knees and then his face in his hands.

Footsteps around him made him realize they'd followed. He

couldn't blame them. "It's over," he said into his hands. "It's got to be over. After all that. I . . . I need it to be over."

"It is. He's in custody."

"But what about the Members? What if their rift with him was all for show and they start back up again?" It was like his mind couldn't stop calculating worst-case scenarios. Each one was more terrifying than the one before.

Scott knelt in front of him. "Carrie said they're already working on the network. Taking it apart piece by piece. Let's take the win for what it is and thank God that Griz is finally in custody."

Tracie sat next to him and wrapped an arm around his waist. "I can't imagine all you've gone through, Mac. I really can't. But I know that Jesus can."

Her warmth seeped into him, breaking through his despairing thoughts. She was right. *How quickly I forget, Lord.*

Mac leaned back and slipped an arm around Tracie. "That's the thing." He lifted his face and stared at the place where the plane had sat. "Without Jesus—without Him getting ahold of me?—I would have taken vengeance for myself. And Griz—Chandler—wouldn't be alive. I can see the consequences of what would have happened if I'd ignored God's tugging on my heart." He grunted. "More like *strain* on my heart, but I don't blame Him for that."

The guys chuckled, and Tracie squeezed her arm around him a little tighter.

"But even knowing that deep down inside . . . knowing that Christ died so that no one should perish . . . I still don't feel like extending grace to that monster." He tried to tamp the anger down inside him, but it rose up his throat. "I wanted revenge for so long. He didn't care who he hurt."

No one said anything as he processed. "I wanted to kill him that day in the park."

"That's understandable." Jason clenched his fists. "I think we have *all* wanted to take this man's life at one point or another."

Scott stepped over and stood in front of Mac. "So now what? He's going to be in prison for the rest of his life. What are you going to do with that?"

He sucked his bottom lip in between his teeth. "That's a tough one. Maybe I'll go visit him once a year . . . so that he knows I'm still—"

"Mac." Tracie's fingertips slipped along his jaw, turning his face to hers. "Part of the deal was that no one could know where he was. Especially you."

"Of course." His sarcastic comment fell flat. *God? Really?* "Okay then. I don't know what I'm going to do." He let his hands fall between his knees.

Tracie stood up, grabbed his arm, and tugged him to his feet. She slipped her hand into his and intertwined their fingers. "I'll tell you what we're going to do. We're going to move forward. One step at a time. Together."

"Together," Jason and Scott chimed.

Mac nodded and gripped Tracie's hand. "Together."

CHAPTER TWENTY-FOUR

One Week and Three Days Sober
July 21—1:37 p.m.
Latitude: 64.84746° N, Longitude: 147.71425° W
Griffin Park

"THIS IS WHERE I SAW him." Mac walked beside her in the park.

"Then I think we need to replace that memory with a good one." Tracie kept her stride slow and easy, a sharp contrast to the nerves bubbling in her stomach. "By the way, I've been meaning to talk to you about the future."

Her heartbeat felt like it was reverberating in her bones. Was she being too bold? Too forward? She bit her lip and tucked a strand of hair behind her ear. No, she'd prayed and sought the Lord with her parents. With Carrie and Darcie. With her pastor. She knew this next step was the right decision.

Taking a deep breath, she bumped his shoulder with hers. "I need a fresh start. After everything that's happened here . . . losing the hospital administrator, Courtney, the NICU, all of it . . . Well, I'm thinking of accepting a job in the Mat-Su Valley."

He stopped and turned toward her. "Really?"

Okay. It wasn't the most exuberant reaction. But at least he wasn't running the other way. "Yes. They need a surgeon. A headhunter called me last night."

"That was quick. You're okay leaving Fairbanks?" He shoved his hands into his pockets, his gaze fixed just over her shoulder.

Her heart cracked just a bit. She loved how he looked like a little boy standing there. She peered up into his handsome face. A face that she had come to love. "Mac, I'm not a spring chicken, and neither are you. And we both know God brought us together. I've learned my lesson."

His right hand went to the back of his neck, rubbing it. Then he raked it through his hair. Shadows lingered in his eyes. "You deserve better, Tracie. I . . . I am still a mess."

Tears stung her eyes. Oh, this beautiful man. "You're not the only one."

"I'll probably struggle with the loss of Sarah and Beth for the rest of my life." The confession hung between them.

Tracie took a deep breath. *Lord, help me show him how much I care.*

She nodded and put a hand on his cheek. "And I'll struggle with alcoholism the rest of mine. And as much as I've heard about your wife and daughter, I'll struggle with you. Together, remember?"

Mac covered her hand with his own for a brief moment. Then he slid his fingers up the length of his arm to her shoulder. Tingles rippled with the path of his touch. "I do care about you, Tracie. A great deal. But I might have to relearn how to be a decent human being." His laugh was light as his gaze penetrated all the way down to her soul.

"I think I can help with that. Besides, I've got a lot invested already. I assure you, I'm in it for the long haul." She took the last step necessary to close the distance between them and raised her other arm to his shoulder, drawing him close. "And . . . to be honest, you might have to teach me how to open up as well. It's been a long time since I've let people in. But after watching your team, meeting and working with Carrie, and then meeting Darcie . . . I want the same thing the other couples have. That depth. You know?"

"I do." It was his turn to put his hands on her face. "I'm a little out of practice, but would you mind terribly if I kissed you?" His head dipped slightly.

Tracie's breath hitched as she followed his lead and tipped her chin up toward him. "I would love it . . ." She breathed against his lips. "But I'm probably more out of practice than you."

His head leaned even closer, and she lifted her mouth to his.

Little sparkles burst on the backs of her eyelids. Her fingers and toes tingled. But more than that, her heart felt like it had found home. As the kiss deepened, Tracie wanted to hold on to this man for dear life. Nothing had ever compared to this moment.

There was no doubt in her mind now . . . she loved Mac.

✦ ✦ ✦

August 14—10:27 a.m.
Latitude: Undisclosed, Longitude: Undisclosed
Secret Federal Detainment Center—Utah

Griz arranged his books on the shelf. It shouldn't be long now before his contact would bring him his pills. Another stipulation of his agreement was that he was allowed two specific visitors: Kirk and Muriel.

She'd come. In time she would understand that his plan was best. And she'd help him escape. If she didn't, she'd never see their son again.

All in perfect timing.

The dry, desert climate made him itch.

But he only had to wait a few more minutes. Everything was going according to plan. He simply needed patience.

His great strength.

The pills would make him feel better—help him focus—and then he could figure out his next steps.

That simpleton DA thought she could stop him. He laughed and rearranged the books by color and size.

Tipping his head, he surveyed his work. Perhaps by color, size, and author. He shifted the books around on the shelves again. There, that was better.

"Hello, Griz." The familiar voice at his cell door was enough to make him grin.

He turned. "Kirk. It's good to see you, old friend." The agreement with the feds also included that his visits would be private, in his own cell. Control was a beautiful thing.

"And you as well." He waited for the guard to open the door.

The giant of a guard didn't even give Griz the time of day. "I'll be back in ten minutes."

"Good. Thank you." Kirk waited for the hulk to walk away. Then he pulled a paper bag out of his pocket. He dumped the contents onto the bed.

Griz counted them. Twelve Tic Tac containers, full. Perfect. He reached for one, popped the little tab, and took two pills. He closed his eyes and swallowed. There. That would help. "Now, let's get down to business." He rubbed his hands together.

Kirk nodded and moved beside him. Then with a quick turn, the younger man grabbed the hair at the back of Griz's head, yanked it back, and jammed a syringe into his neck.

Blood squirted out of the wound. He saw it out of the corner of his eye. Griz coughed and fought with everything in him to push Kirk away, but it did no good.

Then his friend laughed and pulled away.

"What did you do?" He spat the words and dropped to his bed, placing his hand over the injection site.

Kirk turned for the bookshelf and slid his index finger along the spines. He stopped about midway and grabbed the leather-bound journal.

Griz closed his eyes. Muriel. Somehow she'd gotten to him.

"The Members send their regards." Kirk offered a lopsided grin. "*She* wanted me to give you a message." He leaned closer. "Checkmate. Don't worry, she'll find your son." He waved the book in his face, saluted, pulled some keys out of his pocket, and let himself out. Once the door was closed and locked again, he spoke through the slats. "Oh, and I used your own special formula."

Griz slumped over on the bed, trying to get to the secret button that called for help. Another condition of his negotiations. But he had no control of his body anymore. There was nothing he could do.

He'd be dead soon.

Huh.

Looked like he lost after all.

✦ ✦ ✦

One Month Later
September 20—12:00 p.m.
Latitude: 61.691050° N, Longitude: 149.202649° W
Mac's Property, under New Construction—the Mat-Su Valley, Alaska

Mac drove over the rough road, through the thick trees, and then pointed. "We're almost there."

Tracie sat up straighter and bounced in her seat. "All I see is trees. And a few mountain peaks."

"Just be patient." He grabbed her hand, brought it to his lips, and kissed it.

As soon as they rounded the last curve, she saw it and squealed. "Mac!"

He stopped in front of the construction site, turned off the engine, and unbuckled. "Would you like to go see your new house, Mrs. McPherson? Or is that Dr. Mrs. McPherson? Mrs. Dr. McPherson? I'm confused."

She giggled and opened her door.

"Go check it out."

Running up to the front like a little girl, she clapped her hands together.

Mac leaned against the truck and crossed his arms over his chest. It wouldn't be too long until the snow would be in drifts around them. Termination dust already topped the mountains everywhere he looked. But watching the joy light up his wife's face was a moment he'd never forget.

Several of the construction guys came out to see what all the ruckus was about, but when they spotted Mac, they just grinned and went back to work.

It had been a rough road, but God had seen him through. Without Mac's accountability brothers, he probably wouldn't be here. He definitely wouldn't be here without Tracie.

She'd saved his life—in more than one way.

God, I know I don't say it enough, but . . . thank You. You blessed me with Sarah and Beth. Tears pricked his eyes, but the memory of them was sweet. *And now You've blessed me doubly so with Tracie. Help me not to ever take it for granted.*

Life had been hard once the chase was over. But moving on was a remarkable and miraculous thing that only God could have orchestrated.

Tracie's laughter and excitement floated out the open windows to his ears and lifted his heart in a way nothing else could. She bolted out of the house and ran straight into his arms. "I love it so much!"

Pulling her close, he kissed her lips and then her nose, her forehead, then trailed kisses down her neck. "Thank you," he murmured against her skin.

"For what?" She leaned her head back but stayed in his arms.

"For not giving up on me."

She patted his cheek. "I would say it's because you're so cute, but we both know it's because I'm *almost* as stubborn as you."

"Almost?" His laughter rumbled up from his middle.

"Don't worry, I have plenty of time to catch up."

EPILOGUE

Two Years Later

TRACIE WATCHED HER HUSBAND PLAY flag football with the rest of the Cyber Solutions crew and a few others. Get them together and they acted like a bunch of oversize children. Of course, she wouldn't have it any other way. Their jobs were often so stressful, they needed to let off a little steam and bond.

It was their annual company picnic that she had suggested after they were married. A way for the employees and their spouses to bond with the rest of the team. Jason and Darcie had traveled down from Fairbanks with their two kiddos, and even the new team in Juneau had flown up to join in the festivities.

It felt like one giant family. She placed her hand on her rounded belly, gratitude welling within her. Family was a beautiful thing.

Carrie pushed a stroller toward Tracie and sat in the empty camp chair next to her. "Are you surviving your time off from the hospital, or are you going stir-crazy?"

Tracie rolled her eyes. "What do *you* think?"

Her friend laughed as she dug around in the bottom of the stroller. "Here, I brought you this." She pulled out a yellow-and-red board game.

"Operation?" She snorted and then couldn't stop laughing.

"I'm sure the kids would love to play with you." Carrie took a sip of her drink through a straw and looked quite innocent. "It'll help you keep up your skills."

"You know"—Tracie narrowed her eyes at her friend—"it's bad enough that I have to be a 'geriatric pregnancy' and treated like I'm over the hill and fragile at forty. Then there's the fact that now I wouldn't even be able to perform surgery around this huge baby bump if I wanted to. But for my dear friend to poke fun? You do realize that turnabout is fair play, right?" She lifted an eyebrow.

"Oh, keep working on that mom look. You'll need it in the future. Darcie has it down pat, so maybe you should take lessons from her." Carrie laughed. "Besides, I have months before I'm big as a house again. You have plenty of time to think up some sort of revenge. Believe me, the guys at the ABI have given me plenty of grief over the years. I can take it. This last pregnancy, my water broke in the squad room. It served them right. I've already been told I'll be put on maternity leave *early* this time."

Cheering from the field made them both look toward the football matchup. But the guys had simply jumped into a mound to celebrate the end of the game.

Mac disentangled himself from the pile of arms and legs and headed toward her. Tracie handed him a bottle of water, and he leaned down and kissed her cheek.

When the crisis was over and Paul Chandler had been taken into custody, they'd done some deep soul-searching together and many months of counseling. He'd had a hard time letting go of his anger and yearning for revenge. She'd had a hard time accepting how much life she'd missed because she couldn't forgive herself.

But she'd never talk about wasting her life or time now. Mac had reassured her that God had prepared her for such a time as this. If she hadn't been a little obsessive about her patients, he said, he probably wouldn't be here. And over the past couple of years, she'd learned how to pour her passion and love into her work, continue to do the very best she could, and still let go of control. That she placed firmly in God's capable hands. He'd created her with her unique gifts and personality. She would use them for Him. Mac led AA meetings with her, and she hadn't once had another urge to drink since Griz was taken away.

Mac leaned close and whispered in her ear. "You look wistful . . . Whatcha thinking?"

How long had she been staring and wandering down memory lane? She grinned up at him. "Just thinking about how far we've come."

He took the camp chair next to her and groaned. "I'm probably getting too old to be playing around like that." Taking her hand, he lifted it to his lips and kissed it. "I got a call from Fredericks today." He squeezed.

"Oh?"

Carrie leaned forward in her chair too. "And?"

"They've struck a deal with the remaining Members."

Tracie's heart picked up its pace. They hadn't been sure there would ever be closure there. She tucked her bottom lip in between her teeth. "I'm afraid to ask. But I need to know." She put a hand over the baby in her belly as the kicking started up in full exercise mode.

He shrugged. "We're still not allowed to know any details. Just that they've come to a deal of some sort."

"No more word on Griz?" Carrie's brows lowered behind her sunglasses.

"Nope." His hand tensed in Tracie's. "But I chose to forgive, and I'm going to keep choosing that every day."

That had been the hardest part of all of it. They weren't allowed to know anything about the man who had wreaked havoc on an entire state. A man who had murdered more people than she even wanted to grasp. How could someone be that evil, so bent on creating chaos and inflicting pain?

She shook her head. Thoughts on what had happened and the man behind it weren't productive. If they'd learned anything in counseling, it had been to release things. Let them go. Don't dwell on them.

Easier said than done. "Let's hope that chapter is closed for good."

Jason, Scott, and Darcie jogged over. They'd been in the football pile, reveling with the others.

"What chapter?" Jason asked.

Mac groaned.

Darcie swatted at her husband. "The chapter that brought us all together and the same one we'd all love to put far, far behind us."

"Oh, *that* chapter." Jason chugged his water bottle. "How about we all just decide to remember the good parts." He slung an arm over his wife's shoulder. "Chiefly, these three lovely ladies."

Tracie looked to Mac, her eyes tracing his handsome features. She'd be forever grateful that she'd connected with these crazy cyber guys. It had come at such a great cost.

He nodded. "The good parts definitely were good."

"Hear, hear!" Scott knelt beside his wife.

"All right, so how about we do something to celebrate and remember the good? But we'd better do something soon, because this little one isn't going to wait much longer."

"I love that idea," Carrie chimed in. "But look, we're already together today. Let's just keep the celebration going. What do you have in mind?" She lifted an eyebrow and leaned forward.

Tracie looked around the group that had weathered so much together. "You know, you're right. Just being together is perfect." She lifted her water bottle. "Here's to many more years—no, decades—together as friends."

They all lifted water bottles together in the toast.

Mac gripped her hand tight. "To celebrate and remember the good, the first thing that popped into my mind was a favorite verse. Here's to holding each other's feet to the fire. 'Whatever is true, whatever is honorable, whatever is right, whatever is pure, whatever is lovely, whatever is commendable . . . think about these things.'" She watched his Adam's apple bob. "You guys had to remind me over and over that it was a *command* to think on those things, not a suggestion. Because for a long time, I wanted to dwell on my anger. Nothing else." His voice cracked, and he dipped his chin, then lifted it again. "It's a good reminder for all of us to stay focused. To think on truth. And not to get dragged down by the evil in this world."

As Tracie looked around at the beloved friends, tears shimmered in a few eyes, but love was prevalent in every face.

None of them were perfect. They each had long roads ahead. But they would face the future together, holding firm to each other and to God.

She couldn't think of anything better.

✦ ✦ ✦

Six Months Later
One Fellow Member Remains
Langley, Virginia

Muriel's thick heels clicked on the floor as she crossed the lobby and then scanned her ID badge at security.

The deed was done.

It was over.

Absolutely nothing of the Members remained. The ones who'd made deals were gone.

Time for a fresh start. A clean slate.

She'd made a bargain, and she would stick with it.

The only thing that mattered was finding her son. After more than two years, she was desperate. But she knew Griz. Their boy *was* safe. Well taken care of.

Somewhere.

If she had to spend the rest of her life and every resource she had . . .

She *would* find him.

NOTE FROM THE AUTHOR

LET'S TALK ABOUT FORGIVENESS. IT'S a huge component of this story. Not just for Tracie in forgiving herself, but for Mac.

Mac doesn't get the pretty, let's-tie-it-all-up-in-a-nice-neat-bow closure at the end. Of course, as readers, we get to know that Griz is dead. But Mac doesn't. The team doesn't. Why? The whole point for Mac's spiritual journey is that he has to forgive *without* knowing what's going to happen to Griz. Does he have it in him to forgive? To let go of it, to give it over to God? He has to forgive if he wants to move forward and actually live life. We readers get the closure this time. But we know. Life is messy. Sometimes bad guys win here on earth.

Too many times we want our lives to be like a picture-perfect fictional story. Someone does us wrong and we nobly forgive them, but we get to see justice served. Forgiveness is easy in that scenario. But life isn't always like that, and we are called to forgive whether or not the other person ever even acknowledges they've done anything wrong.

That's a challenge, isn't it? To love as God calls us to love—unconditionally. To forgive as God calls us to forgive—freely, without conditions.

The only way to do that is through the supernatural power of Almighty God. Even the most impossible scenario is made possible if we hand over the reins to Him.

This is what I wanted to portray in Mac's story. A plot that most of us would never be able to even fathom. But I can see myself in Mac, can't you? Every time I'm unwilling to forgive an offense—no matter how big or small. Every time someone irks me.

In the Old Testament, we see that murder is wrong.

In the New Testament, Jesus tells us that even hating someone is equivalent to murder.

Ouch.

This is why I pushed Mac to the very limits spiritually, emotionally, and physically. Sometimes that's what it takes to get our attention.

Let's be honest. This world is full of evil. The enemy has a hold and is seeking to devour, kill, and destroy.

But we know who wins, don't we? So, friends, put on that armor. Be vigilant. Be ready.

It has been such a joy to see this series come to life and to hear how it has impacted you. I love to hear from my readers, so feel free to send me a message on social media or through my website:

https://kimberleywoodhouse.com
https://facebook.com/kimberleywoodhouseauthor
https://instagram.com/kimberleywoodhouse

I pray that through it all, you have seen hope that only comes from Jesus Christ.

It. Is. Well.

Until next time,
Kimberley

ACKNOWLEDGMENTS

AFTER FORTY BOOKS, YOU'D THINK I would have this part down to a science. But as I've said many, many times, I couldn't do this without you.

Thank you, readers. Seriously. It is a joy to bring you stories, yes, but it's even more of a joy to see you share them with others.

It takes so many people to put these books into your hands.

The team at Kregel is just wonderful. I have loved this series with them. I kept telling them that I was looking forward to doing a "normal" book with them, because basically, during the writing of this series, I experienced a lot of crazy life events. Most of them involved my dad's health decline and, after he went Home, the grief.

So far there hasn't been a normal book. But I'm thankful for their grace, prayers, and encouragement along the way.

Carrie—my brilliant sidekick, brainstormer, project manager, and friend extraordinaire—has helped shape these stories and also helped keep me from running away and hiding in the woods. Just sayin'. I wouldn't have made it through the last few years without her.

To my little man, who brings me so much joy each and every day. I love getting to watch you grow and the amazing honor of being a part of that. Looks like you'll always be a better bowler than your Nana. And to his little sister, oh boy, does Nana have big plans for you. I am so blessed.

ACKNOWLEDGMENTS

Charity—friend and avid reader—thank you for coming up with the nickname for the killer. It still gives me the creeps.

Rachel K., Emily, Kayliani, Rachel O., Dori, and everyone else at Kregel—thank you so much.

Tracie Peterson—thank you for getting a kick out of the heroine being named after you. I can't believe you've put up with me this long, but thank you for doing it.

My amazing family—Jeremy, Josh, Kayla, Ruth, Steven, and the grandkids. You. Are. The. Best. What a joy that I get to be wife, mom, and Nana the Great every day.

One more big shout-out to Steven, my in-house cyber expert. Even though my eyes glazed over a few times and I simply typed up word for word what you said to put in the book because I didn't fully understand it, you were ever so patient and kind. Thank you.

Dr. McManus—thank you for answering all my crazy questions and for helping with all the medical details.

And to the Author of all—thank You for gifting me with the stories to tell.

ABOUT THE AUTHOR

KIMBERLEY WOODHOUSE IS AN AWARD-WINNING and best-selling author of more than forty books. A lover of suspense, history, and research, she often gets sucked into the past, and then her husband has to lure her out with chocolate and the promise of eighteen holes on the golf course. Married to the love of her life for three-plus decades, she lives and writes in Colorado, where she's traded in her hat of "Craziest Mom" for "Nana the Great." To find out more about Kim's books, follow her on social media. To sign up for her newletter and blog, go to kimberleywoodhouse.com.

The riveting debut of the Alaskan Cyber Hunters trilogy

The gripping sequel in the Alaskan Cyber Hunters trilogy

"Kimberley has done it yet again. What an amazing, breath-stealing, knuckle-biting thrill of a ride. I highly recommend you snatch this one up and make arrangements to read it in one sitting!"

—Lynette Eason, award-winning, best-selling author of the Extreme Measures series